HOLLYWOOD GHOSTS

Volumes in the American Ghosts series:

HOLLYWOOD GHOSTS

Haunting, Spine-Chilling Stories
from America's Film Capital

Edited by
Frank D. McSherry, Jr., Charles G. Waugh,
and Martin H. Greenberg

Rutledge Hill Press
Nashville, Tennessee

Published in Nashville, Tennessee, by Rutledge Hill Press, Inc., 513 Third Avenue South, Nashville, Tennessee 37210

Typography by Bailey Typography, Nashville, Tennessee
Cover design by Harriette Bateman

Library of Congress Cataloging-in-Publication Data

Hollywood ghosts : haunting, spine-chilling stories from
    America's film capital / edited by Frank D. McSherry, Jr.,
    Charles G. Waugh, and Martin H. Greenberg.
        p.   cm.
    ISBN: 1-55853-103-3
    1. Ghost stories, American—California—Los Angeles. 2.
    Motion pictures—Production and direction—Fiction. 3. Hollywood
    (Los Angeles, Calif.)—Fiction. I. McSherry, Frank D. II.
    Waugh, Charles. III. Greenberg, Martin H.
    PS648.G48H6 1991
    813'.08733083279494—dc20   90-25881
                                                                CIP

Manufactured in the United States of America
1 2 3 4 5 6 7 8 — 97 96 95 94 93 92 91

Table of Contents

Shadows of Reality

Ghosts. Filmy things, drifting among tall tombstones in the moonlight, winding down dark stairs in a haunted ruin on a windy night. Mists in the night. Superstition, suggestion.

Or are they shadows of reality? Filmy things. . . .

The stories about ghosts grouped in this anthology are unified with another kind of film: the movies.

With the coming of film, for the first time in history, almost every human being could enjoy great dramas, the sound of symphonies, and the beauty of art. Up until then, only a favored few living in the great capitals of the world were able to attend theaters and museums. Movies became the people's art, easily the most popular art form in all history.

Nearly half of the writers included in this volume know Hollywood at first hand, are screen and television writers as well as award-winning writers of prose. They include Hugo, Nebula, and Edgar winners Harlan Ellison and William F. Nolan; David Morrell of *Rambo* fame; Robert Bloch, author of *Psycho;* August Derleth; scientist Charles Sheffield.

If ghosts are the products of passions so powerful that they live on even after death, we should not be surprised that ghosts should appear in gripping and eerie stories about movies and Hollywood. The major moments in movies are often more memorable than most such moments in many people's lives. ("What is art," said Alfred Hitchcock, "but life with the boring scenes removed?")

Humphrey Bogart, lifting his glass in salute to the beautiful woman he loved, lost, and found again in *Casablanca,* "Here's looking at you, kid."

Scarlett O'Hara, starving in the desolate South after the

Civil War, lifting a fist and crying, "As God is my witness, I'll never be hungry again!"

The luminous, unforgettable Greta Garbo, in *Queen Christina,* face frozen in grief, standing beside her dead lover on deck as their ship moves silently away over the dark sea.

In films, at least, the dead can live on, forever young, immortal. When Mary Astor's finest film, *The Maltese Falcon,* was shown on television, she said:

> Of *course* I'll watch it! It's a wonderful, rich memory. . . . There they all are, Sydney, Peter, Bogie:
> Sidney: But Miss O'Shaughnessy had, by this time, obtained the bird. . . .
> Peter: She shtruck me! She attacked me!
> Bogie:—and then you went down that dark alley, knowing he'd follow you.
> My dear ghosts!

Ghosts. Shadows of reality.

For if emotionally powerful experiences are all it takes to produce *revenants,* then be warned: We have a whole book full of ghosts waiting here for you. Ghosts of the silver screen, luminous and glowing. . . .

—Frank D. McSherry, Jr.
McAlester, Oklahoma

HOLLYWOOD GHOSTS

Calvin thought that stealing the wrong makeup kit was just bad luck until he discovered that the large black box contained the perfect disguise.

ONE

Makeup
Robert McCammon

Stealing the thing was so *easy.* Calvin Doss had visited the Hollywood Museum of Memories on Beverly Boulevard at three A.M., admitting himself through a side door with a hooked sliver of metal he took from the black leather pouch he kept under his jacket, close to the heart.

He'd roamed the long halls—past the chariots used in *Ben-Hur,* past the tent set from *The Sheik,* past the *Frankenstein* lab mock-up—but he knew exactly where he was going. He'd come there the day before, with the paying tourists. And so in ten minutes after he'd slipped into the place he was standing in the Memorabilia Room, foil stars glittering from the wallpaper wherever the beam of his pencil flashlight touched. Before him were locked glass display cases: one of them was full of wigs on faceless mannequin heads; the next held bottles of perfume used as props in a dozen movies by Lana Turner, Loretta Young, Hedy Lamarr; in the next case there were shelves of paste jewelry, diamonds, rubies, and emeralds blazing like Rodeo Drive merchandise.

And then there was the display case Calvin sought, its shelves holding wooden boxes in a variety of sizes and colors. He moved the flashlight's beam to a lower shelf, and there was the large black box he'd come to take. The lid was open, and within it Calvin could see the trays of tubes, little numbered jars, and what looked like crayons wrapped up in waxed paper. Beside the box there was a small white card with a couple of lines of type: *Makeup case once belonging to Jean Harlow. Purchased from the Harlow estate.*

All right! Calvin thought. That's the ticket. He zipped

1

open his metal pouch, stepped around behind the display case to the lock, and worked for a few minutes to find the proper lock-picker from his ample supply.

Easy.

And now it was almost dawn, and Calvin Doss sat in his small kitchenette apartment off Sunset Boulevard, smoking a joint to relax with and staring at the black box that sat before him on a card table. There was nothing to it, really, Calvin thought. Just a bunch of jars and tubes and crayons, and most of those seemed to be so dry they were crumbling to pieces. Even the box itself wasn't attractive. Junk, as far as Calvin was concerned. How Mr. Marco thought he could push the thing to some L.A. collector was beyond him; now, those fake jewels and wigs he could understand, but this. . . ? No way!

The box was chipped and scarred, showing the bare wood beneath the black lacquer at three of the corners. But the lock was unusual: it was a silver claw, a human hand with long sharp fingernails. It was tarnished with age but seemed to work okay. Mr. Marco would appreciate that, Calvin thought. The makeups themselves looked all dried out, but when Calvin unscrewed some of the numbered jars he caught faint whiffs of strange odors: from one a cold, clammy smell, like graveyard dirt; from another the smell of candle wax and metal; from a third an odor like a swamp teeming with reptilian life. None of the makeups carried brand names or any evidence where they'd been bought or manufactured. Some of the crayons crumbled into pieces when he picked them out of their tray, and he flushed the bits down the toilet so Mr. Marco wouldn't find out he'd been tinkering with them.

Gradually the joint overpowered him. He closed the case's lid, snapped down the silver claw, and went to sleep on his sofabed thinking of Deenie.

He awakened with a start. The harsh afternoon sun was streaming through the dusty blinds. He fumbled for his wristwatch. Oh, God! he thought. Two-forty! He'd been told to call Mr. Marco at nine if the job went okay; panic flared within him as he went out to the pay phone at the end of the hall.

Mr. Marco's secretary answered at the antique shop on

2

Rodeo Drive in Beverly Hills. "Who may I say is calling, please?"

"Tell him Cal. Cal Smith."

"Just a moment, please."

Another phone was picked up. "Marco here."

"It's me, Mr. Marco. Cal Doss. I've got the makeup case, and the whole job went like a dream—"

"A dream?" the voice asked softly. There was a quiet murmur of laughter, like water running over dangerous rocks. "Is that what you'd call it, Calvin? If that's the case, your sleep must be terribly uneasy. Have you seen this morning's *Times?*"

"No, sir." Calvin's heart was beating faster. Something had gone wrong; something had been screwed up royally. The noise of his heartbeat seemed to fill the telephone receiver.

"I'm surprised the police haven't visited you already, Calvin. It seems you touched off a concealed alarm when you broke into the display case. Ah. Here's the story, page seven, section two." There was the noise of paper unfolding. "A silent alarm, of course. The police think they arrived at the scene just as you were leaving; one of the officers even thinks he saw your car. A gray Volkswagen with a dented left-rear fender? Does that ring a bell, Calvin?"

"My . . . Volkswagen's light green," Cal said, his throat tightening. "I . . . got the banged fender in the Club Zoom's parking lot. . . ."

"Indeed? I suggest you begin packing, my boy. Mexico might be nice at this time of year. If you'll excuse me now, I have other business to attend to. Have a nice trip—"

"Wait! Mr. Marco! Please!"

"Yes?" The voice was as cold and hard as a glacier now.

"So I screwed up the job. So what? Anybody can have a bad night, Mr. Marco. I've got the makeup case! I can bring it over to you, you can give me the three G's, and then I can pick up my girl and head down to Mexico for—. *What is it?*"

Mr. Marco had started chuckling again, that cold, mirthless laughter that always sent a chill skittering up Calvin's spine. Calvin could envision him in his black leather chair, the armrests carved into faces of growling lions. His broad, moonlike face would be almost expressionless: the eyes dull and deadly, as black as the business end of a double-barreled shotgun, the mouth slightly crooked to one side, parted lips as red as slices of raw liver. "I'm afraid you don't understand, Calvin," he finally said. "I owe you nothing. It seems that you stole the wrong makeup case. . . ."

"*What?*" Calvin said hoarsely.

"It's all in the *Times,* dear boy. Oh, don't blame yourself. *I* don't. It was a mistake made by some hopeless idiot at the museum. Jean Harlow's makeup case was switched with one from the Chamber of Horrors. Her case is ebony with diamonds stitched into a red silk lining, supposedly to signify her love affairs. The one you took belonged to a horror-film actor named Orlon Kronsteen, who was quite famous in the late thirties and forties for his monster makeups. He was murdered . . . oh, ten or eleven years ago, in a Hungarian castle he had rebuilt in the Hollywood hills. Poor devil: I recall his headless body was found dangling from a chandelier. So. Mistakes will happen, won't they? Now, if you'll forgive me. . . ."

"Please!" Cal said, desperation almost choking him. "Maybe . . . maybe you can sell this horror guy's makeup case?"

"A possibility. Some of his better films—*Dracula Rises, Revenge of the Wolf, London Screams*—are still dredged up for late-night television. But it would take time to find a collector, Calvin, and that makeup case is very hot indeed. *You're* hot, Calvin, and I suspect you will be cooling off shortly up at the Chino prison."

"I . . . I need that three thousand dollars, Mr. Marco! I've got plans!"

"Do you? As I say, I owe you nothing. But take a word of warning, Calvin: go far away, and keep your lips sealed about my . . . uh . . . activities. I'm sure you're familiar with Mr. Crawley's methods?"

"Yeah," Calvin said. "Yes, sir." His heart and head were pounding in unison. Mr. Crawley was Marco's "enforcer," a six-foot-five skeleton of a man whose eyes blazed with bloodlust whenever he saw Calvin. "But . . . what am I going to *do?*"

"I'm afraid you're a little man, dear boy, and what little

4

men do is not my concern. I'll tell you instead what you aren't going to do. You aren't going to call this office again. You aren't going to come here again. You aren't ever going to mention my name as long as you live . . . which, if it were up to Mr. Crawley, who is standing just outside my door at this moment, would be less than the time it takes for you to hang up the phone. Which is precisely what *I* am about to do." There was a last chuckle of cold laughter and the phone went dead.

Calvin stared at the receiver for a moment, hoping it might rewaken. It buzzed at him like a Bronx cheer. Slowly he put it back on its cradle, then walked like a zombie toward his room. He heard sirens, and panic exploded within him, but they were far in the distance and receding. What am I going to do? he thought, his brain ticking like a broken record. *What am I going to do?* He closed and bolted his door and then turned toward the makeup case there on the table.

Its lid was open, and Calvin thought that was odd, because he remembered—or thought he remembered—closing it last night. The silver claw was licked with dusty light. Of all the stupid screwups! he thought, anger welling up inside. Stupid, stupid, stupid! He crossed the room in two strides and lifted the case over his head to smash it to pieces on the floor. Suddenly something seemed to bite his fingers and he howled in pain, dropping the case back onto the table; it overturned, spilling jars and crayons.

There was a red welt across Calvin's fingers where the lid had snapped down like a lobster's claw. It bit me! he thought, backing away from the thing.

The silver claw gleamed, one finger crooked as if in invitation.

"I've got to get rid of you!" Calvin said, startled by the sound of his own voice. "If the cops find you here, I'm up the creek!" He stuffed all the spilled makeups back into it, closed the lid, and tentatively poked at it for a minute before picking it up. Then he carried it along the corridor to the back stairway and down to the narrow alley that ran behind the building. He pushed the black makeup case deep inside a garbage can, underneath an old hat, a few empty bottles of Boone's Farm, and a Dunkin Donuts box. Then he returned to the pay phone and, trembling, dialed Deenie's apartment number; there was no answer, so he called the Club Zoom. Mike, the bartender, picked up the phone. "How's it goin', Cal?" In the background the Eagles were on the jukebox, singing about life in the fast lane. "Nope, Cal. Deenie's not comin' in today until six. Sorry. You want to leave a message or something?"

"No," Calvin said. "Thanks anyway." He hung up and returned to his room. Where the hell was Deenie? he wondered. It seemed she was never where she was supposed to be; she never called, never let him know where she was. Hadn't he bought her a nice gold-plated necklace with a couple of diamond specks on it to show her he wasn't mad for stringing along that old guy from Bel-Air? It had cost him plenty, too, and had put him in his current financial mess. He slammed his fist down on the card table and tried to sort things out: somehow he had to get some money. He could hock his radio and maybe collect an old pool-hall debt from Corky McClinton, but that would hardly be enough to carry him and Deenie for very long in Mexico. He had to have that three thousand dollars from Mr. Marco! But what about Crawley? That killer would shave his eyebrows with a .45!

What to do, what to do?

First, Calvin reasoned, a drink to calm my nerves. He opened a cupboard and brought out a bottle of Jim Beam and a glass. His fingers were shaking so much he couldn't pour, so he shoved the glass aside and swigged out of the bottle. It burned like hellfire going down. Damn that makeup case! he thought, and took another drink. Damn Mr. Marco: another drink. Damn Crawley. Damn Deenie. Damn the idiot who switched those lousy makeup cases. Damn me for even taking on this screwy job. . . .

After he'd finished damning his second and third cousins who lived in Arizona, Calvin stretched out on the sofabed and slept.

He came awake with a single terrifying thought: *The cops are here!* But they weren't, there was no one else in the room, everything was okay. His head was throbbing, and through the small, smog-filmed windows the light was graying into night. What'd I do? he thought. Sleep away the whole day? He reached over toward the Jim Beam bottle, there on the card table beside the makeup case, and saw that there was about a half-swallow left in it. He tipped it to his mouth and drank it down, adding to the turmoil in his belly.

When his fogged gaze finally came to rest on the makeup case, he dropped the bottle to the floor.

Its lid was wide open, the silver claw cupping blue shadows.

"What are you doin' here?" he said, his speech slurred. "I got rid of you! Didn't I?" He was trying to think: he seemed to remember taking that thing to the garbage can, but then again, it might've been a dream. "You're a jinx, that's what you are!" he shouted. He struggled up, staggered out into the hallway to the pay phone again, and dialed the antique shop.

A low, cold voice answered: "Marco Antiques and Curios."

Calvin shuddered; it was Crawley. "This is Calvin Doss," he said, summoning up his courage. "Doss. Doss. Let me speak to Mr. Marco."

"Mr. Marco doesn't want to speak to you."

"Listen, I need my three thousand bucks!"

"Mr. Marco is working tonight, Doss. Stop tying up the phone."

"I just . . . I just want what's comin' to me!"

"Oh? Then maybe I can help you, you little punk. How's about two or three forty-five slugs to rattle around in your brain-pan? I dare you to set foot over here!" The phone went dead before Calvin could say another word.

He put his head in his hands. Little punk. Little man. Little jerk. It seemed someone had been calling him those names all his life, from his mother to the juvenile-home creeps to the L.A. cops. I'm not a little punk! he thought. Someday I'll show them all! He stumbled to his room, slamming his shoulder against a wall in the process, and had to turn on the lights before darkness totally filled the place.

And now he saw that the black makeup case had crept closer to the table's edge.

He stared at it, transfixed by that silver claw. "There's something funny about you," he said softly. "Something reeeeallll funny. I put you in the garbage! Didn't I?" And now, as he watched it, the claw's forefinger seemed to . . .

7

move. To bend. To beckon. Calvin rubbed his eyes. It hadn't moved, not really! Or had it? Yes! No. Yes! No. . . .

Had it?

Calvin touched it, then whimpered and drew his hand away. Something had shivered up his arm, like a faint charge of electricity. *"What are you?"* he whispered. He reached out to close the lid, and this time the claw seemed to clutch at his hand, to pull it down into the box itself. He shouted *"Hey!"* and when he pulled his hand back he saw he was gripping one of the jars of makeup, identified by the single number 9.

The lid dropped.

Calvin jumped. The claw had latched itself into place. For a long time he looked at the jar in his hand, then slowly—very slowly—unscrewed the top. It was a grayish-looking stuff, like greasepaint, with the distinct odors of . . . What was it? he thought. Yes. Blood. That and a cold, mossy smell. He dabbed in a finger and rubbed it into the palm of his hand. It tingled, and seemed to be so cold it was hot. He smeared his hands with the stuff. The feeling wasn't unpleasant. No, Calvin decided; it was far from unpleasant. The feeling was of . . . power. Of invincibility. Of wanting to throw himself into the arms of the night, to fly with the clouds as they swept across the moon's grinning face. Feels good, he thought, and smeared some of the stuff on his face. God, if Deenie could only see me now! He began to smile. His face felt funny, filmed with the cold stuff, but different, as if the bone structure had sharpened. His mouth and jaws felt different too.

I want my three thousand dollars from Mr. Marco, he told himself. And I'm going to get it. Yessssssss. I'm going to get it right now.

After a while he pushed aside the empty jar and turned toward the door, his muscles vibrating with power. He felt as old as time, but filled with incredible, wonderful, ageless youth. He moved like an uncoiling serpent to the door, then into the hallway. Now it was time to collect the debt.

He drifted like a haze of smoke through the darkness and slipped into his Volkswagen. He drove through Hollywood, noting the white sickle moon rising over the Capitol Records building, and into Beverly Hills. At a traffic light he could sense someone staring at him from the car beside his; he turned his head slightly, and the young woman at the wheel of her Mercedes froze, terror stitched across her face. When the light changed, he drove on, leaving the Mercedes sitting still.

Yessssss. It was definitely time to collect the debt.

He pulled his car to the curb on Rodeo Drive, two shops down from the royal-blue-and-gold canopy with the lettering MARCO ANTIQUES AND CURIOS. Most of the expensive shops were closed, and there were only a few window-shoppers on the sidewalks. Calvin walked toward the antique shop. Of course the door was locked, a blind pulled down, and a sign that read SORRY WE'RE CLOSED. I should've brought my tool kit! he told himself. But no matter. Tonight he could do magic; tonight there were no impossibilities. He imagined what he wanted to do; then he exhaled and slipped through the doorjamb like a gray, wet mist. Doing it scared the hell out of him, and caused one window-shopper to clutch at his heart and fall like a redwood to the pavement.

Calvin stood in a beige-carpeted display room filled with gleaming antiques: a polished rosewood piano once owned by Rudolph Valentino, a brass bed from the Pickford estate, a lamp with bulbs shaped like roses that had once belonged to Vivien Leigh. Objects of silver, brass, and gold were spotlit by track lights at the ceiling. Calvin could hear Mr. Marco's voice from the rear of the shop, through a door that led back into a short hallway and Marco's office. ". . . that's all well and good, Mr. Frazier," he was saying. "I hear what you're telling me, but I'm not listening. I have a buyer for that item, and if I want to sell it I must make delivery tomorrow afternoon at the latest." There was a few seconds' pause. "Correct, Mr. Frazier. It's not my concern how your people get the Flynn diary. But I'll expect it to be on my desk at two o'clock tomorrow afternoon, is that understood. . . ?"

Calvin begin to smile. He moved across the room as silently as smoke, entered the hallway, and approached the closed door to Marco's office.

He was about to turn the doorknob when he heard Marco put down his telephone. "Now, Mr. Crawley," Marco said. "Where were we? Ah, yes; the matter of Calvin Doss. I very much fear that we cannot trust the man to remain silent in the face of adversity. You know where he lives, Mr. Crawley. I'll have your payment ready for you when you return—"

Calvin reached forward, gripped the doorknob, and wrenched at it. He was amazed and quite pleased when the entire door was ripped from its hinges.

Marco, his three hundred pounds wedged into the chair with the lion faces on the armrests behind a massive mahogany desk, gave out a startled squawk, his black eyes almost popping from his head. Crawley had been sitting in a corner holding a *Hustler* magazine, and now the towering height of him came up like a released spring, his eyes glittering like cold diamonds beneath thick black brows. Crawley's hand went up under his checked sport coat, but Calvin froze him with a single glance.

Marco's face was the color of spoiled cheese. "Who . . . who are you?" he said, his voice trembling. "What do you want?"

"Don't you recognize me?" Calvin asked, his voice as smooth and dark as black velvet. "I'm Calvin Doss, Mr. Marco."

"Cal . . . vin . . . ?" A thread of saliva broke over Marco's double chins and fell onto the lapel of his charcoal-gray Brooks Brothers suit. "No! It can't be!"

"But it is." Calvin grinned and felt his fangs protrude. "I've come for my restitution, Mr. Marco."

"Kill him!" Marco shrieked to Crawley. "Kill him!"

Crawley was still dazed, but he instinctively pulled the automatic from the holster beneath his coat and stuck it into Calvin's ribs. Calvin had no time to leap aside; Crawley's finger was already twitching on the trigger. In the next instant the gun barked twice, and Calvin felt a distant sensation of heat that just as quickly faded. Behind him, through the haze of blue smoke, there were two bullet holes in the wall. Calvin couldn't exactly understand why his stomach wasn't torn open right now, but this was indeed a night of miracles; he grasped the man's collar and with one hand flung him like a scarecrow across the room. Crawley screamed and slammed into the opposite wall, collapsing to the floor in a tangle of arms and legs. He skittered past Calvin like a frantic crab and ran away along the corridor.

"Crawley!" Marco shouted, trying to get out of his chair. "Don't leave me!"

Calvin shoved the desk forward as effortlessly as if it were the matter of dreams, pinning the bulbous Marco in his chair. Marco began to whimper, his eyes floating in wet sockets. Calvin was grinning like a death's-head. "And now," he whispered, "it is time for you to pay." He reached out and grasped the man's tie, slowly tightening it until Marco's face looked like a bloated red balloon. Then Calvin leaned forward, very gracefully, and plunged his fangs into the throbbing jugular vein. A fountain of blood gushed, dripping from the corners of Calvin's mouth. In another few moments Marco's corpse, which seemed to have lost about seventy-five pounds, slumped down in its chair, its shoulders squashed together and the arms up as if in total surrender.

Calvin stared at the body for a moment, a wave of nausea suddenly rising from the pit of his stomach. He felt lightheaded, out of control, lost in a larger shadow. He turned and struggled out to the hallway, where he bent over and retched. Nothing came up, but the taste of blood in his mouth made him wish he had a bar of soap. *What have I done?* he thought, leaning against a wall. Sweat was dripping down his face, plastering his shirt to his back. He looked down at his side, to where there were two holes in his shirt, ringed with powder burns. That should've killed me, he realized. Why didn't it? How did I get in here? Why did I . . . kill Mr. Marco like that? He spat once, then again and again; the taste of blood was maddening. He probed at his gums with a finger. His teeth were all normal now; everything was back to normal.

What did that makeup case turn me into? He wiped the sweat from his face with a handkerchief and stepped back into the office. Yep. Mr. Marco was still dead. The two bullet holes were still in the wall. Calvin wondered where Marco kept his money. Since he was dead, he figured, he wouldn't need it anymore. Right? Calvin leaned over the desk, avoiding the fixed stare from the corpse's eyes, and started going through the drawers. In a lower one, beneath all kinds of papers and other junk, was a white envelope with the name CRAWLEY printed on it. Calvin looked inside. His heart leapt. There was at least five thousand dollars in there; probably the dough Crawley was going to be paid for my murder, Calvin thought. He took the money and ran.

Fifteen minutes later he was pulling into the parking lot beside the Club Zoom. In the red neon-veined light he counted the money, trembling with joy. Fifty-five hundred bucks! It was more money than he had ever seen in his whole life.

He desperately needed some beer to wash away the taste of blood. Deenie would be dancing in there by now, too. He put the money in a back pocket and hurried across the parking lot into the Club Zoom. Inside, strobe lights flashed like crazy lightning. A jukebox thundered from somewhere in the darkness, its bass beat kicking at Calvin's unsettled stomach. A few men sat at the bar or at a scattering of tables, drinking beer and watching the girl onstage who gyrated her hips in a disinterested circle. Calvin climbed onto a bar stool. "Hey, Mike! Gimme a beer! Deenie here yet?"

"Yeah. She's in the back." Mike shoved a mug of beer in front of him and then frowned. "You okay, Cal? You look like you saw a ghost or something."

"I'm fine. Or will be, as soon as I finish this off." He drank most of it in one swallow, swishing it around in his mouth. "That's better."

"What's better, Cal?"

"Nothing. Forget it. Jeez, it's cold in here!"

"You sure you're okay?" Mike asked, looking genuinely concerned. "It must be eighty degrees in here. The air conditioner broke again this afternoon."

"Don't worry about me. I'm just fine. Soon as I see my girl I'll be even better."

"Uh-huh," Mike said quietly. He cleaned up a few splatters of beer from the bar with a rag. "I hear you bought Deenie a present last week. A gold chain. Put you back much?"

"About a hundred bucks. It's worth it, though, just to see that pretty smile. I'm going to ask her to go down to Mexico with me for a few days."

"Uh-huh," Mike said again. Now he was cleaning up

imaginary splatters, and finally he looked Calvin straight in the eyes. "You're a good guy, Cal. You never cause any trouble in here, and I can tell you're okay. I just . . . well, I hate to see you get what's coming."

"Huh? What do you mean by that?"

Mike shrugged. "How long have you known Deenie, Cal? A few weeks? Girls like her come and go, man. Here one day, gone the next. Sure she's good-looking; they all are, and they trade on their looks like their bodies are Malibu beachfront properties. You get my drift?"

"No."

"Okay. This is man-to-man. Friend-to-friend, right? Deenie's a taker, Cal. She'll bleed you dry, and then she'll kick you out with the garbage. She's got about five or six guys on the string."

Calvin blinked, his stomach roiling again. "You're . . . you're lying!"

"God's truth. Dennie's playing you, Cal; reeling you in and out like a fish with a hooked gut—"

"You're lying!" Calvin's face flushed; he rose from his seat and leaned over toward the bartender. "You've got no right saying those things! They're lies! You probably want me to give her up so you can have her! Fat chance! I'm going back to see her right now, and you'd better not try to stop me!" He started to move away from the bar, his brain spinning like a top.

"Cal," Mike said softly, his voice tinged with pity, "Deenie's not alone."

But Calvin was already going back behind the stage, through a black curtain to the dressing rooms. Deenie's room was the third door, and as Calvin was about to knock, he heard the deep roll of a man's laughter. He froze, his hand balled into a fist.

"A diamond ring?" the man said. "You're kidding!"

"Honest to God, Max!" Deenie's voice, warmer than Calvin had ever heard it. "This old guy gave me a diamond ring last week! I think he used to work for NBC or ABC or one of those C's. Anyway, he's all washed-up now. Do you know what he wears in bed? Socks with garters! Ha! He said he wanted me to marry him. He must've been serious because that ring brought six hundred bucks at the pawnshop!"

13

"Oh, yeah? Then where's my share?"

"Later, baby, later. I'll meet you at your place after work, okay? We can do the shower thing and rub each other's backs, huh. . . ?"

There was a long silence in which Calvin could hear his teeth grinding together.

"Sure, babe," Max said finally. "You want to use the black one or the red one tonight?"

Calvin almost slammed his fist through the door. But instead he turned and ran, a volcano about to erupt in his brain; he ran past the bar, past Mike, out the door to his car. *I thought she loved me!* he raged as he screeched out of the parking lot. She *lied!* She played me for a sucker all the way! He floored the accelerator, gripping the wheel with white-knuckled hands.

By the time he locked himself in his apartment, turned his transistor radio up loud, and flopped down on his sofabed, the volcano had exploded, filling his veins with the seething magma of revenge. *Revenge:* now, there's a sweet word, he thought. It was Satan's battle cry, and now seemed branded into Calvin's heart. How to do it? he wondered. How? How? *Why am I always the little punk?*

He turned his head slightly and gazed at the black makeup case.

It was open again, the silver claw beckoning him.

"You're a jinx!" he screamed at it. But he knew now that it was more. Much, much more. It was weird, evil maybe, but there was power in those little jars: power and perhaps also revenge. *No!* he told himself. No, I won't use it! What kind of nutcake am I turning into, to think that makeup could bring me what I want? He stared at the case, his eyes widening. It was unholy, terrible, something from Lucifer's magic shop. He was aware of the roll of money in his back pocket, and aware also of the bullet holes in his shirt. Unholy or not, he thought, it can give me what I want.

Calvin reached into the makeup case and chose a jar at random. It was numbered 13, and when he sniffed at the cream he found it smelled of dirty brick, rain-slick streets, whale-oil lamps. He dabbed his finger into the reddish-brown goop and stared at it for a moment, the odors making him feel giddy and . . . yes, quite mad.

14

He smeared it across his cheeks and worked it into the flesh. His eyes began to gleam with maniacal determination. He scooped out more of it, rubbing it into his face, his hands, his neck. It burned like mad passion.

The lid fell. The claw clicked into place.

Calvin smiled and stood up, stepping to a kitchen drawer. He opened it and withdrew a keen-bladed butcher knife. Now, he thought. Now, me Miss Deenie Roundheels, it's time you got your just desserts, wot? Can't have ladies like you runnin' about in the streets, prancin' and hawkin' your sweet goods to the highest bidder, can we, luv? No, not if I've got a bit to say about it!

And so he hurried out of the apartment and down to his car, a man on an urgent mission of love's revenge.

He waited in the shadows behind the Club Zoom until Deenie came out just after two o'clock. She was alone, and he was glad of that because he had no quarrel with Max; it was the woman—it was Woman—who had betrayed him. She was a beautiful girl with long blond hair, sparkling blue eyes, a sensual pout in a lovely oval face. Tonight she was wearing a green dress, slit to show silky thighs. A sinner's gown, he thought as he watched her slink across the parking lot.

Stepping out of the darkness, he held the knife behind him like a gleaming gift he wanted to surprise her with. "Deenie?" he whispered, smiling. "Deenie, luv?"

She whirled around. "Who's there?"

Calvin stood between darkness and the red swirl of neon. His eyes glittered like pools of blood. "It's your own true love, Deenie," he said. "Your love come to take you to Paradise."

"Calvin?" she whispered, taking a backward step. "What are you doing here? Why . . . does your face look like that?"

"I've brought something for you, luv," he said softly. "Step over here and I'll give it to you. Come on, dearie, don't be shy."

"What's wrong with you, Calvin? You're scaring me."

"Scaring you? Why, whatever for? I'm your own dear Cal, come to kiss you good night. And I've brought a pretty for you. Something nice and bright. Come see."

She hesitated, glancing toward the deserted boulevard.

"Come on," Calvin said. "It'll be the sweetest gift any man ever gave you."

A confused, uncertain smile ripped across her face. "What'd you bring me, Calvin? Huh? Another necklace? Let's see it!"

"I'm holding it behind my back. Come here, luv. Come see."

Deenie stepped forward reluctantly, her eyes as bright as a frightened doe's. When she reached Calvin she held out her hand. "This had better be good, Cal—"

Calvin grasped her wrist and yanked her forward. When her head rocked back, he ripped the blade across her offered throat. She staggered and started to fall, but before she did, Calvin dragged her behind the Club Zoom so he could take his own sweet time. When he was finished, he looked down at the cooling corpse and wished he had a pencil and paper to leave a note. He knew what it would say: You Have to be Smart To catch Me. Smart like a Fox. Yours from the Depths of Hell, Cal the Ripper.

He wiped the blade on her body, got in his car, and drove to Hancock Park, where he threw the murder weapon in the LaBrea tarpits. Then a weak, sick feeling overcame him and he sank down into the grass, clutching his knees up close to his body. He was racked with shudders when he realized there was blood all over the front of his shirt. He pulled up handfuls of grass and tried to wipe most of it away. Then he lay back on the ground, his temples throbbing, and tried to think past the pain.

Oh, God! he thought. What kind of a makeup case have I gotten my hands onto? Who made the box? Who conjured up those jars and tubes and crayons? It was magic, yes: but evil magic, magic gone bad and ugly. Calvin remembered Mr. Marco saying it had belonged to a horror-flick actor named Kronsteen, and that Kronsteen was famous for his monster makeups. Calvin was chilled by a sudden terrible thought: how much was makeup and how much was real? Half and half, maybe? When you put on the makeup, the . . . essence of the monster gripped into you like some kind of hungry leech? And then, when it had fed, when it had gorged itself on evil and blood, it loosened its hold on you and fell away? Back there in Marco's office, Calvin thought, I was really part vampire. And then, in the Club Zoom's parking lot, I was part Jack the Ripper. In those jars, he thought, are not just makeups; in those creams and greasepaints there are real monsters, waiting to be awakened by my desires, my passions, my . . . evil.

I've got to get rid of it, he decided. I've got to throw it out before it destroys me! He rose to his feet and ran across the park to his car.

The hallway on his floor was as dark as a werewolf's dreams at midnight. What happened to the damned light bulbs? Calvin thought as he felt his way toward his door. Weren't they burning when I left?

And then a floorboard creaked very softly, down at the hallway's end.

Calvin turned and stared into the darkness, one hand fumbling with his key. He thought he could make out a vague shape standing over there, but he wasn't sure. His heart whacked against his rib cage as he slid the key home.

And he knew it was Crawley a split second before he saw the orange flare from the .45's muzzle. The bullet hit the doorjamb, pricking his face with wood splinters. He shouted in terror, twisted the doorknob, and threw himself into the room. As he slammed the door shut and locked it, another bullet came screaming through the wood, about an inch from the left side of his skull. He spun away from the door, trying to press himself into the wall.

"Where's that five thousand bucks, Doss!" Crawley shouted from the hallway. "It's mine! Give it to me or I'll kill you, you little punk!" A third bullet punched through the center of the door, leaving a hole as big as a fist. Then Crawley began to kick at the door, making it shudder on its aged hinges. Now there were screams and shouts from all over the building, but the door was about to crash in, and soon Crawley would be inside to deliver those two .45 slugs as promised.

Calvin heard a faint *click*.

He whirled around. The silver claw had unlatched itself; the makeup case stood open. He was shaking like a leaf in a hurricane.

17

The door cracked and whined, protesting the blows from Crawley's shoulder.

Calvin watched it bend inward, almost to the breaking point. Another shot was fired, the bullet shattering a window across the room. He turned and looked fearfully at the makeup case again. It can save me, he thought; that's what I want, and that's what it can do. . . .

"I'm gonna blow out your brains when I get in there, Doss!" Crawley roared.

And then Calvin was across the room; he grabbed a jar numbered 15. The thing practically unscrewed itself, and he could smell the mossy, mountain-forest odor of the stuff. He plunged a forefinger into it, hearing the door begin to split down the middle.

"I'm gonna kill you, Doss!" Crawley said, and with his next kick the door burst open.

Calvin whirled to face his attacker, who froze in absolute terror. As Calvin leapt, he howled in animal rage, his claws striping red lines across Crawley's face. They fell to the floor, Calvin's teeth gnashing at the unprotected throat of his prey. He bent over Crawley's remains on all fours, teeth and claws ripping away flesh to the bone. Then he lifted his head and howled with victory. Beneath him Crawley's body twitched and writhed.

Calvin fell back, breathing hard. Crawley looked like something that had gone through a meat grinder, and now his twitching arms and legs were beginning to stiffen. The building was full of racket, screaming and shouting from the lower floors. He could hear a police siren, fast approaching, but he wasn't afraid; he wasn't afraid at all.

He stood up, stepped over a spreading pool of blood, and peered down into Orlon Kronsteen's makeup case. In there was power. In there were a hundred disguises, a hundred masks. With this thing, he would never be called a little punk again. It would be so easy to hide from the cops. So easy. If he desired, it would be done. He picked up a jar numbered 19. When he unscrewed it he sniffed at the white, almost clear greasepaint and realized it smelled of . . . nothing. He smeared it over his hands and face. Hide me, he thought. Hide me. The siren stopped, right outside the building. Hurry! Calvin commanded whatever force ruled the contents of this box. Make me . . . disappear!

The lid fell.

The silver claw clicked into place with a noise like a whisper.

The two LAPD cops, Ortega and Mullinax, had never seen a man as ripped apart as the corpse that lay on the apartment's floor. Ortega bent over the body, his face wrinkled with nausea. "This guy's long gone," he said. "Better call for the morgue wagon."

"What's this?" Mullinax said, avoiding the shimmering pool of blood that had seeped from the slashed stiff. He unlatched a black box that was sitting on a card table and lifted the lid. "Looks like . . . theatrical makeup," he said quietly. "Hey, Luis! This thing fits the description of what was stolen from the Memory Museum last night!"

"Huh?" Ortega came over to have a look. "Christ, Phil! It is! That stuff belonged to Orlon Kronsteen. Remember him?"

"Nope. Where'd that landlady get off to?"

"I think she's still throwing up," Ortega said. He picked up an open jar and smelled the contents, then dropped it back into the case. "I must've seen every horror flick Kronsteen ever starred in." He looked uneasily at the corpse and shivered. "As a matter of fact, amigo, that poor fella looks like what was left of one of Kronsteen's victims in *Revenge of the Wolf.* What could tear a man up like that, Phil?"

"I don't know. And don't try putting the scare in me, either." He turned his head and stared at something else on the floor, over beyond the unmade sofabed. "My God," he said softly. "Look at that!" He stepped forward a few paces and then stopped, his eyes narrowing. "Luis, did you hear something?"

"Huh? No. What is it over there? Clothes?"

"Yeah." Mullinax bent down, his brow furrowing. Spread out before him, still bearing a man's shape, were a shirt, a pair of pants, and shoes. The shoelaces were still tied, the socks in the shoes; the belt and zipper were still fastened as well. Mullinax untucked the shirttail, noting the bloodstains on it and what looked like two cigarette burns, and saw a pair of underwear still in place in the pants. "That's funny," he said. "That's damned funny. . . ."

Ortega's eyes were as wide as saucers. "Yeah. Funny. Like that flick Kronsteen did, *The Invisible Man Returns.* He left his clothes just like that when he . . . uh . . . vanished. . . ."

"I think we're going to need some help on this one," Mullinax said, and stood up. His face had turned a pasty gray color, and now he looked past Ortega to the rotund woman in a robe and curlers who stood in the doorway. She stared down at the shredded corpse with dreadful fascination. "Mrs. Johnston?" Mullinax said. "Whose apartment did you say this belonged to?"

"Cal . . . Cal . . . Calvin Doss," she stammered. "He never pays his rent on time."

"You're sure this isn't him on the floor?"

"Yes. He's . . . a little man. Stands about under my chin. Oh, I think my stomach's going to blow up!" She staggered away, her house shoes dragging.

"Man, what a mess!" Ortega shook his head. "Those empty clothes . . . that's straight out of *The Invisible Man Returns,* I'm telling you!"

"Yeah. Well, I guess we can send this thing back to where it belongs." Mullinax tapped his finger on the black makeup case. "You say a horror actor owned it?"

"Sure did. A long time ago. Now I guess all that stuff is junk, huh." He smiled faintly. "The stuff dreams are made of, right? I saw most of that guy's flicks twice, when I was a kid. Like the one about the Invisible Man. And there was another one he did that was really something too, called . . . let's see . . . *The Man Who Shrank.* Now, *that* was a classic."

"I don't know so much about horror films," Mullinax said. He ran a finger over the silver claw. "They give me the creeps. Why don't you stay up here with our dead friend and I'll radio for the morgue wagon, okay?" He took a couple of steps forward and then stopped. Something was odd. He leaned against the shattered doorjamb and looked at the sole of his shoe. "Ugh!" he said. "What'd I step on?"

Robert McCammon was born in Alabama in 1952 and reached the bestseller lists with his first novel, Baal, *in 1978. Graduating from the University of Alabama, McCammon worked in advertising and journalism before becoming a full-time writer. Nine novels and one collection of short stories followed* Baal, *all with the same high quality and popularity, all featuring believable people facing appalling terrors, such as in* The Night Boat, Stinger, Usher's Passing, *and* Blue World.

TWO

Laugh Track

Harlan Ellison

I loved my Aunt Babe for three reasons. The first was that even though I was only ten or eleven, she flirted with me as she did with any male of any age who was lucky enough to pass through the heat of her line-of-sight. The second was her breasts—I knew them as "titties"—which left your arteries looking like the Holland Tunnel at rush hour. And the third was her laugh. Never before and never since, in the history of this planet, including every species of life-form extant or extinct, has there been a sound as joyous as my Aunt Babe's laugh which I, as a child, imagined as the sound of the Toonerville Trolley clattering downhill. If you have never seen a panel of that long-gone comic strip, and have no idea what the Toonerville Trolley looked like, forget it. It was some terrific helluva laugh. It could pucker your lips.

My Aunt Babe died of falling asleep and not waking up in 1955, when I was twelve years old.

I first recognized her laugh while watching a segment of *Leave It to Beaver* in November of 1957. It was on the laugh track they'd dubbed in after the show had been shot, but I was only fourteen and thought those were real people laughing at Jerry Mathers's predicament. I yelled for my mother to come quickly, and she came running from the kitchen, her hands all covered with wax from putting up the preserves, and she thought I'd hurt myself or something.

"No . . . no, I'm okay . . . listen!"

She stood there, listening. "Listen to what?" she said after a minute.

"Wait . . . wait . . . *there*! You hear that? It's Aunt Babe. She isn't dead, she's at that show."

My mother looked at me just the way your mother would look at you if you said something like that, and she shook her head, and she said something in Italian my grandmother had no doubt said while shaking her head at *her*, long ago; and she went back to imprisoning boysenberries. *I* sat there and watched The Beav and Eddie Haskell and Whitey Whitney, and broke up every time my Aunt Babe laughed at their antics.

I heard my Aunt Babe's laugh on *The Real McCoys* in 1958; on *Hennessey* and *The Many Loves of Dobie Gillis* in 1959; on *The Andy Griffith Show* in 1960; on *Car 54, Where Are You?* in 1962; and in the years that followed I laughed along with her at *The Dick Van Dyke Show, The Lucy Show, My Favorite Martian, The Addams Family, I Dream of Jeannie,* and *Get Smart!*

In 1970 I heard my Aunt Babe laughing at *Green Acres,* which—though I always liked Eddie Albert and Alvy Moore—I thought was seriously lame; and it bothered me that her taste had deteriorated so drastically. Also, her laugh seemed a little thin. Not as ebulliently Toonerville Trolley going downhill any more.

By 1972 I knew something was wrong because Aunt Babe was convulsing over *Me and the Chimp* but not a sound from her for *My World . . . And Welcome to It.*

By 1972 I was almost thirty, I was working in television, and because I had lived with the sound of my Aunt Babe's laughter for so long, I never thought there was anything odd about it, and I never again mentioned it to anyone.

Then, one night, sitting with a frozen pizza and a Dr. Brown's cream soda, watching an episode of the series I was writing, a sitcom you may remember called *Misty Malone,* I heard my Aunt Babe laughing at a line that the story editor had not understood, that he had rewritten. At that moment, bang! comes the light bulb burning in my brain, comes the epiphany, comes the rude awakening, and I hear myself say, "This is crazy. Babe's been dead and buried lo these seventeen years, and there is strictly *no way* she can be laughing at this moron line that Bill Tidy rewrote from my golden prose, and this is weirder than shit, and *what the hell is going on here!?"*

Besides which, Babe's laugh was now sounding a lot like a 1971 Pinto without chains trying to rev itself out of a snowy rut into which cinders had been shoveled.

And I suppose for the first time I understood that Babe was not alive at the taping of all those shows over the years, but was merely on an old laugh track. At which point I remembered the afternoon in 1953 when she'd taken me to the Hollywood Ranch Market to go shopping, and one of those guys had been standing there handing out tickets to the filming of tv shows, and Babe had taken two tickets to *Our Miss Brooks,* and she'd gone with some passing fancy she was dating at the time, and told us later that she thought Eve Arden was funnier than Lucille Ball.

The laugh track from that 1953 show was obviously still in circulation. Had been, in fact, in circulation for twenty years. And for twenty years my Aunt Babe had been forced to laugh at the same old weary sitcom minutiae, over and over and over. She'd had to laugh at the salt instead of the sugar in Fred MacMurray's coffee; at Granny Clampett sending Buddy Ebsen out to shoot a possum in Beverly Hills; at Bob Cummings trying to conceal Julie Newmar's robot identity; at The Fonz *almost* running a comb through his pompadour; at all the mistaken identities, all the improbable last-minute saves of hopeless situations, all the sophomoric pratfalls from Gilligan to Gidget. And I felt just terrible for her.

Native Americans, what we used to be allowed to call Indians when I was a kid, have a belief that if someone takes their picture with a camera, the box captures their soul. So they shy away from photographers. AmerInds seldom become bank robbers: there are cameras in banks. There was no graduation picture of Cochise in his high school yearbook.

What if—I said to myself—sitting there with that awful pizza growing cold on my lap—what if my lovely Aunt Babe, who had been a Ziegfeld Girl, and who had loved my Uncle Morrie, and who had had such wonderful titties and never let on that she knew *exactly* what I was doing when I'd fall asleep in the car on the way home and snuggle up

25

against them, *what if* my dear Aunt Babe's soul, like her laugh, had been trapped on that goddam track?

And what if she was in there, in there forever, doomed to laugh endlessly at imbecilic shit rewritten by ex-hairdressers, instead of roaming around Heaven, flirting with the angels, which I was certain should have been her proper fate, being that she was such a swell person? What if?

It was the sort of thinking that made my head hurt a lot.

And it made me feel even lower, the more I thought about it, because I didn't know what I could do about it. I just knew that that was what had happened to my Aunt Babe; and there she was in there, condemned to the stupidest hell imaginable. In some arcane way, she had been doomed to an eternity of electronic restimulation. In speech therapy they have a name for it: cataphasia: verbal repetition. But I could tell from the frequency with which I was now hearing Babe, and from the indiscriminate use to which her laugh was being put—not just on *M*A*S*H* and *Maude,* but on yawners like *The Sandy Duncan Show* and a midseason replacement with Larry Hagman called *Here We Go Again,* which didn't—and the way her laugh was starting to slur like an ice skating elephant, that she wasn't having much fun in there. I began to believe that she was like some sort of beanfield slave, *every* now and then being goosed electronically to laugh. She was a video galley slave, one of the pod people, a member of some ghastly high-frequency chain gang. Cataphasia, but worse. Oh, how I wanted to save her; to drag her out of there and let her tormented soul bound free like a snow rabbit, to vanish into great white spaces where the words *Laverne and Shirley* had never trembled in the lambent mist.

Then I went to bed and didn't think about it again until 1978.

By September of 1978 I was working for Bill Tidy again. In years to come I would refer to that pox-ridden period as the Season I Stepped in a Pile of Tidy.

Each of us has one dark eminence in his or her life who somehow has the hoodoo sign on us. Persons so cosmically loathsome that we continually spend our time when in their company silently asking ourselves, *What the hell, what the bloody hell, what the everlasting Technicolor hell am I doing sitting here with this ambulatory piece of offal? This is the worst person who ever got born, and someone ought to wash out his life with a bar of Fels-Naptha.*

But there you sit, and the next time you blink, there you sit again. It was probably the way Catherine the Great felt on her dates with Rasputin.

Bill Tidy had that hold over me.

In 1973 when I'd been just a struggling sitcom writer, getting his first breaks on *Misty Malone,* Tidy had been the story editor. An authoritarian Fascist with all the creative insight of a sump pump. But now, a mere five years later, things were a great deal different: I had created a series, which meant I was a struggling sitcom writer with my name on a parking slot at the studio; and Bill Tidy, direct lineal descendant of The Blob that tried to eat Steve McQueen, had swallowed up half the television industry. He was now the heavy-breathing half of Tidy-Spellberg Productions, in partnership with another ex-hairdresser named Harvey Spellberg, whom he'd met during a metaphysical retreat to Reno, Nevada. They'd become corporate soul mates while praying over the crap tables and in just a few years had built upon their unerring sense of how much debasement the American television-viewing audience could sustain (a much higher gag-reflex level than even the experts had postulated, thereby paving the way for *Three's Company*), to emerge as "prime suppliers" of gibbering lunacy for the three networks.

Bill Tidy was to Art as Pekin, North Dakota, is to wild nightlife.

But he was the fastest money in town when it came to marketing a series idea to one of the networks, and my agent had sent over the prospectus for *Ain't It the Truth,* without my knowing it; and before I had a chance to scream, "Nay, nay, my liege! There are some things mere humans were never meant to know, Doctor Von Frankenstein!" the network had made a development deal with the Rupert Murdoch of mindlessness, and of a sudden I was— as they so aptly put it—in bed with Bill Tidy again.

This is the definition of ambivalence: to have struggled in the ditches for five years, to have created something that was guaranteed to get on the air, and to have that creation masterminded by a toad with the charm of a charnel house and the intellect of a head of lettuce. I thought seriously of moving to Pekin, North Dakota, where the words *coaxial cable* are as speaking-in-tongues to the simple, happy natives; where the blight of Jim Nabors has never manifested itself; where I could open a grain and feed store and never have to sit in the same room with Bill Tidy as he picked his nose and surreptitiously examined the findings.

But I was weak, and even if the series croaked before the season ran its course, I would have a credit that could lead to bigger things. So I pulled down the covers, plumped the pillows, straightened the rubber pishy-pad, and got into bed with Bill Tidy.

By September, I was a raving lunatic. I spent much of my time dreaming about biting the heads off chickens. The deranged wind of network babble and foaming Tidyism blew through the haunted cathedral of my brain. What little originality and invention I'd brought to the series concept—and at best what we're talking about here is primetime network situation comedy, not a PBS tour conducted by Alistair Cooke through the Library of Alexandria—was steadily and firmly leached out of the production by Bill Tidy. Any time a line or a situation with some charm or esthetic value dared to peek its head out of the *merde* of the scripts, Tidy as Grim Reaper would lurch onto the scene swinging the scythe of his demented bad taste, and intellectual decapitation instantly followed.

I developed a hiatic hernia, I couldn't hold down solid food and took to subsisting on strained mung from Gerber's inexhaustible and vomitous larder, I snapped at everyone, sex was a concept whose time had come and gone for me, and I saw my gentle little offering to the Gods of Comedy turned into something best suited for a life under mossy stones.

Had I known that on the evening of Thursday, September 14, 1978, *Ain't It the Truth* was to premiere opposite a new ABC show called *Mork & Mindy,* and that within three weeks a dervish named Robin Williams would be dining on Nielsen rating shares the way sharks devour entire continents, I might have been able to hold onto enough of my sanity to weather the Dark Ages. And I wouldn't have gotten involved with Wally Modisett, the phantom sweetener, and I wouldn't have spoken into the black box, and I wouldn't have found the salvation for my dead Aunt Babe's soul.

But early in September Williams had not yet uttered his first *Nanoo-nanoo* (except on a spinoff segment of *Happy Days* and who the hell watched *that*?) and we had taped the first three segments of *Ain't It the Truth* before a live audience at the Burbank Studios, if you can call those who voluntarily go to tapings of sitcoms "living," and late one night the specter of Bill Tidy appeared in the doorway of my office, his great horse face looming down at me like the demon that emerges from the *Night on Bald Mountain* section of Disney's *Fantasia;* and his sulphurous breath reached across the room and made all the little hairs in my nostrils curl up and try to pull themselves out so they could run away and hide in the back of my head somewhere; and the two reflective puddles of Vegemite he called eyes smoldered at me, and this is what he said. First he said:

"That fuckin' fag cheese-eater director's never gonna work again. He's gonna go two days over, mark my words. I'll see the putzola never works again."

Then he said:

"I bought another condo in Phoenix. Solid gold investment. Better than Picassos."

Then he said:

"I heard it at lunch today. A cunt is just a clam that's wearin' a fright-wig. Good, huh?"

Then he said:

"I want you to stay late tonight. I can't trust anyone else. Guy'll show up here about eight. He'll find you. Just stay put till he gets here. Never mind a name. He'll make himself known to you. Take him over to the mixing studio, run the first three shows for him. Nobody else gets in, *kapeesh, paisan?*"

I was having such a time keeping my gorge from becoming buoyant that I barely heard his directive. Bill Tidy gave new meaning to the words King of the Pig People. The only groups he had failed to insult in the space of thirteen seconds were blacks, Orientals, paraplegics, and Doukhobors, and if I didn't quickly agree to his demands, he'd no doubt round on them, as well. "Got it, Bill. Yessiree, you can count on me. Uh-huh, absolutely, right-on, dead-center, I hear ya talkin', I'm your boy, I loves workin' foah ya, Massa' Tidysuh, you can bank on me!"

He gave me a look. "You know, Angelo, you are gettin' stranger and stranger, like some kind of weird insect."

And he turned and he vanished, leaving me all alone there in the encroaching darkness, just tuning my antennae and rubbing my hind legs together.

I was slumped down on my spine, eyes closed, in the darkened office with just the desk lamp doing its best to rage against the dying of the light, when I heard someone whisper huskily, "Turn off the light."

I opened my eyes. The room was empty. I looked out the window behind my desk. It was night. I was three flights up in the production building. No one was there.

"The light. Turn off the light, can you hear what I'm telling you?"

I strained forward toward the open door and the dark hallway beyond. "You talking to me?" Nothing moved out there.

"The light. Slow; you're a very slow person."

Being Catholic, I respond like a Pavlovian dog to guilt. I turned out the light.

From the deeper darkness of the hallway I saw something shadowy detach itself and glide into my office. "Can I keep my eyes open," I said, "or would a blindfold serve to palliate this unseemly paranoia of yours?"

The shadowy form snorted disdainfully. "At these prices you can use words even bigger than that and I don't give a snap." I heard fingers snap. "You care to take me over to the mixing booth?"

I stood up. Then I sat down. "Don't wanna play." I folded my arms.

The shadowy figure got a petulant tone in his voice. "Okay, c'mon now. I've got three shows to do, and I haven't got all night. The world keeps turning. Let's go."

"Not in the cards, Lamont Cranston. I've been ordered around a lot these last few days; and since I don't know you from a stubborn stain, I'm digging in my heels. Remember the Alamo. Millions for defense, not one cent for tribute. The only thing we have to fear is fear itself. Forty-four forty or fight."

"I think that's fifty-four forty or fight," he said.

We thought about that for a while. Then after a long time I said, "Who the hell are you, and what is it you do that's so illicit and unspeakable that first of all Bill Tidy would hire you to do it, which puts you right on the same level as me, which is the level of graverobbers, dog catchers, and horse-dopers; and second, which is so furtive and vile that you have to do it in the dead of night, coming in here wearing garb fit only for a commando raid? Answer in the key of C#."

He chuckled. It was a nice chuckle. "You're okay, kid," he said. And he dropped into the chair on the other side of my desk where writers pitching ideas for stories sat; and he turned on the desk lamp.

"Wally Modisett," he said, extending a black-gloved hand. "Sound editor." I took the hand and we shook. "Free-lance," he said.

That didn't sound so ominous. "Why the Creeping Phantom routine?"

Then he said the word no one in Hollywood says. He looked intently at all of my face, particularly around the mouth, where lies come from, and he said: "Sweetening."

If I'd had a silver crucifix, I'd have thrust it at him at arm's length. *Be still my heart,* I thought.

There are many things of which one does not speak in the television industry. One does not repeat the name of the NBC executive who was making women writers give him blowjobs in his office in exchange for writing assignments, even though he's been pensioned off with a lucrative production deal at a major studio and the network paid for his psychiatric counseling for several years. One does not talk about the astonishing Digital Dance done by the royalty numbers in a major production company's ledgers, thereby fleecing several superstar participants out of their "points" in the profits, even though it made a large stink on the *World News Tonight* and everybody scampered around trying to settle out of court while *TV Guide* watched. One does not talk about how the studio frightened a buxom ingenue who had become an overnight national sensation into modifying her demands for triple salary in the second season her series was on the air, not even to hint knowingly of a kitchen chair with nails driven up through the seat from the underside.

And one never, never, no never ever talks about the phantom sweeteners.

This show was taped before a live studio audience!

If you've heard it once, you've heard it at least twice. And so when those audiences break up and fall on the floor and roll around and drum their heels and roar so hard they have to clutch their stomachs and tears of hilarity blind them and their noses swell from crying too much and they sound as if they're all genetically selected, high-profile tickleables, you fall right in with them because that ain't canned laughter, it's a live audience, onaccounta *This show was taped before a live studio audience.*

While high in the fly loft of the elegant opera house, the Phantom Sweetener looks down and chuckles smugly.

They're legendary. For years there was only Charlie Douglas, a name never spoken. A laugh man. A sound technician. A sweetener. They say he still uses laughs kidnapped off radio shows from the Forties and Fifties. Golden laughs. Unduplicable originals. Special, rich laughs that blend and support and lift and build a resonance that punches your subliminal buttons. Laughs from *The Jack Benny Show,* from segments of *The Fred Allen Show* down in Allen's Alley, from *The Chase & Sanborn Hour* with Edgar Bergen and Charlie McCarthy (one of the shows on which Charlie mixed it up with W.C. Fields). The laughs that Ed Wynn got, that Goodman and Jane Ace got, that Fanny Brice got. Rich, teak-colored laughs from a time in this country when humor wasn't produced by slugs like Bill Tidy. For a long time Charlie Douglas was all alone as the man who could make even dull thuds go over boffola.

But no one knew how good he was. Except the IRS, which took note of his underground success in the industry by raking in vast amounts of his hard-earned cash.

Using the big Spotmaster cartridges—carts that looked like eight-track cassettes, with thirty cuts per cart—twelve or fourteen per job—Charlie Douglas became a hired gun of guffaws, a highwayman of hee-haws, Zorro of zaniness; a troubleshooter working extended overtime in a specialized craft where he was a secret weapon with a never-spoken code-name.

Carrying with him from studio to studio the sounds of great happy moments stolen from radio signals long-since on their way to Proxima Centauri.

And for a long time Charlie Douglas had it all to himself, because it was a closely guarded secret; not one of the open secrets perhaps unknown in Kankakee or Key West, like Merv Griffin or Ida Lupino or Roger Moore; but common knowledge at the Polo Lounge and Chasen's.

But times got fat and the industry grew and there was more work, and more money, than one Phantom Sweetener could handle.

So the mother of invention called forth more audio soldiers of fortune: Carroll Pratt and Craig Porter and Tom Kafka and two silent but sensational guys from Tokyo and techs at Glen Glenn Sound and Vidtronics. And you never mention their names or the shows they've sweetened, lest you get your buns run out of the industry. It's an open secret, closely held by the community. The networks deny their existence, the production company executives would let you nail them, hands and feet, to their office doors before they'd cop to having their shows shot before a live studio audience sweetened. In the dead of night by the phantoms.

Of whom Wally Modisett is the most mysterious.

And here I sat, across from him. He wore a black turtleneck sweater, jeans, and gloves. And he placed on the desk the legendary black box. I looked at it. He chuckled.

"That's it," he said.

"I'll be damned," I said.

I felt as if I were in church.

In sound editing, the key is equalization. Bass, treble, they can isolate a single laugh, pull it off the track, make a match even twenty years later. They put them on "endless loops" and then lay the show over to a multi-track audio machine, and feed in one laugh on a separate track, meld it, blend it in, punch it up, put that special button-punch giggle right in there with the live studio audience track. They do it, they've always done it, and soon now they'll be able to do it with digital encoding. And he sat right there in front of me with the legendary black box. Legendary, because Wally Modisett was an audio genius, an electronics Machiavelli who had built himself a secret system to do it all through that little black box that he took to the studios in the dead of night when everyone was gone, right into the booth at the mixing room, and he didn't need a multi-track.

If it weren't something to be denied to the grave, the *mensches* and moguls of the television industry would have Wally Modisett's head right up there on Mount Rushmore in the empty space between Teddy Roosevelt and Abe Lincoln.

What took twenty-two tracks for a combined layering on a huge machine, Wally Modisett carried around in the palm of his hand. And looking at his long, sensitive face, with the dark circles under his eyes, I guess I saw a foreshadowing of great things to come. There was laughter in his eyes.

I sat there most of the night, running the segments of *Ain't It the Truth*. I sat down below in the screening room while the Phantom Sweetener locked himself up in the booth. *No one,* he made it clear, watched him work his magic.

And the segments played, with the live audience track, and he used his endless loops from his carts—labeled "Single Giggle 1" and "Single Giggle 2" and slightly larger "Single Giggle 3" and the dreaded "Titter/Chuckle" and the ever-popular "Rim Shot"—those loops of his own design, smaller than those made by Spotmaster, and he built and blended and sweetened the hell out of that laugh track till even I chuckled at moronic material Bill Tidy had bastardized to a level that only the Jukes and Kallikaks could have found uproarious.

And then, on the hundredth playback, after Modisett had added another increment of hilarity, I heard my dead Aunt Babe. I sat straight up in the plush screening room chair, and I slapped the switch on the console that fed into the booth, and I yelled, "Hey! That last one! That last laugh . . . what was that . . . ?"

He didn't answer for a moment. Then, tinnily, through the console intercom, he said, "I call it a wonky."

"Where'd it come from?"

Silence.

"C'mon, man, where'd you get that laugh?"

"Why do you want to know?"

I sat there for a second, then I said, "Listen, either you've got to come down here, or let me come up there. I've got to talk to you."

Silence. Then after a moment, "Is there a coffee machine around here somewhere?"

"Yeah, over near the theater."

"I'll be down in about fifteen minutes. We'll have a cup of coffee. Think you can hold out that long?"

"If you nail a duck's foot down, does he walk in circles?"

It took me almost an hour to convince him. Finally, he decided I was almost as bugfuck as he was, and the idea was so crazy it might be fun to try and work it out. I told him I was glad he'd decided to try it because if he hadn't I'd have followed him to his secret lair and found some way to blackmail him into it, and he said, "Yeah, I can see you'd do that. You're not a well person."

"Try working with Bill Tidy sometimes," I said. "It's enough to turn Mother Teresa into a hooker."

"Give me some time," he said. "I'll get back to you."

I didn't hear from him for a year and a half. *Ain't It the Truth* had gone to the boneyard to join *The Chicago Teddy Bears* and *Angie* and *The Dumplings*. Nobody missed it, not even its creator. Bill Tidy had wielded his scythe with skill.

Then just after two A.M. on a summer night in Los Angeles, my phone rang, and I fumbled the receiver off the cradle and found my face somehow, and a voice said, "I've got it. Come." And he gave me an address; and I went.

The warehouse was large, but all his shit was jammed into one corner. Multi-tracks and oscilloscopes and VCRs and huge 3-mil thick Mylar foam speakers that looked like the rear seats of a 1933 Chevy. And right in the middle of the floor was a larger black box.

"You're kidding?" I said.

He was like a ten-year-old kid. "Would I shit you? I'm telling you, fellah, I've gone where no man has gone before. I has done did it! Jonas Salk and Marie Curie and Lee De Forest and all the rest of them have got to move over, slide

35

aside, get to the back of the bus." And he leaped around, howling, *"I am the king!"*

When I was able to peel him off the catwalks that made a spiderweb tracery above us, he started making some sense. Not a *lot* of sense, because I didn't understand half of what he was saying, but enough *sense* for me to begin to believe that this peculiar obsession of mine might have some toe in the world of reality.

"The way they taped shows back in 1953, when your aunt went to that *Our Miss Brooks,* was they'd use a ¼" machine, reel-to-reel. They'd have directional mikes above the audience, to separate individual laughs. One track for the program, and another track for the audience. Then they'd just pick up what they want, equalize, and sock it onto one track for later use. Sweetened as need be."

He went to a portable fridge and pulled out a Dr. Pepper and looked in my direction. I shook my head. I was too excited for junk food. He popped the can, took a swig, and came back to me.

"The first thing I had to do was find the original tape, the master. Took me a long time. It was in storage with . . . well, you don't need to know that. It was in storage. I must have gone through a thousand old masters. But I found her. Then I had to pull her out. But not just the *sound* of her laugh. The actual laugh itself. The electronic impulses. I used an early model of this to do it." He waved a hand at the big black box.

"She'd started sounding weak to me, over the years," I said. "Slurred sometimes. Scratchy."

"Yeah, yeah, yeah." Impatient to get on with the great revelation. "That was because she was being diminished by fifth, sixth, twentieth generation re-recording. No, I got her at full strength, and I did what I call 'deconvolving.'"

"Which is?"

"Never mind."

"You going to say 'never mind' every time I ask what the hell you did to make it work?"

"As Groucho used to say to contestants, 'You bet your ass.'"

I shrugged. It was his fairy tale.

"Once I had her deconvolved, I put her on an endless

loop. But not just *any* kind of normal standard endless loop. You want to know what kind of endless loop I put her on?"

I looked at him. "You going to tell me to piss off?"

"No. Go ahead and ask."

"All right already: I'm asking. What the hell kind of endless loop did you put her on?"

"A moebius loop."

He looked at me as if he'd just announced the birth of a two-headed calf. I didn't know what the hell he was talking about. That didn't stop me from whistling through my two front teeth, loud enough to cause echoes in the warehouse and I said, "No shit?!?"

He seemed pleased, and went on faster than before. "Now I feed her into the computer, digitally encode her so she never diminishes. Slick, right? Then I feed in a program that says harmonize and synthesize her, get a simulation mapping for the instrument that produced that sound; in other words, your aunt's throat and tongue and palate and teeth and larynx and alla that. Now comes the tricky part. I build a program that postulates an actual physical *situation,* a terrain, a *place* where that voice exists. And I send the computer on a search to bring me back everything that composes that place."

"Hold hold *hold* it, Lamont. Are you trying to tell me that you went in search of the Land of Oz, using that loop of Babe's voice?"

He nodded about a hundred and sixteen times.

"How'd you do *that?* I know: piss off. But that's some kind of weird metaphysical shit. It can't be done."

"Not by drones, fellah. But *I* can do it. I *did* it." He nodded at the black box.

"The tv sitcom land where my dead Aunt Babe is trapped, it's in there, in that cube?"

"Ah calls it a *simularity matrix,*" he said, with an accent that could get him killed in SouthCentral L.A.

"You can call it rosewater if you like, Modisett, but it sounds like the foothills of Bandini Mountain to me."

His grin was the mutant offspring of a sneer and a smirk. I'd seen that kind of look only once, on the face of a failed academic at a collegiate cocktail party. Later that evening the guy used the smirk ploy once too often and a little tweety-bird of an English prof gave him high cause to go see a periodontal reconstructionist.

"I can reconstruct her like a clone, right in the machine," he said.

"How do you know? Tried it yet?"

"It's your aunt, not mine," he said. "I told you I'd get back to you. Now I'm back to you, and I'm ready to run the showboat out to the middle of the river."

So he turned on a lot of things on the big board he had, and he moved a lot of slide-switches up the gain slots, and he did this, and he did that, and a musical hum came from the Quad speakers, and he looked over his shoulder at me, across the tangle of wires and cables that disappeared into the black box, and he said, "Wake her up."

I said, "What?"

He said, "Wake her. She's been an electronic code for almost twenty-five years. She's been asleep. She's an amputated frog leg. Send the current through her."

"How?"

"Call her. She'll recognize your voice."

"How? It's been a long time. I don't sound like the kid I was when she died."

"Trust me," he said. "Call her."

I felt like a goddam fool. "Where do I speak?"

"Just speak, asshole. She'll hear you."

So I stood there in the middle of that warehouse and said, "Aunt Babe?" There was nothing.

"A little louder. Gentle, but louder. Don't startle her."

"You're outta your. . ." His look silenced me. I took a deep breath and said, a little louder, "Hey, Aunt Babe? You in there? It's me, Angelo."

I heard something. At first it sounded like a mouse running toward me across a long blackboard, a blackboard maybe a hundred miles long. Then there was something like the wind you hear in thick woods in the autumn. Then the sound of somebody unwrapping Christmas presents. Then the sound of water, like surf, pouring into a cave at the base of a cliff, and then draining out again. Then the sound of a baby crying and the sound suddenly getting very deep as if it were a three-hundred-pound killer baby that wanted to be fed parts off a freshly killed dinosaur. This kind of torrential idiocy went on for a while, and then, abruptly, out of nowhere, I heard my Aunt Babe clearing her throat, as if she were getting up in the morning. That phlegmy throat-clearing that sounds like quarts of yogurt being shoveled out of a sink.

"Angelo. . . ?"

I crossed myself about eleven times, ran off a few fast Hail Marys and Our Fathers, swallowed hard, and said, "Yeah, Aunt Babe, it's me. How are you?"

"Let me, for a moment here, let me get my bearings." It took more than a moment. She was silent for a few minutes, though she did once say, "I'll be right with you, *mia caro.*"

And finally, I heard her say, "I am really fit to be tied. Do you have any idea what they have put me through? Do you have even the *faintest* idea how many times they've made me watch *The Partridge Family?* Do you have any *idea* how much I hate that kind of music? Never Cole Porter, never Sammy Cahn, not even a little Gus Edwards; I'd settle for Sigmund Romberg after those squalling children. *Caro nipote, quanto mi sei mancato!* Angelo . . . *bello bello.* I want you to tell me everything that's happened, because as soon as I get a chance, I'm going to make a stink you're not going to believe!"

It *was* Babe. My dearest Aunt Babe. I hadn't heard that wonderful mixture of pungent English and lilting Italian with its show biz Yiddish resonances in almost thirty years. I hadn't *spoken* any Italian in nearly twenty years. But I heard myself saying to the empty air, *"Come te la sei passata?"* How've you been?

"Ti voglio bene—bambino caro. I feel just fine. A bit fuzzy, I've been asleep a while but *come sta la famiglia? Anche quelli che non posso sopportare."*

So I told her all about the family, even the ones she couldn't stand, like Uncle Nuncio with breath like a goat, and Carmine's wife, Giuletta, who'd always called Babe a floozy. And after a while she had me try to explain what had happened to her, and I did the best I could, to which she responded, *"Non mi sento come un fantasma."*

So I told her she didn't feel like a ghost because she *wasn't,* strictly speaking, a ghost. More like a random hoot in the empty night. Well, that didn't go over too terrific, because in an instant she'd grasped the truth that if she wasn't going where it is that dead people go, she'd never meet up with my Uncle Morrie again; and that made her very sad. *"Oh, dio!"* and she started crying.

So I tried to jolly her out of it by talking about all the history that had transpired since 1955, but it turned out she knew most of it anyhow. After all, hadn't she been stuck there, inside the biggest blabbermouth the world had *ever* known? Even though she'd been in something like an alpha state of almost-sleep, her essence had been *saturated* with news and special reports, docudramas and public service announcements, talk shows and panel discussions, network extra alerts and hour-by-hour live coverage of fast-breaking events.

Eventually I got around to explaining how I'd gotten in touch with her, about Modisett and the big black box, about how the Phantom Sweetener had deconvolved her, and about Bill Tidy.

She was not unfamiliar with the name.

After all, hadn't she been stuck there, inside the all-talking, all-singing, all-dancing electromagnetic pimp for Tidy's endless supply of brain-damaged, insipid persiflage?

I painted Babe a loving word-portrait of my employer and our unholy liaison. She said: *"Stronzo! Figlio di una mignotta! Mascalzone!"* She also called him *bischero,* by which I'm sure she meant the word in its meaning of goof, or simpleton, rather than literally: "man with erection."

Modisett, who spoke no Italian, stared wildly at me, seeming to bask in the unalloyed joy of having tapped a line in some Elsewhere. Yet even he could tell from the tone of revulsion in Babe's disembodied voice that she had suffered long under the exquisite tortures of swimming in a sea of Tidy product.

What Tidy had been doing to me seemed to infuriate her. She was still my loving Aunt Babe.

So I spent all that night, and the next day, and the next night—while Modisett mostly slept and emptied Dr. Pepper down his neck—chatting at leisure with my dead Aunt Babe.

You'll never know how angry someone can get from prolonged exposure to Gary Coleman.

*　　*　　*

The Phantom Sweetener can't explain what followed. He says it defies the rigors of Boolean logic, whatever the hell that means. He says it transcends the parameters of Maxwell's Equation, which ought to put Maxwell in a bit of a snit. He says (and with more than a touch of the gibber in his voice) it deflowers, rapes & pillages, breaks & enters Minkowski's Covariant Tensor. He says it is enough to start Philo T. Farnsworth spinning so hard in his grave that he would carom off Vladimir K. Zworykin in his. He says it would get Marvin Minsky up at M.I.T. speaking in tongues. He says—and this one *really* turned me around and opened my eyes—he says it (wait for it), "Distorts Riemannian geometry." To which I said, "You have *got* to be shitting me! Not Riemannian gefuckingometry!?!"

This is absolute babble to me, but it's got Modisett down on all fours, foaming at the mouth and sucking at the electrical outlets.

Apparently, Babe has found pathways in the microwave comm-system. The Phantom Sweetener says it might have happened because of what he calls "print-through," that phenomenon that occurs on audio tape when one layer magnetizes the next layer, so you hear an echo of the word or sound that is next to be spoken. He says if the tape is wound "heads out" and is stored that way, then the signal will jump. The signal that is my dead Aunt Babe has jumped. And keeps jumping. She's loose in the comm-system and she ain't asking where's the beef: *she knows!* And Modisett says the reason they can't catch her and wipe her is that old tape *always* bleeds through. Which is why, when Bill Tidy's big multimillion dollar sitcom aired last year, instead of the audience roaring with laughter, there was the voice of this woman shouting above the din, "That's stupid! Worse than stupid! That's *bore*-ing! Ka-ka! C'mon folks, let's have a good old-fashioned Bronx cheer for crapola like this! Let's show 'em what we *really* think of this flopola!"

And then, instead of augmented laughter, instead of yoks, came a raspberry that could have floated the *Titanic* off the bottom.

Well, they pulled the tape, and they tried to find her, but she was gone, skipping off across the simularity matrix like

Bambi, only to turn up the next night on another Tidy-Spellberg abomination.

Well, there was no way to stop it, and the networks got very leery of Tidy and Company, because they couldn't even use the millions of billions of dollars worthy of shitty rerun shows they'd paid billions and millions for syndication rights to, and they sued the hell out of Bill Tidy, who went crazy as a soup sandwich not too long ago, and I'm told he's trying to sell ocean view lots in some place like Pekin, North Dakota, and living under the name Silas Marner or some-such because half the civilized world is trying to find him to sue his ass off.

And I might have a moment of compassion for the creep, but I haven't the time. I have three hit shows running at the moment, one each on ABC, NBC, and CBS.

They are big hits because somehow, in a way that no one seems able to figure out, there are all these little subliminal buttons being pushed by my shows, and they just soar to the top of the Nielsen ratings.

And I said to Aunt Babe, "Listen, don't you want to go to Heaven, or wherever it is? I mean, don't you want out of that limbo existence?"

And with love, because she wanted to protect her *bambino caro,* because she wanted to make up for the fact that I didn't have her wonderful bosom to fall asleep on anymore, she said, "Get out of here, Angelo, my darling? What . . . and leave show business?"

Harlan Ellison has won award after award for his powerful, often controversial, fiction, essays, and screenplays. His best known works include the award-winners " 'Repent, Harlequin!' Said the Tick-Tock Man," "Jeffty Is Five," "The Whimper of Whipped Dogs," and "Soft Monkey." Some of his best fiction is collected in Deathbird and Other Stories, *while one of his widest known works is the popular* Star Trek *script, "City at the Edge of Forever." An* Edge in My Voice *features some of his best essays, and* The Essential Ellison *is an extensive career perspective.*

Everybody believed that Wes Crane was repeating the career of James Deacon.
They conveniently forgot that Deacon had died after making only three films.

THREE

Dead Image
David Morrell

"You know who he looks like, don't you?"

Watching the scene, I just shrugged.

"Really, the resemblance is amazing," Jill said.

"Mmm."

We were in the studio's screening room, watching yesterday's dailies. The director—and I use the term loosely—had been having troubles with the leading actor, if acting's what you could say that good-looking bozo does. It wasn't enough that Mr. Beefcake wanted eight million bucks and fifteen points to do the picture. It wasn't enough that he changed my scene so the dialogue sounded as if a moron had written it. No, he had to keep dashing to his trailer, snorting more coke (for "creative inspiration," he said), then sniffling after every sentence in the big speech of the picture. If this scene didn't work, the audience wouldn't understand his motivation for leaving his girlfriend after she became a famous singer, and believe me, nothing's more unforgiving than an audience when it gets confused. The word-of-mouth would kill us.

"Come on, you big dumb sonofabitch," I muttered. "You make me want to blow my nose just listening to you."

The director had wasted three days doing retakes, and the dailies from yesterday were worse than the ones from the two days before. Sliding down in my seat, I groaned. The director's idea of fixing the scene was to have a team of editors work all night patching in reaction shots from the girl and the guys in the country-western band she sang with. Every time Mr. Wonderful sniffled—cut, we saw somebody staring at him as if he was Jesus.

43

"Jesus," I moaned to Jill. "Those cuts distract from the speech. It's supposed to be one continuous shot."

"Of course, this is rough, you understand," the director told everyone from where he sat in the back row of seats. Near the door. To make a quick getaway, if he had any sense. "We haven't worked on the dubbing yet. That sniffling won't be on the release print."

"I hope to God not," I muttered.

"Really. Just like him," Jill said next to me.

"Huh? Who?" I turned to her. "What are you talking about?"

"The guitar player. The kid behind the girl. Haven't you been listening?" She kept her voice low enough that no one else could have heard her.

That's why I blinked when the studio v.p. asked from somewhere in the dark to my left, "Who's the kid behind the girl?"

Jill whispered, "Watch the way he holds that beer can."

"There. The one with the beer can," the v.p. said.

Except for the lumox sniffling on the screen, the room was silent.

The v.p. spoke louder. "I said who's the—?"

"I don't know." Behind us, the director cleared his throat.

"He must have told you his name."

"I never met him."

"How the hell, if you—"

"All the concert scenes were shot by the second-unit director."

"What about the reaction shots?"

"Same thing. The kid only had a few lines. He did his bit and went home. Hey, I had my hands full making Mr. Nose Candy feel like the genius he thinks he is."

"There's the kid again," Jill said.

I was beginning to see what she meant now. The kid looked a lot like—

"James Deacon," the v.p. said. "Yeah, that's who he reminds me of."

Mr. Muscle Bound had managed to struggle through the speech. I'd recognized only half of it—partly because the lines he'd added made no sense, mostly because he mumbled. At the end, we had a closeup of his girlfriend, the singer,

44

crying. She'd been so heartless clawing her way to the top that she'd lost the one thing that mattered—the man who'd loved her. In theory, the audience was supposed to feel so sorry for her that they were crying along with her. If you ask me, they'd be in tears all right, from rolling around in the aisles with laughter. On the screen, Mr. Beefcake turned and trudged from the rehearsal hall, as if his underwear was too tight. He had his eyes narrowed manfully, ready to pick up his Oscar.

The screen went dark. The director cleared his throat again. He sounded nervous. "Well?"

The room was silent.

The director sounded more nervous. "Uh . . . So what do you think?"

The lights came on, but they weren't the reason I suddenly had a headache.

Everybody turned toward the v.p., waiting for the word of God.

"What I think," the v.p. said. He nodded wisely. "Is we need a re-write."

"This fucking town." I gobbled Dy-Gel as Jill drove us home. The Santa Monica freeway was jammed as usual. We had the top down on the Porsche so we got a really good dose of car exhaust.

"They won't blame the star. After all, he charged eight million bucks, and next time he'll charge more if the studio pisses him off." I winced from heartburn. "They'd never think to blame the director. He's a goddamned artist as he keeps telling everybody. So who does that leave? The underpaid schmuck who wrote what everybody changed."

"Take it easy. You'll raise your blood pressure." Jill turned off the freeway.

"Raise my blood pressure? Raise my—? It's already raised! Any higher, I'll have a stroke!"

"I don't know what you're so surprised about. This happens on every picture. We've been out here fifteen years. You ought to be used to how they treat writers."

"Whipping boys. That's the only reason they keep us around. Every director, producer, and actor in town is a better writer. Just ask them, they'll tell you. The only problem is they can't read, let alone write, and they just don't seem to have the time to sit down and put all their wonderful thoughts on paper."

"But that's how the system works, hun. There's no way to win, so either you love this business or leave it."

I scowled. "About the only way to make a decent picture is to direct as well as write it. Hell, I'd star in it too if I wasn't losing my hair from pulling it out."

"And twenty million bucks," Jill said.

"Yeah, that would help too—so I wouldn't have to grovel in front of those studio heads. But hell, if I had twenty million bucks to finance a picture, what would I need to be a writer for?"

"You know you'd keep writing, even if you had a hundred million."

"You're right. I must be nuts."

"Wes Crane," Jill said.

I sat at the word processor, grumbling as I did the re-write. The studio v.p. had decided that Mr. Biceps wasn't going to leave his girlfriend. Instead his girlfriend was going to realize how much she'd been ignoring him and give up her career for love. "There's an audience out there dying for a movie against women's lib," he said. It was all I could do not to throw up.

"Wes what?" I kept typing on the keyboard.

"Crane. The kid in the dailies."

I turned to where she stood at the open door to my study. I must have blinked stupidly because she got that patient look on her face.

"The one who looks like James Deacon. I got curious. So for the hell of it, I phoned the casting office at the studio."

"All right, so you found out his name. So what's the point?"

"Just a hunch."

"I still don't get it."

"Your script about mercenary soldiers."

I shrugged. "It still needs a polish. Anyway it's strictly on spec. When the studio decides we've ruined this picture sufficiently, I have to do that Napoleon mini-series for ABC."

"You wrote that script on spec because you believed in the story, right? It's something you really wanted to do."

"The subject's important. Soldiers of fortune employed by the CIA. Unofficially, America's involved in a lot of foreign wars."

"Then fuck the mini-series. I think the kid would be wonderful as the young mercenary who gets so disgusted that he finally shoots the dictator who hired him."

I stared. "You know, that's not a bad idea."

"When we were driving home, didn't you say that the only way to film something decent was to direct the thing yourself?"

"And star in it." I raised my eyebrows. "Yeah, that's me. But I was just making a joke."

"Well, lover, I know you couldn't direct any worse than that asshole who ruined your stuff this morning. I've got the hots for you, but you're not good-looking enough for even a character part. That kid is, though. And the man who discovers him—"

"—can write his own ticket. If he puts the package together properly."

"You've had fifteen years of learning the politics."

"But if I back out on ABC . . ."

"Half the writers in town wanted that assignment. They'll sign someone else in an hour."

"But they offered a lot of dough."

"You just made four hundred thousand on a story the studio ruined. Take a flyer, why don't you? This one's for your self-respect."

"I think I love you."

"When you're sure, come down to the bedroom."

She turned and left. I watched the doorway for a while, then swung my chair to face the picture window and thought about mercenaries. We live on a bluff in Pacific Palisades. You can see the ocean forever. But what I saw in my head was the kid in the dailies. How he held that beer can.

Just like James Deacon.

Deacon. If you're a film buff, you know who I'm talking about. The farm boy from Oklahoma. Back in the middle sixties. At the start a juvenile delinquent, almost went to reform school for stealing cars. But a teacher managed to get him interested in high school plays. Deacon never graduated. Instead he borrowed a hundred bucks and hitchhiked to New York where he camped on Lee Strasberg's doorstep till Strasberg agreed to give him a chance in the method acting school. A lot of brilliant actors had come out of that school. Brando, Newman, Clift, Gazzara, McQueen. But some say Deacon was the best of the lot. A bit part on Broadway. A talent scout in the audience. A screen test. The rest as they say is history. The part of the younger brother in *The Prodigal Son*. The juvenile delinquent in *Revolt on Thirty-Second Street*. Then the wildcat oil driller in *Birthright* where he upstaged half a dozen major stars. There was something about him. Intensity, sure. You could sense the pressure building in him, swelling inside his skin, wanting out. And authenticity. God knows, you could tell how much he believed the parts he was playing. He actually was those characters.

But mostly the camera simply loved him. That's the way they explain a star out here. Some good-looking guys come across as plain on the screen. And plain ones look gorgeous. It's a question of taking a three-dimensional face and making it one-dimensional for the screen. What's distinctive in real life gets muted, and vice versa. There's no way to figure if the camera will like you. It either does or doesn't. And it sure liked Deacon.

What's fascinating is that he also looked as gorgeous in real life. A walking movie. Or so they say. I never met him, of course. He's before my time. But the word in the industry was that he couldn't do anything wrong. That's even before his three movies were released. A guaranteed superstar.

And then?

Cars. If you think of his life as a tragedy, cars were the flaw. He loved to race them. I'm told his body had practically distintegrated when he hit the pickup truck at a hundred miles an hour on his way to drive his modified Corvette at a race track in northern California. Maybe you heard the legend. That he didn't die but was so disfigured that he's in a rest home somewhere to spare his fans the disgust of how he looks. But don't believe it. Oh, he died, all right. Just like a shooting star, he exploded. And the irony is that, since his three pictures hadn't been released by then, he never knew how famous he became.

But what I was thinking, if a star could shine once. . . .

"I'm looking for Wes. Is he around?"

I'd phoned the Screen Actor's Guild to get his address. For the sake of privacy, sometimes all an actor will give the Guild is the name and the phone number of his agent, and what I had in mind was so tentative that I didn't want the hassle of dealing with an agent right then.

But I got lucky. The Guild had an address.

The place was in a canyon out near the desert. A dusty winding road led up to an unpainted house with a sundeck supported on stilts and a half-dozen junky cars in front along with a dune buggy and a motorcycle. Seeing those clunkers, I felt self-conscious in the Porsche.

Two guys and a girl were sitting on the steps. The girl had a butch cut. The guys had hair to their shoulders. They wore sandals, shorts, and that's all. The girl's breasts were as brown as nutmeg.

The three of them stared right through me. Their eyes looked big and strange.

I opened my mouth to repeat the question.

But the girl beat me to it. "Wes?" She sounded groggy. "I think . . . out back."

"Hey, thanks." But I made sure I had the Porsche's keys in my pocket before I plodded through sand past sagebrush around the house.

The back had a sundeck too, and as I turned the corner, I saw him up there, leaning against the rail, squinting toward the foothills.

I tried not to show surprise. In person, Wes looked even more like Deacon. Lean, intense, hypnotic. Around twenty-one, the same age Deacon had been when he made his first movie. Sensitive, brooding, as if he suffered secret tortures. But tough-looking too, projecting the image of someone who'd been emotionally savaged once and wouldn't allow it to happen again. He wasn't tall, and he sure was thin, but he radiated such energy that he made you think he was big and powerful. Even his clothes reminded me of Deacon.

49

Boots, faded jeans, a denim shirt with the sleeves rolled up and a pack of cigarettes tucked in the fold. And a battered stetson with the rims curved up to meet the sides.

Actors love to pose, of course. I'm convinced that they don't even go to the bathroom without giving an imaginary camera their best profile. And the way this kid leaned against the rail, staring moodily toward the foothills, was certainly photogenic.

But I had the feeling that it wasn't a pose. His clothes didn't seem a deliberate imitation of Deacon. He wore them too comfortably. And his brooding silhouette didn't seem calculated either. I've been in the business long enough to know. He dressed and leaned that way naturally. That's the word they use for a winner in this business. He was a natural.

"Wes Crane?" I asked.

He turned and looked down at me. At last, he grinned. "Why not?" He had a vague country-boy accent. Like Deacon.

"I'm David Sloane."

He nodded.

"Then you recognize the name?"

He shrugged. "Sounds awful familiar."

"I'm a screenwriter. I did *Broken Promises,* the picture you just finished working on."

"I remember the name now. On the script."

"I'd like to talk to you."

"About?"

"Another script." I held it up. "There's a part in it that I think might interest you."

"So you're a producer, too?"

I shook my head.

"Then why come to me? Even if I like the part, it won't do us any good."

I thought about how to explain. "I'll be honest. It's a big mistake as far as negotiating goes, but I'm tired of bullshit."

"Cheers." He raised a beer can to his lips.

"I saw you in the dailies this morning. I liked what I saw. A lot. What I want you to do is read this script and tell me if you want the part. With your commitment and me as director, I'd like to approach a studio for financing. But that's the package. You don't do it if I don't direct. And I don't do it unless you're the star."

"So what makes you think they'd accept me?"

"My wife's got a hunch."

He laughed. "Hey, I'm out of work. Anybody offers me a job I take it. Why should I care who directs? Who are you to me?"

My heart sank.

He opened another beer can. "Guess what, though? I don't like bullshit either." His eyes looked mischievous. "Sure, what have I got to lose? Leave the script."

My number was on the front of it. The next afternoon, he called.

"This script of yours? I'll tell you the same thing you said about my acting. I liked it. A lot."

"The script still needs a polish."

"Only where the guy's best friend gets killed. The hero wouldn't talk so much about what he feels. The fact is, he wouldn't say anything. No tears. No outburst. This is a guy who holds himself in. All you need is a closeup on his eyes. That says it all. He stares down at his buddy. He picks up his M-16. He turns toward the palace. The audience'll start to cheer. They'll know he's set to kick ass."

Most times when an actor offers suggestions, my stomach cramps. They get so involved in their parts that they forget about the story's logic. They want more lines. They want to emphasize their role till everybody else in the picture looks weak. Now here was an actor who wanted his largest speech cut out. He was thinking story, not ego. And he was right. That speech had always bothered me. I'd written it ten different ways and still hadn't figured out what was wrong.

Till now.

"The speech is out," I said. "It won't take fifteen minutes to redo the scene."

"And then?"

"I'll go to the studio."

"You're really not kidding me? You think there's a chance I can get the part?"

"As much chance as I have to direct it. Remember the arrangement. We're a package. Both of us, or none."

51

"And you don't want me to sign some kind of promise?"

"It's called a binder. And you're right. You don't have to sign a thing."

"Let me get this straight. If they don't want you to direct but they offer me the part, I'm supposed to turn them down. Because I promised you?"

"Sounds crazy, doesn't it?" The truth was, even if I had his promise in writing, the studio's lawyers could have it nullified if Wes claimed he'd been misled. This town wouldn't function if people kept their word.

"Yeah, crazy," Wes said. "You've got a deal."

In the casting office at the studio, I asked the woman behind a counter, "Have you got any film on an actor named Crane? Wes Crane?"

She looked at me strangely. Frowning, she opened a filing cabinet and sorted through some folders. She nodded, relieved. "I knew that name was familiar. Sure, we've got a screen test on him."

"What? Who authorized it?"

She studied a page. "Nope. Doesn't say."

And I never found out, and that's one of the many things that bother me. "Do you know who's seen the test?"

"Oh, sure, we have to keep a record." She studied another page. "But I'm the only one who looked at it."

"You?"

"He came in here one day to fill out some forms. We got to kidding around. It's hard to describe. There's something about him. So I thought I'd take a look at his test."

"And?"

"What can I say? I recommended him for that bit part in *Broken Promises*."

"If I want to see that test, do you have to check with anybody?"

She thought about it. "You're still on the payroll for *Broken Promises,* aren't you?"

"Right."

"And Crane's in the movie. It seems to me a legitimate request." She checked a schedule. "Use screening room four. In thirty minutes. I'll send down a projectionist with the reel."

*   *   *

So I sat in the dark and watched the test and first felt the shiver that I'd soon know well. When the reel was over, I didn't move for a while.

The projectionist came out. "Are you all right, Mr. Sloane? I mean, you're not sick or anything?"

"No. But thanks. I'm . . ."

"What?"

I took a deep breath and went back to the casting office. "There's been a mistake. That wasn't Crane's test."

She shook her head. "There's no mistake."

"But that was a scene from *The Prodigal Son.* James Deacon's movie. There's been a switch."

"No, that was Wes Crane. It's the scene he wanted to do. The set department threw together something that looked like the hayloft in the original."

"Wes . . . ?"

"Crane," she said. "Not Deacon."

We stared.

"And you liked it?" I asked.

"Well, I thought he was ballsy to choose that scene—and pull it off. One wrong move, he'd have looked like an idiot. Yeah, I liked it."

"You want to help the kid along?"

"Depends. Will it get me in trouble?"

"Exactly the opposite. You'll earn brownie points."

"How?"

"Just phone the studio v.p. Tell him I was down here asking to watch a screen test. Tell him you didn't let me because I didn't have authorization. But I acted upset, so now you've had second thoughts, and you're calling him to make sure you did the right thing. You don't want to lose your job."

"So what will that accomplish?"

"He'll get curious. He'll ask whose test it was. Just tell him the truth. But use these words. 'The kid who looks like James Deacon.'"

"I still don't see. . . ."

"You will." I grinned.

I called my agent and told him to plant an item in *Daily Variety* and *Hollywood Reporter.* "Oscar-winning scribe,

David Sloane, currently prepping his first behind-the-lens chore on *Mercenaries,* toplining James Deacon lookalike, Wes Crane."

"What's going on? Is somebody else representing you? I don't know from chicken livers about *Mercenaries.*"

"Lou, trust me."

"Who's the studio?"

"All in good time."

"You sonofabitch, if you expect me to work for you when somebody else is getting the commission—"

"Believe me, you'll get your ten percent. But if anybody calls, tell them they have to talk to me. You're not allowed to discuss the project."

"Discuss it? How the hell can I discuss it when I don't know a thing about it?"

"There. You see how easy it'll be."

Then I drove to a video store and bought a tape of *The Prodigal Son.*

I hadn't seen the movie in years. That evening, Jill and I watched it fifteen times. Or at least a part of it that often. Every time the hayloft scene was over, I rewound the tape to the start of the scene.

"For God's sake, what are you doing? Don't you want to see the whole movie?"

"It's the same." I stared in astonishment.

"What do you mean the same? Have you been drinking?"

"The hayloft scene. It's the same as in Wes Crane's screen test."

"Well, of course. You said that the set department tried to imitate the original scene."

"I don't mean the hayloft." I tingled again. "See, here in *The Prodigal Son,* Deacon does most of the scene sprawled on the floor of the loft. He has the side of his face pressed against those bits of straw. I can almost smell the dust and the chaff. He's talking more to the floor than he is to his father behind him."

"I see it. So what are you getting at?"

"That's identical in Wes Crane's test. One continuous shot with the camera at the floor. Crane has his cheek against the wood. Every movement, every pause, even that choking noise right here as if the character's about to start sobbing— they're identical."

"But what's the mystery about it? Crane must have studied this section before he decided to use it in his test."

I rewound the tape.

"No, not again," Jill said.

The next afternoon, the studio v.p. phoned. "I'm disappointed in you, David."

"Don't tell me you didn't like the rewrite on *Broken Promises.*"

"The rewrite? The . . . ? Oh, yes, the rewrite. Great, David, great. They're shooting it now. Of course, you understand I had to make a few extra changes. Don't worry, though. I won't ask to share the writing credit with you." He chuckled.

I chuckled right back. "Well, that's a relief."

"What I'm calling about are the trades today. Since when have you become a director?"

"I was afraid of this. I'm not allowed to talk about it, Walt."

"I asked your agent. He says he didn't handle the deal."

"Well, yeah, it's something I set up on my own."

"Who with?"

"Walt, really I can't talk about it. Those items in the trades surprised the hell out of me. They might screw up the deal. I haven't finished the negotiations yet."

"With this kid who looks like James Deacon."

"Honestly, I've said as much as I can, Walt."

"I'll tell you flat out. I don't think it's right for you to try to sneak him away from us. I'm the one who discovered him, remember. I had a look at his screen test yesterday. He's got the making of a star."

I knew when he'd screened that test. Right after the girl in the casting department phoned him to ask if I had the right to see the test. One thing you can count on in this business. They're all so paranoid that they want to know what everybody else is doing. If they think a trend is developing, they'll stampede to follow it.

"Walt, I'm not exactly trying to sneak him away from you. You don't have him under contract, do you?"

"And what's this project called *Mercenaries*?" Walt demanded. "What's that all about?"

"It's a script I did on spec. I got the idea when I heard about the ads at the back of *Soldier of Fortune* magazine."

"*Soldier of*—David, I thought we had a good working relationship."

"Sure. That's what I thought too."

"Then why didn't you talk to me about this story? Hey, we're friends, after all. Chances are you wouldn't have had to write it on spec. I could have given you some development money."

And after you'd finished mucking with it, you'd have turned it into a musical, I thought. "Well, I guess I figured it wasn't for you. Since I wanted to direct and use an unknown in the lead."

Another thing you can count on in this business. Tell a producer that a project isn't for him, and he'll feel so left out that he'll want to see it. That doesn't mean he'll buy it. But at least he'll have the satisfaction of knowing that he didn't miss out on a chance for a hit.

"Directing, David? You're a writer. What do you know about directing? I'd have to draw the line on that. But using the kid as a lead. I considered that yesterday after I saw his test."

Like hell you did, I thought. The test only made your curious. The items in the trades today are what gave you the idea.

"You see what I mean?" I asked. "I figured you wouldn't like the package. That's why I didn't take it to you."

"Well, the problem's hypothetical. I just sent the head of our legal department out to see him. We're offering the kid a long-term option."

"In other words, you want to fix it so no one else can use him, but you're not committing yourself to star him in a picture, and you're paying him a fraction of what you think he might be worth."

"Hey, ten thousand bucks isn't pickled herring. Not from his point of view. So maybe we'll go to fifteen."

"Against?"

"A hundred and fifty thousand if we use him in a picture."

"His agent won't go for it."

"He doesn't have one."

That explained why the Screen Actor's Guild had given me Wes's home address and phone number instead of an agent's.

"I get it now," I said. "You're doing all this just to spite me."

"There's nothing personal in this, David. It's business. I tell you what. Show me the script. Maybe we can put a deal together."

"But you won't accept me as director."

"Hey, with budgets as high as they are, the only way I can justify our risk with an unknown actor is by paying him next to nothing. If the picture's a hit, he'll screw us next time anyhow. But I won't risk money I'm saving by using an inexperienced director who'd probably run the budget into the stratosphere. I see this picture coming in at five million tops."

"But you haven't even read the script. It's got several big action scenes. Explosions. Helicopters. Expensive special effects. Ten million minimum."

"That's just my point. If we used a major star, the budget would go up to twenty million, not to mention the percs he'd demand. And you're so close to the concept that you wouldn't want to compromise on the special effects. You're not directing."

"Well, as you said before, it's hypothetical. I've taken the package to somebody else."

"Not if we put him under option. David, don't fight me on this. Remember, we're friends."

Paramount phoned an hour later. Trade gossip travels fast. They'd heard I was having troubles with my studio and wondered if we could take a meeting to discuss the project they'd been reading about.

I said I'd get back to them. But now I had what I wanted—I could truthfully say that Paramount had been in touch with me. I could play the studios off against each other.

Walt phoned back that evening. "What did you do with the kid? Hide him in your closet?"

"Couldn't find him, huh?"

"The head of our legal department says the kid lives with a bunch of freaks way the hell out in the middle of nowhere. The freaks don't communicate too well. The kid isn't there, and they don't know where he went."

"I'm meeting him tomorrow."

"Where?"

"Can't say, Walt. Paramount's been in touch."

Wes met me at a taco stand he liked on Sunset. He'd been racing his motorcycle in a meet, and when he pulled up in his boots and jeans, his tee-shirt and leather jacket, I shivered from *déjà vu*. He looked exactly as Deacon had looked in *Revolt on Thirty-Second Street*.

"Did you win?"

He grinned and raised his thumb. "Yourself?"

"Some interesting developments."

He barely had time to park his bike before two men in suits came over. I wondered if they were cops, but their suits were too expensive. Then I realized. The studio. I'd been followed from my house.

"Mr. Hepner would like you to look at this," the blue suit told Wes. He set a document on the roadside table.

"What is it?"

"An option for your services. Mr. Hepner feels that the figure will interest you."

Wes shoved it over to me. "What's it mean?"

I read it quickly. The studio had raised the fee. They were offering fifty thousand now against a quarter million.

I told him the truth. "In your position, it's a lot of cash. I think that at this point you need an agent."

"You know a good one?"

"My own. But that might be too chummy."

"So what do you think I should do?"

"The truth? How much did you make last year? Fifty grand's a serious offer."

"Is there a catch?"

I nodded. "Chances are you'll be put in *Mercenaries*."

"And?"

"I don't direct."

Wes squinted at me. This would be the moment I'd always cherish. "You're willing to let me do it?" he asked.

"I told you I can't hold you to our bargain. In your place, I'd be tempted. It's a good career move."

"Listen to him," the gray suit said.

"But do you *want* to direct?"

I nodded. Till now, all the moves had been predictable. But Wes himself was not. Most unknown actors would grab at the chance for stardom. They wouldn't care what private agreements they ignored. Everything depended on whether Wes had a character similar to Deacon's.

"And no hard feelings if I go with the studio?" he asked.

I shrugged. "What we talked about was a fantasy. This is real."

He kept squinting at me. All at once he turned to the suits and slid the option toward them. "Tell Mr. Hepner, my friend here has to direct."

"You're making a big mistake," the blue suit said.

"Yeah, well, here today, gone tomorrow. Tell Mr. Hepner that I trust my friend to make me look good."

I exhaled slowly. The suits looked grim.

I'll skip the month of negotiations. There were times when I sensed that Wes and I had both thrown away our careers. The key was that Walt had taken a stand, and pride wouldn't let him budge. But when I offered to direct for union scale (and let the studio have the screenplay for the minimum the Writer's Guild would allow, and Wes agreed to the Actor's Guild minimum), Walt had a deal he couldn't refuse. Greed budged him in our favor. He bragged about how he'd out-maneuvered us.

We didn't care. I was making a picture I believed in, and Wes was on the verge of being a star.

I did my homework. I brought the picture in for seven million. These days, that's a bargain. The rule of thumb says that you multiply the picture's cost by three (to account for studio overhead and bank interest, this and that), and you've got the break-even point.

So we were aiming for twenty-one million in ticket sales. Worldwide, we did a hundred and twenty million. Now a lot of that went to the distributors, the folks that sell you pop-corn. And a lot of that went into some mysterious black hole of theater owners who don't report all the tickets they sold, and foreign chains that suddenly go bankrupt. But after the sale to Showtime and CBS, after the income from tapes and discs and showings on airlines, the studio had a solid thirty million profit in the bank. And that, believe me, qualifies as a hit.

We were golden. The studio wanted another Wes Crane picture yesterday. The reviews were glowing. Both Wes and I were nominated for—but didn't receive—an Oscar. "Next time," I told Wes.

And now that we were hot, we demanded fees that were large enough to compensate for the pennies we'd been paid on the first one.

Then the trouble started.

You remember that Deacon never knew he was a star. He died with three pictures in the can and a legacy that he never knew would make him immortal. But what you prob-ably don't know is that Deacon became more difficult as he went from picture to picture. The theory is that he sensed the power he was going to have, and he couldn't handle it. Because he was making up for his troubled youth. He was showing people that he wasn't the fuckup his foster parents and his teachers (with one exception) said he was. But Dea-con was so intense—and so insecure—that he started re-verting. Secretly he felt he didn't deserve his predicted success. So he did become a fuckup as others had pre-dicted.

On his next-to-last picture, he started showing up three hours late for the scenes he was supposed to be in. He played expensive pranks on the set, the worst of which was lacing the crew's lunch with a laxative that shut down pro-duction for the rest of the day. His insistence on racing cars forced the studio to pay exorbitant premiums to the insur-ance company that covered him during shooting. On his last picture, he was drunk more often than not, swilling beer and tequila on the set. Just before he died in the car crash, he looked twenty-two going on sixty. Most of his visuals had been completed, just a few closeups remaining, but since a good deal of *Birthright* was shot on location in the Texas oilfields, his dialogue needed re-recording to eliminate background noises on the soundtrack. A friend of his who'd learned to imitate Deacon's voice was hired to dub several key speeches. The audience loved the finished print, but they didn't realize how much of the film depended on careful editing, emphasizing other characters in scenes where Deacon looked so wasted that his footage couldn't be used.

So naturally I wondered—if Wes Crane looked like Deacon and sounded like Deacon, dressed like Deacon and had Deacon's style, would he start to behave like Deacon? What would happen when I came to Wes with a second project?

I wasn't the only one offering stories to him. The scripts came pouring in to him.

I learned this from the trades. I hadn't seen him since Oscar night in April. Whenever I called his place, either I didn't get an answer or a spaced-out woman's voice told me that Wes wasn't home. In truth, I'd expected him to have moved from that dingy house near the desert. The gang that lived there reminded me of the Manson clan. But then I remembered that he hadn't come into big money yet. The second project would be the gold mine. And I wondered if he was going to stake the claim out only for himself.

His motorcycle was parked outside our house when Jill and I came back from a Writer's Guild screening of a new Clint Eastwood movie. This was at sunset with sailboats silhouetted against a crimson ocean. Wes was sitting on the steps that wound up through a rose garden to our house. He held a beer can. He was wearing jeans and a tee-shirt again, and the white of that tee-shirt contrasted beautifully with his tan. But his cheeks looked gaunter than when I'd last seen him.

Our exchange had become a ritual.

"Did you win?"

He grinned and raised a thumb. "Yourself?"

I grinned right back. "I've been trying to get in touch with you."

He shrugged. "Well, yeah, I've been racing. I needed some down-time. All that publicity, and. . . . Jill, how are you?"

"Fine, Wes. You?"

61

"The second go-around's the hardest."

I thought I understood. Trying for another hit. But now I wonder.

"Stay for supper?" Jill asked.

"I'd like to, but—"

"Please, do. It won't be any trouble."

"Are you sure?"

"The chili's been cooking in the crockpot all day. Tortillas and salad."

Wes nodded. "Yeah, my mom used to like making chili. That's before my dad went away and she got to drinking."

Jill's eyebrows narrowed. Wes didn't notice, staring at his beer can.

"Then she didn't do much cooking at all," he said. "When she went to the hospital. . . . This was back in Oklahoma. Well, the cancer ate her up. And the city put me in a foster home. I guess that's when I started running wild." Brooding, he drained his beer can and blinked at us as if remembering we were there. "A home-cooked meal would go good."

"It's coming up," Jill said.

But she still looked bothered, and I almost asked her what was wrong. She went inside.

Wes reached in a paper sack beneath a rose bush. "Anyway, buddy." He handed me a beer can. "You want to make another movie?"

"The trades say you're much in demand." I sat beside him, stared at the ocean, and popped the tab on the beer can.

"Yeah, but aren't we supposed to be a team? You direct and write. I act. Both of us, or none." He nudged my knee. "Isn't that the bargain?"

"It is if you say so. Right now, you've got the clout to do anything you want."

"Well, what I want is a friend. Someone I trust to tell me when I'm fucking up. Those other guys, they'll let you do anything if they think they can make a buck, even if you ruin yourself. I've learned my lesson. Believe me, this time I'm doing things right."

"In that case," I said, vaguely puzzled.

"Let's hear it."

"I've been working on something. We start with several givens. The audience likes you in an action role. But you've got to be rebellious, anti-establishment. And the issue has to be controversial. What about a bodyguard—he's young, he's tough—who's supposed to protect a famous movie actress? Someone who reminds us of Marilyn Monroe. Secretly he's in love with her, but he can't bring himself to tell her. And she dies from an overdose of sleeping pills. The cops say it's suicide. The newspapers go along. But the bodyguard can't believe she killed herself. He discovers evidence that it was murder. He gets pissed at the coverup. From grief, he investigates further. A hit team nearly kills him. Now he's twice as pissed. And what he learns is that the man who ordered the murder—it's an election year, the actress was writing a tell-it-all about her famous lovers—is the President of the United States."

"I think"—he sipped his beer—"it would play in Oklahoma."

"And Chicago and New York. It's a backlash about big government. With a sympathetic hero."

He chuckled. "When do we start?"

And that's how we made the deal on *Grievance.*

I felt excited all evening, but later—after we'd had a pleasant supper and Wes had driven off on his motorcycle—Jill stuck a pin in my swollen optimism.

"What he said about Oklahoma, about his father running away, his mother becoming a drunk and dying from cancer, about his going to a foster home . . ."

"I noticed it bothered you."

"You bet. You're so busy staring at your keyboard that you don't keep up on the handouts about your star."

I set down the bowl I'd taken from the dryer. "So?"

"Wes comes from Indiana. He's a foundling, raised in an orphanage. The background he gave you isn't his."

"Then whose . . . ?"

Jill stared at me.

"My God, not Deacon's."

So there is was, like a hideous face popping out of a box to leer at me. Wes's physical resemblance to Deacon was accidental, an act of fate that turned out to be a godsend for him. But the rest—the mannerisms, the clothes, the voice—were truly deliberate. I know what you're thinking—I'm contradicting myself. When I first met him, I thought that his style was too natural to be a conscious imitation. And when I realized that his screen test was identical in every respect to Deacon's hayloft scene in *The Prodigal Son,* I didn't believe that Wes had callously reproduced the scene. The screen test felt too natural to be an imitation. It was a homage.

But now I knew better. Wes was imitating, all right. But chillingly, what Wes had done went beyond conventional imitation. He'd accomplished the ultimate goal of every method actor. He wasn't playing a part. He wasn't pretending to be Deacon. He actually *was* his model. He'd so immersed himself in a role which at the start was no doubt consciously performed that now he *was* the role. Wes Crane existed only in name. His background, his thoughts, his very identity, weren't his own anymore. They belonged to a dead man.

"What the hell is this?" I asked. *"The Three Faces of Eve? Sybil?"*

Jill looked at me nervously. "As long as it isn't *Psycho.*"

What was I to do? Tell Wes he needed help? Have a heart-to-heart and try to talk him out of his delusion? All we had was the one conversation to back up our theory, and anyway he wasn't dangerous. The opposite. His manners were impeccable. He always spoke softly, with humor. Besides, actors used all kinds of ways to psych themselves up. By nature, they're eccentric. The best thing to do, I thought, was wait and see. With another picture about to start, there wasn't any sense in making trouble. If his delusion became destructive. . . .

But he certainly wasn't difficult on the set. He showed up a half hour early for his scenes. He knew his lines. He spent several evenings and weekends—no charge—rehearsing with the other actors. Even the studio v.p. admitted that the dailies looked wonderful.

About the only sign of trouble was his mania for racing cars and motorcycles. The v.p. had a fit about the insurance premiums.

"Hey, he needs to let off steam," I said. "There's a lot of pressure on him."

And on me. I'll admit. I had a budget of eighteen million this time, and I wasn't going to ruin things by making my star self-conscious.

Halfway through the shooting schedule, Wes came over. "See, no pranks. I'm being good this time."

"Hey, I appreciate it." What the fuck did he mean by "this time"?

You're probably thinking that I could have stopped what happened if I'd cared more about him than I did for the picture. But I did care—as you'll see. And it didn't matter. What happened was as inevitable as a tragedy.

Grievance became an even bigger success than *Mercenaries*. A worldwide hundred and fifty million gross. *Variety* predicted an even bigger gross for the next one. Sure, the next one—number three. But at the back of my head, a nasty voice was telling me that for Deacon three had been the unlucky number.

I left a conference at the studio, walking toward my new Ferrari in the executive parking lot, when someone shouted my name. Turning, I peered through the Burbank smog at a longhaired, bearded man wearing beads, a serape, and sandals, running over to me. I wondered what he wore, if anything, beneath the dangling serape.

I recognized him—Donald Porter, the friend of Deacon who'd played a bit part in *Birthright* and imitated Deacon's voice on some of the soundtrack after Deacon had died. Porter had to be in his forties now, but he dressed as if the sixties had never ended and hippies still existed. He'd starred and directed in a hit youth film twenty years ago—a lot of drugs and rock and sex. For a while, he'd tried to start his own studio in Santa Fe, but the second picture he directed was a flop, and after fading from the business for a while, he'd made a comeback as a character actor. The way he was dressed, I didn't understand how he'd passed the security guard at the gate. And because we knew each other—I'd done a rewrite on a television show he was featured in—I had the terrible feeling that he was going to ask me for a job.

"I heard you were on the lot. I've been waiting for you," he said.

I stared at his bare legs beneath his serape.

"*This,* man?" He gestured comically at himself. "I'm in the new TV movie they're shooting here. *The Electric Kool-Aid Acid Test.*"

I nodded. "Tom Wolfe's book. Ken Kesey. Don't tell me you're playing—"

"No. Too old for Kesey. I'm Neal Cassidy. After he split from Kerouac, he joined up with Kesey, driving the bus for the Merry Pranksters. You know, it's all a load of crap, man. Cassidy never dressed like this. He dressed like Deacon. Or Deacon dressed like him."

"Well, good. Hey, great. I'm glad things are going well for you." I turned toward my Ferrari.

"Just a second, man. That's not what I wanted to talk to you about. Wes Crane. You know?"

"No, I—"

"Deacon, man. Come on. Don't tell me you haven't noticed. Shit, man. I dubbed Deacon's voice. I knew him. I was his *friend.* Nobody else knew him better. Crane sounds more like Deacon than I did."

"So?"

"It isn't possible."

"Because he's better?"

"Cruel, man. Really. Beneath you. I have to tell you something. I don't want you thinking I'm on drugs again. I swear I'm clean. A little grass. That's it." His eyes looked as bright as a nova. "I'm into horoscopes. Astrology. The stars. That's a good thing for a movie actor, don't you think? The stars. There's a lot of truth in the stars."

"Whatever turns you on."

"You think so, man? Well, listen to this. I wanted to see for myself, so I found out where he lives, but I didn't go out there. Want to know why?" He didn't let me answer. "I didn't have to. 'Cause I recognized the address. I've been there a hundred times. When Deacon lived there."

I flinched. "You're changing the subject. What's that got to do with horoscopes and astrology?"

"Crane's birth date."

"Well?"

"It's the same as the day Deacon died."

I realized I'd stopped breathing. "So what?"

"More shit, man. Don't pretend it's coincidence. It's in the stars. You know what's coming. Crane's your bread and butter. But the gravy train'll end four months from now."

I didn't ask.

"Crane's birthday's coming up. The anniversary of Deacon's death."

And when I looked into it, there were other parallels. Wes would be twenty-three—Deacon's age when he died. And Wes would be close to the end of his third movie—about the same place in Deacon's third movie when he. . . .

We were doing a script I'd written, *Rampant,* about a young man from a tough neighborhood who comes back to teach there. A local street gang harasses him and his wife until the only way he can survive is by reverting to the violent life (he once led his own gang) that he ran away from.

It was Wes's idea to have the character renew his fascination with motorcycles. I have to admit that the notion had commercial value, given Wes's well-known passion for motorcycle racing. But I also felt apprehensive, especially when he insisted on doing his own stunts.

I couldn't talk him out of it. As if his model behavior on the first two pictures had been too great a strain on him, he snapped to the opposite extreme: showing up late, drinking on the set, playing expensive pranks. One joke involving fire crackers started a blaze in the costume trailer.

It all had the makings of a death wish. His absolute identification with Deacon was leading him to the ultimate parallel.

And just like Deacon in his final picture, Wes began to look wasted. Hollow-cheeked, squinty, stooped from lack of food and sleep. His dailies were shameful.

"How the hell are we supposed to ask an audience to pay to see this shit?" the studio v.p. asked.

"I'll have to shoot around him. Cut to reaction shots from the characters he's talking to." My heart lurched.

"That sounds familiar," Jill said beside me.

I knew what she meant. I'd become the director I'd criticized on *Broken Promises.*

"Well, can't you control him?" the v.p. asked.

"It's hard. He's not quite himself these days."

"Dammit, if you can't, maybe another director can. This garbage is costing us twenty million bucks."

The threat made me seeth. I almost told him to take his twenty million bucks and—

Abruptly I understood the leverage he'd given me. I straightened. "Relax. Just let me have a week. If he hasn't improved by then, I'll back out gladly."

"Witnesses heard you say it. One week, pal, or else."

In the morning, I waited for Wes in his trailer when as usual he showed up late for his first shot.

At the open trailer door, he had trouble focusing on me. "If it isn't teach." He shook his head. "No, wrong. It's me who's supposed to play the teach in—what's the name of this garbage we're making?"

"Wes, I want to talk to you."

"Hey, funny thing. The same goes for me with you. Just give me a chance to grab a beer, okay?" Fumbling, he shut the trailer door behind him and lurched through shadows toward the miniature fridge.

"Try to keep your head clear. This is important," I said.

"Right. Sure." He popped the tab on a beer can and left the fridge door open while he drank. He wiped his mouth. "But first I want a favor."

"That depends."

"I don't have to ask, you know. I can just go ahead and do it. I'm trying to be polite."

"What is it?"

"Monday's my birthday. I want the day off. There's a motorcycle race up near Sonora. I want to make a long weekend out of it." He drank more beer.

"We had an agreement once."

He scowled. Beer dribbled down his chin.

"I write and direct. You star. Both of us, or none."

"Yeah. So? I've kept the bargain."

"The studio's given me a week. To shape you up. If not, I'm out of the project."

He sneered. "I'll tell them I don't work if you don't."

"Not that simple, Wes. At the moment, they're not that

eager to do what you want. You're losing your clout. Remember why you liked us as a team?"

He listed bleerily.

"Because you wanted a friend. To keep you from making what you called the same mistakes again. To keep you from fucking up. Well, Wes, that's what you're doing. Fucking up."

He finished his beer and crumbled the can. He curled his lips, angry. "Because I want a day off on my birthday?"

"No, because you're getting your roles confused. You're not James Deacon. But you've convinced yourself that you are, and Monday you'll die in a crash."

He blinked. Then he sneered. "So what are you, a fortune teller now?"

"A half-baked psychiatrist. Unconsciously, you want to complete the legend. The way you've been acting, the parallel's too exact."

"I told you the first time we met—I don't like bullshit!"

"Then prove it. Monday, you don't go near a motorcycle, a car, hell even a go-cart. You come to the studio sober. You do your work as well as you know how. I drive you over to my place. We have a private party. You and me and Jill. She promises to make your favorite meal. Homemade birthday cake. The works. You stay the night. In the morning, we put James Deacon behind us and—"

"Yeah? What?"

"You achieve the career Deacon never had."

His eyes looked uncertain.

"Or you go to the race and destroy yourself and break the promise you made. You and me together. A team. Don't back out of our bargain."

He shuddered as if he was going to crack.

In a movie, that would have been the climax—how he didn't race on his birthday, how he had the private party, and he hardly said a word and went to sleep in our guest room.

And survived.

But this is what happened. On the Tuesday after his birthday, he couldn't remember his lines. He couldn't play to the camera. He couldn't control his voice. Wednesday was worse.

But I'll say this. On his birthday, the anniversary of Deacon's death, when Wes showed up sober and treated our bargain with honor, he did the most brilliant acting of his career. A zenith of tradecraft. I often watch the video of those scenes with profound respect.

And the dailies were so truly brilliant that the studio v.p. let me finish the picture.

But the v.p. never knew how I faked the rest of it. Overnight, Wes had totally lost his technique. I had enough in the can to deliver a print—with a lot of fancy editing and some uncredited but very expensive help from Donald Porter. He dubbed most of Wes's final dialogue.

"I told you. Horoscopes. Astrology," Donald said.

I didn't believe him till I took four scenes to an audio expert I know. He specializes in voice prints.

He spread the graphs in front of me. "Somebody played a joke on you. Or else you're playing one on me."

I felt so unsteady that I had to press my hands on his desk when I asked him, "How?"

"Using Deacon's scene from *The Prodigal Son* as the standard, this other film is close. But this third one doesn't have any resemblance."

"So where's the joke?"

"In the fourth. It matches perfectly. Who's kidding who?"

Donald Porter had been the voice on the second clip. Close to Deacon's, dubbing for Wes in *Rampant*. Wes himself had been the voice on the third clip—the dialogue in *Rampant* that I couldn't use because he didn't sound like Deacon at all.

And the fourth clip? The voice that was identical to Deacon's, authenticated, verifiable. Wes again. His screen test. The imitated scene from *The Prodigal Son.*

So what's the bottom line?

Wes dropped out of sight. For sure, his technique had collapsed so badly that he would never again be a shining star.

I began to hear rumors, though. So for a final time I drove out to his dingy place near the desert. The Manson lookalikes were gone. Only one motorcycle stood outside. I climbed the steps to the sun porch, knocked, received no answer, and opened the door.

The blinds were closed. The place was in shadow. I went down a hall and heard strained breathing. Turned to the right. And entered a room.

The breathing was louder, more strident and forced.

"Wes?"

"Don't turn on the lights."

"I've been worried about you, friend."

"Don't—"

But I did. And what I saw made me swallow vomit.

He was slumped in a chair. Seeping into it would be more accurate. Rotting. Decomposing. His cheeks had holes that showed his teeth. A pool that stank of leaking potatoes spread on the floor around him.

"I should have gone racing on my birthday, huh?" His voice whistled through the gaping flesh in his throat.

"Oh, shit, friend." I started to cry. "Jesus Christ, I should have let you."

"Do me a favor, huh? Turn off the light now. Let me finish this in peace."

I had so much to say to him. But I couldn't. My heart broke.

"And buddy," he said, "I think we'd better forget about our bargain. We won't be working together anymore."

I stumbled out of there, blinded by the sun, unable to clear my nostrils of the stench. I threw up beside the car.

And this is how it ended, the final dregs of his career. His talent was gone, but how his determination lingered.

Movies. Immortality.

See, special effects are expensive. Studios will grasp at any means to cut the cost.

He'd told me, "Forget about our bargain." I later found out what he meant—he worked without me in one final feature. He wasn't listed in the credits, though. *Zombies from Hell.* Remember how awful Bela Lugosi looked in his last exploitation movie before they buried him in his Dracula cape?

Bela looked great compared to Wes. I saw the Zombie

movie in a four-plex out in the valley. It did great business. Jill and I almost didn't get a seat.

Jill wept as I did.

This fucking town. Nobody cares how it's done, as long as it packs them in.

The audience cheered when Wes stalked toward the leading lady.

And his jaw fell off.

The creator of the famous Rambo, David Morrell was born in Ottawa, Canada, in 1943. Educated at the University of Waterloo and Pennsylvania State University, he is currently Professor of American Literature at the University of Iowa. His first novel, First Blood, *was followed by other Rambo novels as well as a suspense trilogy,* The Brotherhood of the Rose, The Fraternity of the Stone, *and* The League of Night and Fog. *His shorter works often deal with the darkness of the supernatural, such as "But at My Back I Will Always Hear," included in* Ghosts of the Heartland.

Lud agreed to check out the rumors that Maggie Marable's house was haunted because he needed the money. He never realized that a ghost could have so much to offer.

FOUR

House of Secrets

Ron Goulart

The charges brought against him were somewhat unusual. They included assaulting a mystic and attempting to dig up a rock star's basement. Things could've been worse, though, since Lud Jardinian had also been planning to blackmail a former president of the United States. But that didn't work out.

Lud was a lean, dark man, thirty-seven years old and two and a half inches shorter than he wanted to be. He was supposedly a television and motion picture scriptwriter, although he hadn't had any assignments for seventeen months. Since neither his wife nor his main lady friend wanted anything to do with him at the moment, he was living in a rented cottage in a weedy part of Westwood. The day he realized he was two months behind on his rent and most of his bills, Lud decided to visit his oldest friend in Hollywood.

That was why he had been sitting in the executive waiting room at the Monogram-International Pictures studios out in Burbank two weeks ago. It was a fuzzy Tuesday afternoon, and Lud had watched it wane and gradually approach twilight from a stiff metal and leather chair.

He shifted his weight again, causing many of his more important bones to make weary creaking sounds.

The incredibly lovely blonde receptionist smiled sympathetically. "Mr. Erdlatz ought to be able to see you any minute now."

"It'll be an honor."

"He's quite busy."

"I've been able to deduce that during my stay here."

After rearranging a small stack of memos, the receptionist said, "I understand you and Mr. Erdlatz have been friends since college days."

"Chums," agreed Lud.

"You were in the same fraternity at USC?"

Nodding, he said, "We were frat brothers, yes. We shared many a good time. And Kane also shared my car, several of my women, most of my part-time income, and a goodly portion of my allowance from home."

She smiled. "I went to business college."

"That's not as much fun," Lud told her. "For real fun, you need a buddy like Kane Erdlatz and a college such—"

"Of course, of course. Sitting here bitching and moaning." The large, sun-brown blond man who'd opened the door to the right of the receptionist's desk was gazing out. "What else would you—"

"Helps while away the hours." Lud stood, not holding out his hand.

Kane Erdlatz jerked a thumb at his immense office. "C'mon in," he invited. "Hold my calls, Elana."

"You can't categorize it as a fall from grace." Erdlatz was behind his large, silvery desk, tapping his fingers on a scattering of magazines. "Since you were never that high on the ladder to begin with, Lud. But to end up writing articles for mags like *Naked People, Disgusting,* and *Hots* is to have betrayed what little early promise you did have. Cheap girlie mags published in places like Glendale and—"

"*Disgusting* is a humor magazine."

"And to sign your own name to this stuff is—"

"Kane, I need some kind of job. Since you're now head of Monogram, I was hoping you—"

"It isn't hope that wins ball games. You—"

"They're going to toss me in the street if I don't come up with the rent by—"

"Where've you been living since your wife booted you out?"

"Westwood. I have a small yet palatial—"

"Well, nobody pays much attention to what happens in

Westwood. So when you do get thrown into the street, nobody will even notice or—"

"You just signed Coke Dakers to a multipicture contract," cut in Lud, rising some out of his deep, wide chair. "One of the hottest rock stars in America, and he's going to do his first feature film for you. When I was over at Alch Films, I scripted *Study Hall, Final Exam, Study Hall II,* and—"

"Turkeys all," remarked Erdlatz. "I heard the Civil Defense people were considering using *Study Hall II* as a surefire way to evacuate towns in case of—"

"I can write down a damn good script with adolescent angst and—"

"Because you never grew up. Mentally, you're still in the acne stage." He patted the top of his desk, located a pale blue memo, and held it up. "Here's something that pays a thousand . . . make that twelve hundred, for old times' sake . . . per week."

"For how many weeks?"

"Two."

"That's not enough time to write a—"

"There's nothing for you here in the writing end."

"But what about the Coke Dakers movie?"

"Deal's all set. We got, and were darn lucky to snag him, Elroy Flurch to write it."

"Never heard of him. What are his credits?"

"So far none, but he understands youth. Which he ought to, since he's just fourteen."

After making a small strangled sound, Lud inquired, "About this twelve-hundred-a-week job?"

Rubbing the memo slip across his chin, Erdlatz said, "Many talented people are superstitious."

"I know that, yes."

"One such is Coke Dakers," he went on. "He feels especially uneasy about ghosts."

Lud straightened up. "Wait now, I heard he was going to buy Maggie Marable's old mansion, that enormous Moorish place in Beverly Hills where she carried on with statesmen, literary lights, and show business luminaries before—"

"It's also where she killed herself some thirteen years ago."

75

"That's a long time, especially in Hollywood. Coke Dakers doesn't believe that her ghost is still haunting—"

"He's heard rumors," said Erdlatz. "Rumors helped along by the fact that the last tenant—some weenie who made two hot karate movies in 1980—ran screaming from the place one evening and never returned."

"When was that?"

"Three years ago, and no one has lived there since. Coke is getting the place for a hell of a price—just $900,000."

"But he's afraid to move in?"

"He'd prefer to have someone test the waters first."

"They do something similar to this in India, to catch wild tigers."

Erdlatz said, "Look, you live in the mansion for two weeks. Check everything out; see if it's haunted or not. You make yourself $2,400, a lot more than *Naked People* pays you for compromising what few—"

"You've never been at all charitable. So this isn't some idea you came up with to slip me money."

"It's exactly what I'm telling you it is," said the tanned movie executive. "Coke is very anxious to move in. He's going to be living with Mintzy Whyte-Melville soon as she gets back from Montreal."

"What's she doing there?"

"Shooting *Chicago*."

Shaking his head slowly, Lud said, "I don't know. This sounds like some dumb comic book story I read as a kid. Something from an issue of *House of Secrets* or *House of Mystery*. Spend-a-night-in-the-old-dark-house stuff."

"Except, the pay is better."

"In the stories, the nitwit who does it ends up either stone-cold dead the next morning, or they find him wandering the moors, baying like a loon, with his hair turned to silver."

"You're practically a loon now, and there isn't all that much hair to worry about." Erdlatz fluttered the memo. "So?"

"Half the money in front?"

"A third."

"Done," said Lud.

*   *   *

A chill rain and a harsh wind attacked Lud as he ran from his five-year-old Toyota along the gravel drive toward the wide oaken front door of the gray Moorish-style mansion. The wind wrenched one of the red tiles off the slanting roof, sent it hurtling down to smack into his only usable suitcase.

Huddled on the red tile porch, Lud fished out the door key. Erdlatz had attached a little tag to it that read *Haunted House.*

"Whimsy." After about a minute of struggle, he got the door unlocked.

Creaking impressively, the thick old door swung inward at his push. He stumbled across the threshold out of the rain-swept night.

Dropping his suitcase next to a heavy redwood table, he reached out and turned on all the light switches—six of them—available.

Orange bulbs in gnarled wrought-iron holders blossomed on the pale peach stucco walls of the long hallway. More dusty light came on in the wrought iron chandelier dangling midway along the corridor.

The house smelled of dust, old smoke, and mildew.

Taking a careful deep breath, Lud picked up his rain-spattered suitcase and carried it along the hall into the main living room.

Four more black light switches here. There were still Navajo rugs on the hardwood floor, as well as a low black leather sofa and two matching armchairs. The stone fireplace was deep and shadowy; rain was coming down it to splatter a mound of very old ashes.

Putting his suitcase down on the dusty hearth, Lud began a slow circuit of the large, chill room.

"Yike!"

The phone on the tile and wrought-iron coffee table had commenced ringing.

After another deep breath, he answered it. "Hello?"

"What sort of dippy phone number is this?"

"Beverly Hills. I'm sort of house-sitting as a favor to—"

"I know it's Beverly Hills. Isn't it my business to know things like that? Don't millions of people across the country read my syndicated 'Hollywood Dirt' column in 463 newspapers because I know all—"

"Pearl, the reason I tried to call you earlier is—"

"That's another thing. I was just starting to live down the fact I'm married to you. We've been separated a year and a half; people are starting to forget. But then you tell my service to have me call my husband at this mysterious dippy number in Beverly Hills, and it looks—"

"Pearl, I need a little help from you about—"

"No, nope, absolutely not. I won't loan you another dollar," said his estranged wife in that voice he had, somehow, once found charming. "Well, wait a minute. If you happen to be dying of an incurable disease and could swear to me—actually, a notarized statement would be better—could assure me you have only weeks to live—days would be better—then I might loan you up to two hundred dollars. And I'll see you to a headstone. A small one."

"I'm not dying, Pearl."

"And what other bad news do you have for me? I have a dinner date, two screenings, and an assignation on for tonight, so—"

"Maggie Marable," he managed to put in.

"Hum?"

"It's her house I'm sitting."

His wife's voice gentled. "Oh, so? I sense a story here."

"Not yet."

"What do you mean 'not yet'? You have to give me what you have ahead of any other—"

"Eventually, sure. Now, though, Pearl, just attend to me for a moment. The reason—"

"There you go again, Lud. Pulling your my-wife-never-listens-to-me act. Honestly, that's the dippiest—"

"Coke Dakers has bought the Maggie Marable place here, and I—"

"I know that. It was in my column last Tuesday, and if you read it regularly, you wouldn't be so—"

"Dakers has the notion the mansion is haunted."

"Everybody's heard that dippy rumor. It's nothing but publicity crap, started by her washed-up agent to—"

"I'm supposed to live here for a couple weeks, see if a ghost or a demon or anything else is in residence."

"That might make an interesting item. Fifty, sixty words about—"

"What I wanted from you was a little background on Maggie Marable. Her career, her romances," said Lud. "And the reason for her suicide."

"It may not've been suicide."

"Meaning?"

"I'll have Jody send you some material on MM," promised his wife. "Meanwhile, call me if you get anything else on what Coke is—"

"I don't even know him. This job—"

"And if you do see a ghost, tell me before you tell anybody. Get pictures, but use something better than that clunky camera you—"

"I don't intend to see ghosts," he told her. "The reason I want to know something more about Maggie Marable is so I can carry on intelligent conversations with Kane Erdlatz and whoever else asks me about—"

"Right now I have to go. Jody'll send you the stuff. Bye."

He hung up.

The rain was coming down harder, and there was a new smell in the room.

"Perfume," said Lud, sniffing.

He decided he wasn't going to let that unsettle him.

Lud didn't have a real encounter until his third midnight. He'd been sitting up in the big four-poster bed, reading through the fat folder of material on Maggie Marable that his wife had sent over by messenger that afternoon.

"Andrew Willis, too?" he was murmuring. "Did I know that about her? He was Senator Willis then, didn't become president until after she was dead. Interesting."

Rain returned a few minutes shy of twelve, a light rain hitting gently on the tile roof.

Yawning, Lud slumped, his head sinking into the pillow. The folder shut, dropped to his lap with his forefinger making a marker.

He always slept in pajama tops only. Now, as he drifted closer into sleep, Lud became aware of a warmth growing along his bare left leg.

Blinking, he glanced over to his left and then sat up again. "Pearl, would that be you?"

There was a woman under the covers next to him. Body

and head hidden by the pale blue comforter. But that backside wasn't familiar, wasn't his wife's. Pearl's was much sparser.

"Pardon me, miss." He reached toward the covered figure stretched out beside him. "I don't know how you sneaked in here, but—"

When he tried to tap her on the shoulder, the blanket all at once collapsed. He was patting nothing but firm mattress.

"Yow!" he remarked. He leaped free of the wide bed, sending the gossip file on Maggie Marable spinning into the air and scattering its pages.

He didn't get quite clear of the satin sheets, and he fell on one knee to the floor. After sliding on a throw rug, he came to a stop against the louvered door of the wide wardrobe closet.

"Her." He eyed the now seemingly empty bed. "That was her. Maggie Marable. Sure, I should've recognized her body right off."

He walked, slowly and backward, out of there. The sofa in the living room wasn't comfortable at all. He stayed stretched out on it for all the drizzling, restless night.

The next night she talked to him.

That happened in the large, white, beam-ceilinged kitchen. He was dawdling in there, brewing some hot cocoa in hopes it'd ease his second night on the grim sofa. In addition to cocoa, he spooned in some Ovaltine he'd located at the back of a pantry shelf. Long ago, in his youth, his mother had come close to convincing him Ovaltine helped you sleep. For good measure, he was going to add rum from the pint he'd bought in a liquor store down on the Strip that afternoon.

Lud was watching the milk in the saucepan, wearing a candy-striped apron he'd uncovered in the broom closet.

"Hey, you can help me."

He turned away from the milk to stare at the dark doorway into the hall. There was no sign of anyone.

"Otherwise I'm doomed to roam this dump forever. And that's really very boring," said the voice that was coming from out in the hall. "It's a drag. Or do people still say things are a drag? I'm sort of out of touch."

80

"Most people don't, I guess," he replied in a thin voice that sounded much more youthful than usual.

"Most of the schmucks who've lived here run off before I ever got to explain what I want."

Lud asked, "Are you going to come in here?"

"Not tonight. It's a real strain to materialize, and I'm going to save that until tomorrow, probably."

"Good, fine."

"The other problem is that, you know, I can communicate for only a few minutes each night. So, please, don't be a putz and go screaming into the night. O.K.?"

"How exactly can I help you, Miss Marable?" He had no doubt that this was the ghost of Maggie Marable he was chatting with.

"Call me Maggie. And you're . . . ?"

"Lud Jardinian."

"That's an Armenian name."

"My father's Armenian, yes."

"O.K., enough small talk. Here's the situation; pay attention. Since I was murdered, I have to haunt this dump until—"

"Murdered?"

Only silence from the long, dark hallway.

"Did you say you'd been murdered, Miss Marable? Maggie?"

There was no response.

It took him approximately three minutes to walk from the stove to the open doorway.

He did some complicated breathing before thrusting his head out into the hall.

It was empty, although a strong, musky perfume lingered.

He was sitting in the living room late the next afternoon, once again going over the notes Pearl had provided.

"Andrew Willis seems the most likely suspect," he said to himself. "Married, considering a presidential run. Is that the way things work in real life, though? Sure, in a script the most likely suspect always turns out to be completely innocent, unless you're going to pull a switch and—"

The phone rang, and he answered it.

"That skinny bitch," said the voice of Kane Erdlatz.

"Which skinny bitch?"

"Your wife, Pearl Seabride. Don't you see 'Hollywood Dirt' every day?"

"I skip now and then. What exactly—"

"She's got an item about Coke. Says he's afraid of ghosts, fearful of moving into his new house."

"Oh, so?"

"Did you happen to mention this new assignment of yours to that underfed bimbo or—"

"She's still my wife. Naturally, I'm going to share my triumphs and my—"

"Coke is ticked off; this hurts his image."

"Lots of people have faith in the spirit world. Admitting a belief in spooks may well improve his—"

"The guy I'm going to star in *Slaughter's Revenge* can't admit to being afraid of anything," Erdlatz pointed out. "He's extremely unhappy."

"Suffering is good for artists, helps them to—"

"Coke's going to do something drastic if I don't get the guy calmed down. If, for instance, I could assure him that you haven't encountered so much as a hint of a ghost during your lengthy and expensive stay there, that'd help."

Lud didn't immediately reply.

"Old buddy?"

"I haven't exactly encountered anything," Lud lied. "But I do sense something. Tell you what: when my two weeks are up, I'm sure I'll be able to give the mansion a clean bill of health. Just don't want to commit myself right at the—"

"You may not have two weeks. Coke's damn uneasy about that item in your skinny wife's column, and he may try to—"

"Pearl is slender. When you earn as much as she does, you can't be classed as skinny. Only poor people are—"

"Get some results," advised Erdlatz, and hung up.

Lud put down the phone, then went trotting upstairs to the master bedroom.

Halting next to the big bed, he glanced around. "Maggie," he said aloud. "I may get tossed out of here anytime now. So if there's, you know, anything you'd like to tell me from the great beyond . . . well, the sooner the better."

He paused, shoulders hunched.
Nothing occurred.

A minute shy of midnight, he saw her at last.
He was in the kitchen, making cocoa.
"Are you dumb or what? A writer, you sure ought to know ghosts can communicate only at the witching hour." The pretty blonde young woman was framed in the doorway, wearing what appeared to be a simple black cocktail dress.
"That's a nice dress."
"It's the dumb thing my agent had me buried in," Maggie Marable said. "For some reason, don't ask me why, I always have it on when I materialize. Personally, I'd like to have a little more variety in my wardr—"
"It's nice meeting you, finally. I was a great fan of your movies, especially *The Naked Gun* and *Which Blonde Has the—*"
"Listen, I don't have all that much time. Go easy on the gush."
He nodded. "Right, you better tell me about your murder."
"You're really married to that skinny gossip columnist, huh?"
"Slender, and we're separated. Who exactly did you in?"
"It was Andy."
"Andrew Willis?"
"Him, yes." The dead actress took a step into the kitchen. "Who would've thought? I know I nagged him a lot, urged him to leave that dim-witted wife of his—funny how many otherwise rational men marry dimwits. I made what was, in retrospect, a dumb move. Threatened to make our affair public if he didn't dump her. A politician like Andy—"
"That wasn't wise, since he was getting ready about then to run for—"
"Don't I know it wasn't wise, Lud?" She pointed a thumb at her chest. "He slipped a couple dozen sleeping pills in my scotch, and—bam!—I go to sleep and wake up in glory. And I'm not even a full-fledged citizen of the hereafter, be-

cause they have this dim-witted rule that every spirit has to avenge his or her murder before being—"

"To do a really efficient job of avenging you, Maggie, we'll have to have proof of what Willis did."

"I don't actually have any proof that he doped my drink. Once I got on the other side, of course, I heard him talking about it to one of his associates. That, though, is only hearsay evidence."

"You've kept up with politics, haven't you? Andrew Willis was president. Two terms. Before we can accuse a former president of the United—"

"I know damn well that bastard was president of the country. When you're doomed to roam this level of existence, you watch a lot of television. Not that I much like the dimwit who's in office now, but nobody made duller speeches than Andy. He could—Hey! My diaries."

"Hum?" He eased closer to her.

"I kept a journal, ever since I was a gawky kid back in Iola, Wisconsin," explained the spectral actress. "Some of the later entries are pretty steamy. I mentioned Andy a lot."

"That wouldn't prove Willis did you in, but it would sure link him to you. From there we—"

"I recall writing down a few of the arguments we had, some of the threats he made."

"Where are these diaries?"

"I hid them here in this damn house, hid them well enough so that nobody would be able to find them."

"Fine, then just tell me where you—Maggie?"

She was grimacing, bending slightly and clutching at her midsection. "We have to wait until my next—"

"Where are they?"

She pointed at the floor. "You have to go down into. . . ."

Then she wasn't with him.

Her image snapped away, and he was alone.

"Maggie?"

Completely alone.

The sunlight glared off the ocean. Pearl, standing near the wide window of the studio in her beachfront house, was outlined in a harsh yellow-gold light. "Don't be a goon. Where are the damn books?"

"I'll find out tonight," Lud assured her. "What I want to know from you is, what would those diaries of hers be worth?"

"Maggie Marable's love diaries? One hell of a lot. Millions." His wife turned her back on the bright afternoon Pacific. "First off, we auction the book rights and get all those dorks in Manhattan fighting over them. I can sell the newspaper rights to my syndicate for a whole enormous stewpot of dough. There's also a movie in them, a TV special, a Broadway play. Hell, and that's only the start."

"We," he corrected. "*We* can sell them."

"That's what I meant, Lud."

"What about President Willis?"

"He's not president any longer, so he can't—"

"He's back with his old law firm up in San Francisco. What I mean is—how close can we come to suggesting he murdered Maggie Marable?"

"Pretty close," his wife answered. "Once we have the diaries and can show she was fooling around with him—You're absolutely certain she didn't tell you where they were?"

He shook his head. "Nope, she was just coming to that part."

"O.K., tonight," decided Pearl. "I better come over to the mansion, too."

"No, you stick here. I've established a relationship with Maggie. Having a gossip columnist there would only futz it up."

"Me? Don't I interview the most aloof, the crankiest celebrities in the world and get them to open up, to blurt out their innermost secrets?"

"Ghosts are different."

His wife eyed him. "You wouldn't be contemplating swiping those diaries all for yourself?"

"I wanted your advice. Naturally, I'll share the profits with you."

"You may not be as big a dodo as I thought." Pearl smiled at him. "Why not stay for dinner?"

He lectured himself during most of the long drive from the beach back to Beverly Hills.

"Dumb, exceedingly dumb," Lud said, checking his

watch yet again and discovering that midnight was almost upon him. "Not to mention gauche. Sleeping with your own wife. Worse, dawdling around her place so long you'll probably miss your meeting with Maggie tonight."

A light rain commenced as he began the climb up the final twisting, hilly road.

"And Pearl doesn't even trust you," he added. "Thinks you're going to keep the journals all to yourself."

He turned the windshield wipers on.

"During dinner she suggested that I was so low that I might even take the damn diaries and try to blackmail President Willis with them." He laughed disdainfully. "Her opinion of me is even lower than. . . . Matter of fact, he isn't president anymore. So if you did approach him, the Secret Service couldn't take a shot at you or anything. And the guy's a multimillionaire, isn't he? All the money he made from writing his memoirs—and he already had family money."

Driving through the wrought iron gates of the Maggie Marable estate, he headed for the garages.

"You could sell to Willis just the volumes that mentioned him—No, not even the volumes. Just his pages. Sure, and keep the rest of them for book publication and all the other perks you and Pearl were talking about tonight. Willis would pay—maybe a million to cover his reputation. That, plus all the book money, would—Hey!"

A battered pink van was parked right smack in front of the garages.

Hitting the brakes, he parked his car in the drive, turned off the ignition, and dived out into the rainy night.

It was now eleven minutes beyond midnight.

He tripped on the slippery tile steps, fell to his knees. Before he got up, the front door of the house opened.

A thickset man in a rumpled tan suit emerged. He was pink-faced, had crinkly gray sideburns, and his plastic-framed spectacles were patched with two Band-Aids. Clutched in his plump right hand was a very battered black attaché case.

"Shall I present you with the bill, good sir? Or simply mail it to Mr. Coke Dakers?"

"Bill for what?"

Reaching down with his free hand, the plump, pinkish man assisted Lud to rise. "My services."

"What kind of services could you have been performing at this ungodly hour?"

"Ah, good sir, this is exactly the right time for this sort of thing." Grunting, he reached inside his wrinkled coat and produced a folded sheet of yellow paper. "There's a charge for paraphernalia, of course. Incantations I throw in free, but my time I bill you at $150 an hour or any portion thereof."

An odd pungent odor was wafting out of the house. "What is it you do, exactly?"

"Forgive me, I haven't, good sir, introduced myself. Encountering you arse over teakettle on the stoop here quite robbed me of my manners, I fear," he said. "I am Abdul the Mystic. My business name, you understand."

"What did you do in there, Abdul?"

"Why, exorcised the uneasy spirit of Maggie Marable," he replied. "Only took me seven minutes, but I have to charge you for the full hour, because that's the way I—"

"Exorcised her? She's gone?"

"For all eternity. There's a warranty stamped at the bottom of the bill explaining that, for legal purposes, eternity is defined as—"

"Why in the hell did you do a half-witted thing like—"

"Mr. Dakers insisted. Since he'd been made a fool in the press, he vowed he must move in at once," explained Abdul the Mystic. "Since he didn't want to face a ghost, he did what he should have done at the offset, and hired a crackerjack exorcist."

"But she was going to tell me where . . . tell me something important."

"Ha, that must be what she was shrieking about just prior to my dispatching her off to her well-deserved eternal rest."

Lud took hold of the mystic by the shoulders. "What? What did she say?"

"Something about the basement, as I recall, but I didn't pay that much attention. On a job like this, I work solo, and keeping the sulfur burning and reciting all the spells call for a heck of a lot of concentra—"

"Think, Abdul."

"I fear that's all I remember, good sir." He waggled the sheet of yellow paper. "Perhaps I'd best leave this with you, since you're no doubt the custodian I was told would—"

"You half-wit. You've cost me millions, and now you want me to pay you $150 for—"

"Not $150. That's just my hourly wage. I also billed you for the sulfur, the—Oof!"

Lud whacked him over the skull several times with his own briefcase. As soon as Abdul the Mystic had dropped to the hall floor, Lud leaped over him and went stomping down into the basement.

"Maggie? Are you here at all?"

She didn't answer him.

He located a shovel and a pick in the chill, musty shadows. "That's what she must've meant. She buried the diaries down here someplace."

He was still in the basement, almost through the thick concrete, when Erdlatz and the police arrived two hours later.

Noted for his superb parody and the satirical bite of his humorous mysteries and science fiction, Rob Goulart sets many of his books in Hollywood. Born in California in 1933, he graduated from the University of California at Berkeley and worked as an advertising copywriter until 1968. His many series include those featuring Hollywood occult detective Max Kearny or private eye John Easy, a twelve-book continuation of the Avenger pulp novels, and science fiction series such as The Chameleon Corps and Other Shape Changers. *He has also written perceptive popular histories of comic strips and pulp fiction such as* The Dime Detectives.

Who but Cecil B. DeMille could direct the biggest epic of all time? If only he could get his Producer to listen to reason. . . .

FIVE

The Making of Revelation, Part I

Philip José Farmer

God said, "Bring me Cecil B. DeMille."

"Dead or alive?" the angel Gabriel said.

"I want to make him an offer he can't refuse. Can even *I* do this to a dead man?"

"Oh, I see," said Gabriel, who didn't. "It will be done."

And it was.

Cecil Blount DeMille, confused, stood in front of the desk. He didn't like it. He was used to sitting behind the desk while others stood. Considering the circumstances, he wasn't about to protest. The giant, divinely handsome, bearded, pipe-smoking man behind the desk was not one you'd screw around with. However, the gray eyes, though steely, weren't quite those of a Wall Street banker. They held a hint of compassion.

Unable to meet those eyes, DeMille looked at the angel by his side. He'd always thought angels had wings. This one didn't, though he could certainly fly. He'd carried DeMille in his arms up through the stratosphere to a city of gold somewhere between the Earth and the moon. Without a space suit, too.

God, like all great entities, came right to the point.

"This is 1980 A.D. In twenty years it'll be time for The Millennium. The day of judgment. The events as depicted in the Book of Revelation or the Apocalypse by St. John the Divine. You know, the seven seals, the four horsemen, the moon dripping blood, Armageddon, and all that."

DeMille wished he'd be invited to sit down. Being dead

89

for twenty-one years, during which he'd not moved a muscle, had tended to weaken him.

"Take a chair," God said. "Gabe, bring the man a brandy." He puffed on his pipe; tiny lightning crackled through the clouds of smoke.

"Here you are, Mr. DeMille," Gabriel said, handing him the liqueur in a cut quartz goblet. "Napoleon 1880."

DeMille knew there wasn't any such thing as a one-hundred-year-old brandy, but he didn't argue. Anyway, the stuff certainly tasted like it was. They really lived up here.

God sighed, and he said, "The main trouble is that not many people really believe in Me any more. So My powers are not what they once were. The old gods, Zeus, Odin, all that bunch, lost their strength and just faded away, like old soldiers, when their worshippers ceased to believe in them.

"So, I just can't handle the end of the world by Myself any more. I need someone with experience, know-how, connections, and a reputation. Somebody people know really existed. You. Unless you know of somebody who's made more biblical epics than you have."

"That'll be the day," DeMille said. "But what about the unions? They really gave me a hard time, the commie bas . . . uh, so-and-so's. Are they as strong as ever?"

"You wouldn't believe their clout nowadays."

DeMille bit his lip, then said, "I want them dissolved. If I only got twenty years to produce this film, I can't be held up by a bunch of gold-brickers."

"No way," God said. "They'd all strike, and we can't afford any delays."

He looked at his big railroad watch. "We're going to be on a very tight schedule."

"Well, I don't know," DeMille said. "You can't get anything done with all their regulations, interunion jealousies, and the featherbedding. And the wages! It's no wonder it's so hard to show a profit. It's too much of a hassle!"

"I can always get D. W. Griffith."

DeMille's face turned red. "You want a grade-B production? No, no, that's all right! I'll do it, do it!"

God smiled and leaned back. "I thought so. By the way, you're not the producer, too; I am. My angels will be the executive producers. They haven't had much to do for several millennia, and the devil makes work for idle hands, you know. Haw, haw! You'll be the chief director, of course. But this is going to be quite a job. You'll have to have at least a hundred thousand assistant directors."

"But . . . that means training about 99,000 directors!"

"That's the least of our problems. Now you can see why I want to get things going immediately."

DeMille gripped the arms of the chair and said, weakly, "Who's going to finance this?"

God frowned. "That's another problem. My Antagonist has control of all the banks. If worse comes to worse, I could melt down the heavenly city and sell it. But the bottom of the gold market would drop all the way to hell. And I'd have to move to Beverly Hills. You wouldn't believe the smog there or the prices they're asking for houses.

"However, I think I can get the money. Leave that to Me."

The men who really owned the American banks sat at a long mahogany table in a huge room in a Manhattan sky-scraper. The Chairman of the Board sat at the head. He didn't have the horns, tail, and hooves which legend gave him. Nor did he have an odor of brimstone. More like Brut. He was devilishly handsome and the biggest and best-built man in the room. He looked like he could have been the chief of the angels and in fact once had been. His eyes were evil but no more so than the others at the table, bar one.

The exception, Raphael, sat at the other end of the table. The only detractions from his angelic appearance were his bloodshot eyes. His apartment on the West Side had paper-thin walls, and the swingers' party next door had kept him awake most of the night. Despite his fatigue, he'd been quite effective in presenting the offer from above.

Don Francisco "The Fixer" Fica drank a sixth glass of wine to up his courage, made the sign of the cross, most offensive to the Chairman, gulped, and spoke.

"I'm sorry, Signor, but that's the way the vote went. One hundred percent. It's a purely business proposition, legal, too, and there's no way we won't make a huge profit from it. We're gonna finance the movie, come hell or high water!"

Satan reared up from his chair and slammed a huge but well-manicured fist onto the table. Glasses of vino crashed over; plates half-filled with pasta and spaghetti rattled. All but Raphael paled.

"*Dio motarello! Lecaculi! Cacasotti! Non romperci i coglioni!* I'm the Chairman, and I say no, no, no!"

Fica looked at the other heads of the families. Mignotta, Fregna, Stronza, Loffa, Recchione, and Bocchino seemed scared, but each nodded the go-ahead at Fica.

"I'm indeed sorry that you don't see it our way," Fica said. "But I must ask for your resignation."

Only Raphael could meet The Big One's eyes, but business was business. Satan cursed and threatened. Nevertheless, he was stripped of all his shares of stock. He'd walked in the richest man in the world, and he stormed out penniless and an ex-member of the Organization.

Raphael caught up with him as he strode mumbling up Park Avenue.

"You're the father of lies," Raphael said, "so you can easily be a great success as an actor or politician. There's money in both fields. Fame, too. I suggest acting. You've got more friends in Hollywood than anywhere else."

"Are you nuts?" Satan snarled.

"No. Listen. I'm authorized to sign you up for the film on the end of the world. You'll be a lead, get top billing. You'll have to share it with The Son, but we can guarantee you a bigger dressing room than His. You'll be playing yourself, so it ought to be easy work."

Satan laughed so loudly that he cleared the sidewalks for two blocks. The Empire State Building swayed more than it should have in the wind.

"You and your Boss must think I'm pretty dumb! Without me the film's a flop. You're up a creek without a paddle. Why should I help you? If I do I end up at the bottom of a flaming pit forever. Bug off!"

Raphael shouted after him, "We can always get Roman Polanski!"

Raphael reported to God, who was taking His ease on His jasper and cornelian throne above which glowed a rainbow.

"He's right, Your Divinity. If he refuses to co-operate, the whole deal's off. No real Satan, no real Apocalypse."

God smiled. "We'll see."

Raphael wanted to ask Him what He had in mind. But an angel appeared with a request that God come to the special effects department. Its technicians were having trouble with the roll-up-the-sky-like-a-scroll machine.

"Schmucks!" God growled. "Do I have to do everything?"

Satan moved into a tenement on 121st Street and went on welfare. It wasn't a bad life, not for one who was used to hell. But two months later, his checks quit coming. There was no unemployment any more. Anyone who was capable of working but wouldn't was out of luck. What had happened was that Central Casting had hired everybody in the world as production workers, stars, bit players, or extras.

Meanwhile, all the advertising agencies in the world had spread the word, good or bad depending upon the viewpoint, that the Bible was true. If you weren't a Christian, and, what was worse, a sincere Christian, you were doomed to perdition.

Raphael shot up to Heaven again.

"My God, You wouldn't believe what's happening! The Christians are repenting of their sins and promising to be good forever and ever, amen! The Jews, Moslems, Hindus, Buddhists, scientologists, animists, you name them, are lining up at the baptismal fonts! What a mess! The atheists have converted, too, and all the communist and Marxian socialist governments have been overthrown!"

"That's nice," God said. "But I'll really believe in the sincerity of the Christian nations when they kick out their present administrations. Down to the local dogcatcher."

"They're doing it!" Raphael shouted. "But maybe You don't understand! This isn't the way things go in the Book of Revelation! We'll have to do some very extensive rewriting of the script! Unless You straighten things out!"

God seemed very calm. "The script? How's Ellison coming along with it?"

Of course, God knew everything that was happening, but He pretended sometimes that He didn't. It was His excuse for talking. Just issuing a command every once in a while made for long silences, sometimes lasting for centuries.

He had hired only science fiction writers to work on the

script since they were the only ones with imaginations big enough to handle the job. Besides, they weren't bothered by scientific impossibilities. God loved Ellison, the head writer, because he was the only human he'd met so far who wasn't afraid to argue with Him. Ellison was severely handicapped, however, because he wasn't allowed to use obscenities while in His presence.

"Ellison's going to have a hemorrhage when he finds out about the rewrites," Raphael said. "He gets screaming mad if anyone messes around with his scripts."

"I'll have him up for dinner," God said. "If he gets too obstreperous, I'll toss around a few lightning bolts. If he thinks he was burned before . . . Well!"

Raphael wanted to question God about the tampering with the book, but just then the head of Budgets came in. The angel beat it. God got very upset when He had to deal with money matters.

The head assistant director said, "We got a big problem now, Mr. DeMille. We can't have any Armageddon. Israel's willing to rent the site to us, but where are we going to get the forces of Gog and Magog to fight against the good guys? Everybody's converted. Nobody's willing to fight on the side of Antichrist and Satan. That means we've got to change the script again. I don't want to be the one to tell Ellison. . . ."

"Do I have to think of everything?" DeMille said. "It's no problem. Just hire actors to play the villains."

"I already thought of that. But they want a bonus. They say they might be persecuted just for *playing* the guys in the black hats. They call it the social-stigma bonus. But the guilds and the unions won't go for it. Equal pay for all extras or no movie and that's that."

DeMille sighed. "It won't make any difference anyway as long as we can't get Satan to play himself."

The assistant nodded. So far, they'd been shooting around the devil's scenes. But they couldn't put it off much longer.

DeMille stood up. "I have to watch the auditions for The Great Whore of Babylon."

The field of 100,000 candidates for the role had been narrowed to a hundred, but from what he'd heard none of these could play the part. They were all good Christians now, no matter what they'd been before, and they just didn't have their hearts in the role. DeMille had intended to cast his brand-new mistress, a starlet, a hot little number—if promises meant anything—100 percent right for the part. But just before they went to bed for the first time, he'd gotten a phone call.

"None of this hankypanky, C.B.," God had said. "You're now a devout worshipper of Me, one of the lost sheep that's found its way back to the fold. So get with it. Otherwise, back to Forest Lawn for you, and I use Griffith."

"But—but I'm Cecil B. DeMille! The rules are O.K. for the common people, but—"

"Throw that scarlet woman out! Shape up or ship out! If you marry her, fine! But remember, there'll be no more divorces!"

DeMille was glum. Eternity was going to be like living forever next door to the Board of Censors.

The next day, his secretary, very excited, buzzed him.

"Mr. DeMille! Satan's here! I don't have him for an appointment, but he says he's always had a long-standing one with you!"

Demoniac laughter bellowed through the intercom.

"C.B., my boy! I've changed my mind! I tried out anonymously for the part, but your shithead assistant said I wasn't the type for the role! So I've come to you! I can start work as soon as we sign the contract!"

The contract, however, was not the one the great director had in mind. Satan, smoking a big cigar, chuckling, cavorting, read the terms.

"And don't worry about signing in your blood. It's unsanitary. Just ink in your John Henry, and all's well that ends in hell."

"You get my soul," DeMille said weakly.

"It's not much of a bargain for me. But if you don't sign it, you won't get me. Without me, the movie's a bomb. Ask The Producer, He'll tell you how it is."

"I'll call Him now."

"No! Sign now, this very second, or I walk out forever!"
DeMille bowed his head, more in pain than in prayer.
"Now!"

DeMille wrote on the dotted line. There had never been any genuine indecision. After all, he was a film director.

After snickering Satan had left, DeMille punched a phone number. The circuits transmitted this to a station which beamed the pulses up to a satellite which transmitted these directly to the heavenly city. Somehow, he got a wrong number. He hung up quickly when Israfel, the angel of death, answered. The second attempt, he got through.

"Your Divinity, I suppose You know what I just did? It *was* the only way we could get him to play himself. You understand that, don't You?"

"Yes, but if you're thinking of breaking the contract or getting Me to do it for you, forget it. What kind of an image would I have if I did something unethical like that? But not to worry. He can't get his hooks into your soul until I say so."

Not to worry? DeMille thought. I'm the one who's going to hell, not Him.

"Speaking of hooks, let Me remind you of a clause in your contract with The Studio. If you *ever* fall from grace, and I'm not talking about that little bimbo you were going to make your mistress, you'll die. The Mafia isn't the only one that puts out a contract. *Capice?*"

DeMille, sweating and cold, hung up. In a sense, he was already in hell. All his life with no women except for one wife? It was bad enough to have no variety, but what if whoever he married cut him off, like one of his wives—what was her name?—had done?

Moreover, he couldn't get loaded out of his skull even to forget his marital woes. God, though not prohibiting booze in His Book, had said that moderation in strong liquor was required and no excuses. Well, maybe he could drink beer, however disgustingly plebeian that was.

He wasn't even happy with his work now. He just didn't get the respect he had in the old days. When he chewed out the camerapeople, the grips, the gaffers, the actors, they stormed back at him that he didn't have the proper Christian humility, he was too high and mighty, too arrogant. God would get him if he didn't watch his big fucking mouth.

This left him speechless and quivering. He'd always thought, and acted accordingly, that the director, not God, was God. He remembered telling Charlton Heston that when Heston, who after all was *only* Moses, had thrown a temper tantrum when he'd stepped in a pile of camel shit during the filming of *The Ten Commandments.*

Was there more to the making of the end-of-the-world than appeared on the surface? Had God seemingly forgiven everybody their sins and lack of faith but was subtly, even insidiously, making everybody pay by suffering? Had He forgiven but not forgotten? Or vice versa?

God marked even the fall of a sparrow, though why the sparrow, a notoriously obnoxious and dirty bird, should be significant in God's eye was beyond DeMille.

He had the uneasy feeling that everything wasn't as simple and as obvious as he'd thought when he'd been untimely ripped from the grave in a sort of Caesarean section and carried off like a nursing baby in Gabriel's arms to the office of The Ultimate Producer.

From the *Playboy* Interview feature, December, 1990.

Playboy: Mr. Satan, why did you decide to play yourself after all?

Satan: Damned if I know.

Playboy: The rumors are that you'll be required to wear clothes in the latter-day scenes but that you steadfastly refuse. Are these rumors true?

Satan: Yes indeed. Everybody knows I never wear clothes except when I want to appear among humans without attracting undue attention. If I wear clothes it'd be unrealistic. It'd be phony, though God knows there are enough fake things in this movie. The Producer says this is going to be a PG picture, not an X-rated. That's why I walked off the set the other day. My lawyers are negotiating with The Studio now about his. But you can bet your ass that I won't go back unless things go my way, the right way. After all, I am an artist, and I have my integrity. Tell me, if you had a prong this size, would you hide it?

Playboy: The Chicago cops would arrest me before I got a block from my pad. I don't know, though, if they'd charge me with indecent exposure or being careless with a natural resource.

Satan: They wouldn't dare arrest me. I got too much on the city administration.

Playboy: That's *some* whopper. But I thought angels were sexless. You are a fallen angel, aren't you?

Satan: You jerk! What kind of researcher are you? Right there in the Bible, Genesis 6:2, it says that the sons of God, that is, the angels, took the daughters of men as wives and had children by them. You think the kids were test tube babies? Also, you dunce, I refer you to Jude 7 where it's said that the angels, like the Sodomites, committed fornications and followed unnatural lusts.

Playboy: Whew! That brimstone! There's no need getting so hot under the collar, Mr. Satan. I only converted a few years ago. I haven't had much chance to read the Bible.

Satan: I read the Bible every day. All of it. I'm a speed-reader, you know.

Playboy: You read the Bible? (Pause). Hee, hee! Do you read it for the same reason W. C. Fields did when he was dying?

Satan: What's that?

Playboy: Looking for loopholes.

DeMille was in a satellite and supervising the camerapeople while they shot the takes from ten miles up. He didn't like at all the terrific pressure he was working under. There was no chance to shoot *every* scene three or four times to get the best angle. Or to reshoot if the actors blew their lines. And, oh, sweet Jesus, they were blowing them all over the world!

He mopped his bald head. "I don't care what The Producer says! We have to retake at least a thousand scenes. And we've a million miles of film to go yet!"

They were getting close to the end of the breaking-of-the-seven-seals sequences. The Lamb, played by The Producer's Son, had just broken the sixth seal. The violent worldwide earthquake had gone well. The sun-turning-black-as-a-funeral-pall had been a breeze. But the moon-all-red-as-blood had had some color problems. The rushes looked more like Colonel Sanders' orange juice than hemoglobin. In DeMille's opinion the stars-falling-to-earth-like-figs-shaken-down-by-a-gale scenes had been excellent, visually speaking. But everybody knew that the stars were not little blazing stones set in the sky but were colossal balls of atomic fires each of which was many times bigger than Earth. Even one of them, a million miles from Earth, would destroy it. So where was the credibility factor?

"I don't understand you, boss," DeMille's assistant said. "You didn't worry about credibility when you made *The Ten Commandments.* When Heston, I mean, Moses, parted the Red Sea, it was the fakiest thing I ever saw. It must've made unbelievers out of millions of Christians. But the film was a box-office success."

"It was the dancing girls that brought off the whole thing!" DeMille screamed. "Who cares about all that other bullshit when they can see all those beautiful long-legged snatches twirling their veils!"

His secretary floated from her chair. "I quit, you male chauvinistic pig! So me and my sisters are just snatches to you, you bald-headed cunt?"

His hotline to the heavenly city rang. He picked up the phone.

"Watch your language!" The Producer thundered. "If you step out of line too many times, I'll send you back to the grave! And Satan gets you right then and there!"

Chastened but boiling near the danger point, DeMille got back to business, called Art in Hollywood. The sweep of the satellite around Earth included the sky-vanishing-as-a-scroll-is-rolled-up scenes, where every-mountain-and-island-is-removed-from-its-place. If the script had called for a literal removing, the tectonics problem would have been terrific and perhaps impossible. But in this case the special effects departments only had to simulate the scenes.

Even so, the budget was strained. However, The Producer, through his unique abilities, was able to carry these off. Whereas, in the original script, genuine displacements of Greenland, England, Ireland, Japan, and Madagascar had been called for, not to mention thousands of smaller islands, these were only faked.

"Your Divinity, I have some bad news," Raphael said.

The Producer was too busy to indulge in talking about something he already knew. Millions of the faithful had backslid and taken up their old sinful ways. They believed that since so many events of the Apocalypse were being faked, God must not be capable of making any really big catastrophes. So, they didn't have anything to worry about.

The Producer, however, had decided that it would not only be good to wipe out some of the wicked but it would strengthen the faithful if they saw that God still had some muscle.

"They'll get the real thing next time," He said. "But we have to give DeMille time to set up his cameras at the right places. And we'll have to have the script rewritten, of course."

Raphael groaned. "Couldn't somebody else tell Ellison? He'll carry on something awful."

"I'll tell him. You look pretty pooped, Rafe. You need a little R&R. Take two weeks off. But don't do it on Earth. Things are going to be very unsettling there for a while."

Raphael, who had a tender heart, said, "Thanks, Boss. I'd just as soon not be around to see it."

The seal was stamped on the foreheads of the faithful, marking them safe from the burning of a third of Earth, the turning of a third of the sea to blood along with the sinking of a third of the ships at sea (which also included the crashing of a third of the airplanes in the air, something St. John had overlooked), the turning of a third of all water to wormwood (a superfluous measure since a third was already thoroughly polluted), the failure of a third of daylight, the release of giant mutant locusts from the abyss, and the release of poison-gas-breathing mutant horses, which slew a third of mankind.

DeMille was delighted. Never had such terrifying scenes been filmed. And these were nothing to the plagues which followed. He had enough film from the cutting room to make a hundred documentaries after the movie was shown. And then he got a call from The Producer.

"It's back to the special effects, my boy."

"But why, Your Divinity? We still have to shoot the-Great-Whore-of-Babylon sequences, the two-Beasts-and-the-marking-of-the-wicked, the Mount-Zion-and-The-Lamb-with-His-one-hundred-and-forty-thousand-good-men-who-haven't-defiled-themselves-with-women, the—"

"Because there aren't any wicked left by now, you dolt! And not too many of the good, either!"

"That couldn't be helped," DeMille said. "Those gas-breathing, scorpion-tailed horses kind of got out of hand. But we just *have* to have the scenes where the rest of mankind that survives the plagues still doesn't abjure its worship of idols and doesn't repent of its murders, sorcery, fornications, and robberies."

"Rewrite the script."

"Ellison will quit for sure this time."

"That's all right. I already have some hack from Peoria lined up to take his place. And cheaper, too."

DeMille took his outfit, one hundred thousand strong, to the heavenly city. Here they shot the war between Satan and his demons and Michael and his angels. This was not in the chronological sequence as written by St. John. But the logistics problems were so tremendous that it was thought best to film these out of order.

Per the rewritten script, Satan and his host were defeated, but a lot of nonbelligerents were casualties, including De-Mille's best cameraperson. Moreover, there was a delay in production when Satan insisted that a stuntperson do the part where he was hurled from heaven to earth.

"Or use a dummy!" he yelled. "Twenty thousand miles is a hell of a long way to fall! If I'm hurt badly I might not be able to finish the movie!"

The screaming match between the director and Satan took place on the edge of the city. The Producer, unnoticed, came up behind Satan and kicked him from the city for the second time in their relationship with utter ruin and furious combustion.

Shrieking, "I'll sue! I'll sue!" Satan fell towards the planet below. He made a fine spectacle in his blazing entrance into the atmosphere, but the people on Earth paid it little attention. They were used to fiery portents in the sky. In fact, they were getting fed up with them.

DeMille screamed and danced around and jumped up and down. Only the presence of The Producer kept him from using foul and abusive language.

"We didn't get it on camera! Now we'll have to shoot it over!"

"His contract calls for only one fall," God said. "You'd better shoot the War-between-The-Faithful-and-True-Rider-against-the-beast-and-the-false-prophet while he recovers."

"What'll I do about the fall?" DeMille moaned.

"Fake it," The Producer said, and He went back to His office.

Per the script, an angel came down from heaven and bound up the badly injured and burned and groaning Satan with a chain and threw him into the abyss, the Grand Canyon. Then he shut and sealed it over him (what a terrific sequence that was!) so that Satan might seduce the nations no more until a thousand years had passed.

A few years later the devil's writhings caused a volcano to form above him, and the Environmental Protection Agency filed suit against Celestial Productions, Inc., because of the resultant pollution of the atmosphere.

Then God, very powerful now that only believers existed on Earth, performed the first resurrection. In this, only the martyrs were raised. And Earth, which had had much elbow room because of the recent wars and plagues, was suddenly crowded again.

Part I was finished except for the reshooting of some scenes, the dubbing in of voice and background noise, and the synchronization of the music, which was done by the cherubim and seraphim (all now unionized).

The great night of the premiere in a newly built theater in Hollywood, six million capacity, arrived. DeMille got a standing ovation after it was over. But *Time* and *Newsweek* and *The Manchester Guardian* panned the movie.

"There are some people who may go to hell after all," God growled.

DeMille didn't care about that. The film was a box-office success, grossing ten billion dollars in the first six months. And when he considered the reruns in theaters and the TV rights . . . well, had anyone ever done better?

He had a thousand more years to live. That seemed like a long time. Now. But . . . what would happen to him when Satan was released to seduce the nations again? According

102

to John the Divine's book, there'd be another worldwide battle. Then Satan, defeated, would be cast into the lake of fire and sulphur in the abyss.

(He'd be allowed to keep his Oscar, however.)

Would God let Satan, per the contract DeMille had signed with the devil, take DeMille with him into the abyss? Or would He keep him safe long enough to finish directing Part II? After Satan was buried for good, there'd be a second resurrection and a judging of those raised from the dead. The goats, the bad guys, would be hurled into the pit to keep Satan company. DeMille should be with the saved, the sheep, because he had been born again. But there was that contract with The Tempter.

DeMille arranged a conference with The Producer. Ostensibly, it was about Part II, but DeMille managed to bring up the subject which really interested him.

"I can't break your contract with him," God said.

"But I only signed it so that You'd be sure to get Satan for the role. It was a self-sacrifice. Greater love hath no man and all that. Doesn't that count for anything?"

"Let's discuss the shooting of the new heaven and the new Earth sequences."

At least I'm not going to be put into hell until the movie is done, DeMille thought. But after that? He couldn't endure thinking about it.

"It's going to be a terrible technical problem," God said, interrupting DeMille's gloomy thoughts. "When the second resurrection takes place, there won't be even Standing Room Only on Earth. That's why I'm dissolving the old Earth and making a new one. But I can't just duplicate the old Earth. The problem of Lebensraum would still remain. Now, what I'm contemplating is a Dyson sphere."

"What's that?"

"A scheme by a 20th-century mathematician to break up the giant planet Jupiter into large pieces and set them in orbit at the distance of Earth from the sun. The surfaces of the pieces would provide room for a population enormously larger than Earth's. It's a Godlike concept."

"What a documentary its filming would be!" DeMille said. "Of course, if we could write some love interest in it, we could make a he . . . pardon me, a heaven of a good story!"

God looked at his big railroad watch.

"I have another appointment, C.B. The conference is over."

DeMille said goodby and walked dejectedly towards the door. He still hadn't gotten an answer about his ultimate fate. God was stringing him along. He felt that he wouldn't know until the last minute what was going to happen to him. He'd be suffering a thousand years of uncertainty, of mental torture. His life would be a cliff-hanger. Will God relent? Or will he save the hero at the very last second?

"C.B.," God said.

DeMille spun around, his heart thudding, his knees turned to water. Was this it? The fatal finale? Had God, in His mysterious and subtle way, decided for some reason that there'd be no Continued in Next Chapter for him? It didn't seem likely, but then The Producer had never promised that He'd use him as the director of Part II nor had He signed a contract with him. Maybe, like so many temperamental producers, He'd suddenly concluded that DeMille wasn't the right one for the job. Which meant that He could arrange it so that his ex-director would be thrown now, right this minute, into the lake of fire.

God said, "I can't break your contract with Satan. So. . . ."

"Yes?"

DeMille's voice sounded to him as if he were speaking very far away.

"Satan can't have your soul until you die."

"Yes?"

His voice was only a trickle of sound, a last few drops of water from a clogged drainpipe.

"So, if you don't die, and that, of course, depends upon your behavior, Satan can't ever have your soul."

God smiled and said, "See you in eternity."

A science fiction writer of unusual and powerful imagination, Philip José Farmer was born in Indiana in 1918. He entered Bradley College in 1935, but long periods of steel mill work needed to support his family kept him from graduating until 1950. An influential writer, Farmer brought a new maturity to science fiction with his 1953 Hugo-winning tragedy, "The

Lovers." Many of his novels feature adventures of famous literary and historical figures such as Tarzan, Doc Savage, and Phileas Fogg. The first novel of his Riverworld series, To Your Scattered Bodies Go, *appeared in 1971. Farmer continues the Doc Savage series with* Escape from Loki.

When Alex finally got to meet Elisabeth Kent, star of a 1960s television series and the woman of his dreams, he didn't realize how real some television characters can be.

SIX

Old Loves

Karl Edward Wagner

He had loved her for twenty years, and today he would meet her for the first time. Her name was Elisabeth Kent, but to him she would always be Stacey Steele.

Alex Webley had been an undergraduate in the mid-1960s when *The Agency* premiered on Saturday night television. This had been at the height of the fad for spy shows—James Bond and imitations beyond counting, then countermoves toward either extreme of realism or parody. Upon such a full sea *The Agency* almost certainly would have sunk unnoticed, had it not been for the series' two stars—or more particularly, had it not been for Elisabeth Kent.

In the role of Stacey Steele she played the delightfully eccentric—"kooky" was the expression of the times—partner of secret agent Harrison Dane, portrayed by actor Garrett Channing—an aging matinee idol, to use the expression of an earlier time. The two were employed by an enigmatic organization referred to simply as The Agency, which dispatched Dane and Miss Steele off upon dangerous assignments throughout the world. Again, nothing in the formula to distinguish *The Agency* from the rest of the pack—except for the charisma of its costars and for a certain stylish audacity to its scripts that became more outrageous as the series progressed.

Initially it was to have been a straight secret agent series: strong male lead assisted by curvaceous ingénue whose scatterbrained exploits would provide at least one good capture and rescue per episode. The role of Harrison Dane went to Garrett Channing—a fortuitous piece of contrary-to-type casting of an actor best remembered as the suave villain or debonair hero of various forgettable 1950s programmers. Channing had once been labeled "the poor man's James Mason," and perhaps the casting director had recalled that James Mason had been an early choice to portray James Bond. The son of a Bloomsbury greengrocer, Channing's Hollywood-nurtured sophistication and charm seemed ideal for the role of American super-spy, Harrison Dane.

Then, through a casting miracle that could only have been through chance and not genius, the role of Stacey Steele went to Elisabeth Kent. Miss Kent was a tall, leggy dancer whose acting experience consisted of several on-and-off-Broadway plays and a brief role in the most recent James Bond film. *Playboy,* as was its custom, ran a pictorial feature on the lovelies of the latest Bond film and devoted two full pages to the blonde Miss Kent—revealing rather more of her than was permitted in the movies of the day. It brought her to the attention of the casting director, and Elisabeth Kent became Stacey Steele.

Became Stacey Steele almost literally.

Later they would say that the role destroyed Elisabeth Kent. Her career dwindled miserably afterward. Some critics suggested that Miss Kent had been blackballed by the industry after her unexpected departure from the series resulted in *The Agency's* plummeting in the ratings and merciful cancellation after a partial season with a forgettable DD-cup Malibu blonde stuffed into the role of female lead. The consensus, however, pointed out that after her role in *The Agency* it was Stacey Steele who was in demand, and not Elisabeth Kent. Once the fad for secret agent films passed, there were no more roles for Stacey Steele. Nor for Elisabeth Kent. A situation comedy series flopped after three episodes. Two films with her in straight dramatic roles were noteworthy bombs, and a third was never released. Even if Elisabeth Kent succeeded in convincing some producer or director that she was not Stacey Steele, her public remained adamant.

Her only film appearance within the past decade had been as the villainess in a Hong Kong chop-fooey opus,

Tiger Fists Against the Dragon. Perhaps it lost some little in translation.

Inevitably, *The Agency* attracted a dedicated fan following, and Stacey Steele became a cult figure. The same was true to a lesser extent for Garrett Channing, although that actor's death not long after the series' cancellation spared him both the benefits and the hazards of such a status. The note he left upon his desk: "Goodbye, World—I can no longer accept your tedium." was considered an enviable exit line.

The Agency premiered in the mid-1960s, just catching the crest of the Carnaby Street mod-look craze. Harrison Dane, suave super-spy and mature man of the world though he was, was decidedly hip to today's swinging beat, and the promos boldly characterized him as a "mod James Bond." No business suits and narrow ties for Harrison Dane: "We want to take the stuffiness out of secret agenting," to quote one producer. As the sophisticated counterpart to the irrepressible Miss Steele, Dane saved the day once a week attired in various outfits consisting of bell-bottom trousers, paisley shirts, Nehru jackets, and lots of beads and badges. If one critic described Harrison Dane as "a middleaged Beatle," the public applauded this "anti-establishment super-spy."

No such criticism touched the image of Stacey Steele. Stacey Steele was the American viewing public's ideal of the Swinging London Bird—her long-legged physique perfectly suited to vinyl minidresses and thigh-high boots. Each episode became a showcase for her daring fashions—briefest of miniskirts, hip-hugging leather bell-bottoms, see-through (as much as the censors would permit) blouses, cut-out dresses, patent boots, psychedelic jewelry, groovy hats, all that was marvy, fab, and gear. There was talk of opening a franchise of Stacey Steele Boutiques, and Miss Steele became a featured model in various popular magazines seeking to portray the latest fashions for the Liberated Lady of the Sixties. By this time Elisabeth Kent's carefully modulated BBC accent would never betray her Long Island birthright to the unstudied ear.

Stacey Steele was instant pin-up material, and stills of the miniskirted secret agent covered many a dorm wall beside blow-ups of Bogie and black-light posters. Later detractors argued that *The Agency* would never have lasted its first season without Stacey Steele's legs, and that the series was little more than an American version of one of the imported British spy shows. Fans rebutted such charges with the assertion that it had all started with James Bond anyway, and *The Agency* proved that the Americans could do it best. Pin-up photos of Stacey Steele continue to sell well twenty years after.

While *The Agency* may have been plainly derivative of a popular British series, American viewers made it their favorite show against formidable primetime competition from the other two networks. For three glorious seasons *The Agency* ruled Saturday nights. Then, Elisabeth Kent's sudden departure from the series: catastrophe, mediocrity, cancellation. But not oblivion. The series passed into syndication and thus into the twilight zone of odd-hour reruns on local channels and independent networks. Old fans remembered, new fans were born. *The Agency* developed a cult following, and Stacey Steele became its goddess.

In that sense, among its priesthood was Alex Webley. He had begun his worship two decades ago in the TV lounge of a college dorm, amidst the incense of spilled beer and tobacco smoke and an inspired choir of whistles and guffaws. The first night he watched *The Agency* Webley had been blowing some tangerine with an old high school buddy who had brought a little down from Antioch. Webley didn't think he'd gotten off, but when the miniskirted Miss Steele used dazzling karate chops to dispatch two baddies, he knew he was having a religious experience. After that, he watched *The Agency* every Saturday night without fail. It would have put a crimp in his dating if Webley had been one who dated. His greatest moment in college was the night when he stood off two drunken jocks, either of whom could have folded Webley in half, who wanted to switch channels from *The Agency* to watch a basketball game. They might have stuffed Webley into a wastebasket had not other *Agency* fans added their voices to his protest. Thus did Alex Webley learn the power of fans united.

It was a power he experienced again with news of Elisabeth Kent's departure from the series, and later when *The*

110

Agency was cancelled. Webley was one of the thousands of fans who wrote to the network demanding that Stacey Steele be brought back to the show (never mind how). With the show's cancellation, Webley helped circulate a petition that *The Agency* be continued, with or without Stacey Steele. The producers were impressed by such show of support, but the network pointed out that 10,000 signatures from the lunatic fringe do not cause a flicker on the Nielsen ratings. Without Stacey Steele, *The Agency* was out of business, and that was that. Besides, the fad for overdone spy shows was over and done.

Alex Webley kept a file of clippings and stills, promotional items, comic books and paperbacks, anything at all pertaining to *The Agency* and to the great love of his life, Elisabeth Kent. From the beginning there were fanzines—crudely printed amateur publications devoted to *The Agency*—and one or two unofficial fan clubs. Webley joined and subscribed to them all. Undergraduate enthusiasms developed into a lifelong hobby. Corresponding with other diehard fans and collecting *Agency* memorabilia became his preoccupying outside interest in the course of taking a doctorate in neurobiology. He was spared from Viet Nam by high blood pressure, and from any longterm romantic involvement by a highly introverted nature. Following his doctorate, Webley landed a research position at one of the pharmaceutical laboratories, where he performed his duties efficiently and maintained an attitude of polite aloofness toward his coworkers. Someone there dubbed him "the Invisible Man," but there was no malice to the *mot juste.*

At his condo, the door to the spare bedroom bore a brass-on-walnut plaque that read *HQ.* Webley had made it himself. Inside were filing cabinets, bookshelves, and his desk. The walls were papered with posters and stills, most of them photos of Stacey Steele. A glass-fronted cabinet held videocassettes of all *The Agency* episodes, painstakingly acquired through trades with other fans. The day he completed the set, Webley drank most of a bottle of Glenfiddich—Dane and Miss Steele's favorite potation—and afterward became quite ill.

By now Webley's enthusiasm had expanded to all of the spy shows and films of the period, but old loves die hard, and *The Agency* remained his chief interest. Webley was editor/publisher of *Special Assignment,* a quarterly amateur magazine devoted to the spy craze of the 60s. *Special Assignment* was more than a cut above the mimeographed fanzines that Webley had first begun to collect; his magazine was computer-typeset and boasted slick paper and color covers. By its tenth issue, *Special Assignment* had a circulation of several thousand, with distribution through specialty bookshops here and abroad. It was a hobby project that took up all of Webley's free time and much of his living space, and Webley was content.

Almost content. *Special Assignment* carried photographs and articles on every aspect of the old spy shows, along with interviews of many of the actors and actresses. Webley, of course, devoted a good many pages each issue to *The Agency* and to Stacey Steele—but to his chagrin he was unable to obtain an interview with Elisabeth Kent. Since her one disastrous comeback attempt, Miss Kent preferred the life of a recluse. There was some dignity to be salvaged in anonymity. Miss Kent did not grant interviews, she did not make public appearances, she did not answer fan mail. After ten years the world forgot Elisabeth Kent, but her fans still remembered Stacey Steele.

Webley had several years prior managed to secure Elisabeth Kent's address—no mean accomplishment in itself— but his rather gushing fan letters had not elicited any sort of reply. Not easily daunted, Webley faithfully sent Miss Kent each new issue of *Special Assignment* (personally inscribed to her), and with each issue he included a long letter of praise for her deathless characterization of Stacey Steele, along with a plea to be granted an interview. Webley never gave up hope, despite Miss Kent's unbroken silence.

When he at last did receive a letter from Miss Kent graciously granting him the long-sought interview, Webley knew that life is just and that the faithful shall be rewarded.

He caught one of those red-eye-special flights out to Los Angeles, but was too excited to catch any sleep on the way. Instead he reread a wellworn paperback novelization of one of his favorite *Agency* episodes, *"The Chained Lightning Caper,"* and mentally reviewed the questions he would ask

Miss Kent—still not quite able to believe that he would be talking with her in another few hours.

Webley checked into a Thrifti-Family Motel near the airport, unpacked, tried without success to sleep, got up, showered and shaved. The economy flight he had taken hadn't served a meal, but then it had been all Webley could manage just to finish his complimentary soft beverage. The three-hour time change left his system rather disordered in any event, so that he wasn't certain whether he actually should feel tired or hungry were it not for his anxiousness over the coming interview. He pulled out his notes and looked over them again, managing to catch a fitful nap just before dawn. At daylight he made himself eat a dismal breakfast in the motel restaurant, then returned to his room to shave again and to put on the clothes he had brought along for the interview.

It was the best of Webley's several Harrison Dane costumes, carefully salvaged from various thrift shops and yard sales. Webley maintained a wardrobe of vintage mod clothing, and he had twice won prizes at convention masquerades. The pointed-toe Italian boots were original to the period—a lovingly maintained treasure discovered ten years before at Goodwill Industries. The suede bell-bottoms were custom-made by an aging hippy at an aging leathercrafts shop that still had a few psychedelic posters tacked to its walls. Webley tried them on at least once a month and adjusted his diet according to snugness of fit. The jacket, a sort of lavender thing that lacked collar or lapels, was found at a vintage clothing store and altered to his measurements. The paisley shirt, mostly purples and greens, had been discovered at a yard sale, and the beads and medallions had come from here and there.

Webley was particularly proud of his Dane Cane, which he himself had constructed after the secret agent's famous weapon. It appeared to be a normal walking stick, but it contained Dane's arsenal of secret weapons and paraphernalia—including a radio transmitter, recording device, tear gas, and laser. Harrison Dane was never without his marvelous cane, and good thing, too. Alex Webley had caused rather a stir at the airport check-in, before airline officials finally permitted him to transport his Dane Cane via baggage.

Webley still clung to the modified Beatles haircut that Harrison Dane affected. He combed it now carefully, and he studied his reflection in the room's ripply mirror. The very image of Harrison Dane. Stacey Steele—Miss Kent—would no doubt be impressed by the pains he had taken. It would have been great to drive out in a Shelby Cobra like Dane's, but instead he called for a cab.

Not a Beverly Hills address, Webley sadly noted, as the taxi drove him to one of those innumerable canyon neighborhoods tottering on steep hillsides and the brink of shabbiness. Her house was small and featureless, a little box propped up on the hillside beside a jagged row of others like it—distinguishable one from another chiefly by the degree of seediness and the cars parked in front. Some cheap development from the 1950s, Webley judged, and another ten years likely would see the ones still standing bought up and the land used for some cheap condo development. He felt increasingly sad about it all; he had been prepared to announce his arrival to some uniformed guard at the subdivision's entrance gate.

Well, if it were within his power to do so, Webley intended to bring to bear the might and majesty of *Special Assignment* to pressure these stupid producers into casting Elisabeth Kent in new and important roles. That made this interview more important than ever to Webley—and to Miss Kent.

He paid off the cab—tipping generously, as Harrison Dane would have done. This was perhaps fortuitous, as the driver shouted after him that he had forgotten his attaché case. Webley wondered how Dane would have handled such an embarrassing lapse—of course, Dane would never have committed such a blunder. Webley's case—also modelled after Dane's secret agent attaché case, although Webley's lacked the built-in machine gun—contained a bottle of Glenfiddich, his notes, cassette recorder, and camera. It was essential that he obtain some photographs of Miss Kent at home: since her appearance in the unfortunate *Tiger Fists* film, current photos of Elisabeth Kent were not made available. Webley had heard vicious rumors that the actress had lost her looks, but he put these down to typical show biz backstabbing, and he prayed it wasn't so.

He rang the doorbell, using the tip of his cane, just as Dane always did, and waited—posing jauntily against his cane, just as Dane always did. The seconds dragged on eternally, and there was no response. He rang again, and waited. Webley looked for a car in the driveway; saw none, but the carport was closed. He rang a third time.

This time the door opened.

And Alex Webley knew his worship had not been in vain.

"Hullo, Dane," she said. "I've been expecting you."

"How very good to see you, Miss Steele," said Webley. "I hope I haven't kept you waiting."

And she *was* Stacey Steele. Just like in *The Agency*. And Webley felt a thrill at knowing she had dressed the part just for the interview—just for him.

The Hollywood gossip had been all lies, because she hardly looked a day older—although part of that was no doubt due to her appearance today as Stacey Steele. It was perfect. It was all there, as it should be: the thigh-length boots of black patent leather, the red leather minidress with *LOVE* emblazoned across the breastline (the center of the O was cut out, revealing a daring glimpse of braless cleavage), the blonde bangs-and-ironed-straight Mary Travers hair, the beads and bells. Time had rolled back, and she *was* Stacey Steele.

"Come on in, luv," Miss Steele invited, in her so-familiar throaty purr.

Aerobics really can do wonders, Webley thought as he followed her into her living room. Twenty years may have gone by, but if *The Agency* were to be revived today, Miss Kent could step right into her old role as the mod madcap Miss Steele. Exercise and diet, probably—he must find some discreet way of asking her how she kept her youthful figure.

The living room was a close replica of Stacey Steele's swinging London flat, enough so that Webley guessed she had removed much of the set from the Hollywood sound-stage where the series was actually shot. He sat down, not without difficulty, on the inflatable day-glo orange chair—Dane's favorite—and opened his attaché case.

"I brought along a little libation," he said, presenting her with the Glenfiddich.

Miss Steele gladly accepted the dark-green triangular bottle. "Ah, luv! You always remember, don't you!"

She quickly poured a generous level of the pale amber whisky into a pair of stemmed glasses and offered one to Webley. Webley wanted to protest that it was too early in the day for him to tackle straight scotch, but he decided he'd rather die than break the spell of this moment.

Instead, he said: "Cheers." And drank.

The whisky went down his throat smoothly and soared straight to his head. Webley blinked and set down his glass in order to paw through the contents of his case. Miss Steele had recharged his glass before he could protest, but already Webley was thinking how perfect this all was. This would be one to tell to those scoffers who had advised him against wearing his Harrison Dane costume to the interview.

"Here's a copy of our latest issue. . . ." Webley hesitated only slightly, ". . . Miss Steele."

She took the magazine from him. The cover was a still of Stacey Steele karate-chopping a heavy in a pink foil spacesuit. "Why, that's me! How groovy!"

"Yes. From 'The Mod Martian Caper,' of course. And naturally you'll be featured on our next cover, along with the interview and all." The *our* was an editorial plural, inasmuch as Webley was the entire staff of *Special Assignment*.

"Fab!" said Miss Steele, paging through the magazine in search of more photos of herself.

Webley risked another sip of Glenfiddich while he glanced around the room. However the house might appear from the outside, inside Miss Kent had lovingly maintained the *ambiance* of *The Agency*. The black lights and pop-art posters, the psychedelic color schemes, the beaded curtains, the oriental rugs. Indian music was playing, and strewn beside the vintage KHL stereo Webley recognized early albums from the Beatles and the Stones, from the Who and the Yardbirds, from Ultimate Spinach and Thirteenth Floor Elevator. He drew in a deep breath; yes, that was incense burning on the mantelpiece—cinnamon, Miss Steele's favorite.

"That's the platinum bird you used in 'The Malted Falcon Caper,' isn't it?"

Miss Steele touched the silver falcon statuette Webley had spotted. "The very bird. Not really made of platinum, sorry to report."

"And that must be the chastity belt they locked you into in 'The Medieval Mistress Caper.'" Again Webley pointed.

"One and the same. And not very comfy on a cold day, I assure you."

Webley decided he was about to sound gushy, so he finished his second whisky. It didn't help collect his thoughts, but it did restore a little calmness. He decided not to argue when Miss Steele refreshed their drinks. His fingers itched for his camera, but his hands were trembling too much.

"You seem to have kept quite a few props from *The Agency*," he suggested. "Isn't that the steel mask they put over your head in 'The Silent Cyborg Caper?' Not very comfortable either, I should imagine."

"At times I did find my part a trifle confining," Miss Steele admitted. "All those captures by the villains."

"With Harrison Dane always there in the nick of time," Webley said, raising his glass to her. If Miss Steele was in no hurry to get through the interview, then neither was he.

"It wasn't all that much fun waiting to be rescued every time," Miss Steele confided. "Tied out in the hot sun across a railroad track, or stretched out on a rack in a moldly old dungeon."

"'The Uncivil Engineer Caper,'" Webley remembered, and "'The Dungeon to Let Caper.'"

"Or being strapped to a log in a sawmill."

"'The Silver Scream Caper.'"

"I was brushing sawdust out of my hair for a week."

"And in 'The Missing Mermaid Caper' they handcuffed you to an anchor and tossed you overboard."

"Yes, and I still have my rubber fishtail from that one."

"Here?"

"Certainly. I've held on to a museum's worth of costumes and props. Would you like to see the lot of it?"

"Would I ever!" Webley prayed he had brought enough film.

117

"Then I'll just give us a refill."

"I really think I've had enough just now," Webley begged.

"Why, Dane! I never knew you to say no."

"But one more to top things off," agreed Webley, unable to tarnish the image of Harrison Dane.

Miss Steele poured. "Most of it's kept downstairs."

"After all, Miss Steele, this is a special occasion." Webley drank.

He had a little difficulty with the stairs—he vaguely felt he was floating downward, and the Dane Cane kept tripping him—but he made it to the lower level without disgracing himself. Once there, all he could manage was a breathless: "Out of sight!"

Presumably the downstairs had been designed as a sort of large family room, complete with fireplace, cozy chairs, and at one time probably a ping pong table or such. Miss Kent had refurnished the room with enough props and sets to reshoot the entire series. Webley could only stand and stare. It was as if an entire file of *Agency* stills had been scattered about and transformed into three-dimensional reality.

There was the stake the natives had tied her to in "The No Atoll At All Caper," and there was the man-eating plant that had menaced her in "The Venusian Vegetarian Caper." In one corner stood—surely a replica—Stacey Steele's marvelous VW Beetle, sporting its wild psychedelic paint scheme and harboring a Porche engine and drivetrain. There was the E.V.O.L. interrogation chair from "The Earth's End Caper," and behind it one of the murderous robots from "The Angry Android Caper." Harrison Dane's circular bed, complete with television, stereo, bar, machine guns, and countless other built-in devices, was crowded beside the very same torture rack from "The Dungeon to Let Caper." Cataloging just the major pieces would be an hour's work, even for Webley, and a full inventory of all the memorabilia would take at least a couple of days.

"Impressed, luv?"

Webley closed his mouth. "It's like the entire *Agency* series come to life in one house," he finally said.

"Do browse about all you like, luv."

Webley stumbled across the room, trying not to touch any of the sacred relics, scarcely able to concentrate upon any one object for longer than its moment of recognition. It was all too overpowering an assault upon his sensory mechanisms.

"A toast to us, luv."

Webley didn't remember whether Miss Steele had brought along their glasses or poured fresh drinks from Harrison Dane's art nouveau bar, shoved against one wall next to the mind transfer machine from "The Wild, Wild Bunch Caper." He gulped his drink without thinking and moments later regretted it.

"I think I'd better sit down for a minute," Webley apologized.

"Drugged drinks!" Miss Steele said brightly. "Just like in 'The Earth's End Caper.' Quick, Dane! Sit down here!"

Webley collapsed into the interrogation chair as directed—it was closest, and he was about to make a scene if he didn't recover his balance. Automatic cuffs instantly secured his arms, legs, and body to the chair.

"Only in 'The Earth's End Caper,'" said Miss Steele, "I was the one they drugged and fastened into this chair. There to be horribly tortured, unless Harrison Dane came to the rescue."

Webley turned his head as much as the neck restraints would permit. Miss Steele was laying out an assortment of scalpels and less obvious instruments, recognized by Webley as props from the episode.

"Groovy," he managed to say.

Miss Steele was assembling some sort of dental drill. "I was always the victim." She smiled at him with that delightful madcap smile. "I was always the one being captured, humiliated, helplessly awaiting your last minute mock heroics."

"Well, not all the time," Webley protested, going along with the joke. He hoped he wasn't going to be ill.

"Are these clamps very tight?"

"Yes. Very. The prop seems in perfect working order. I think I really ought to stretch out for a while. Most embarrassing, but I'm afraid that drinking this early. . . ."

"It wasn't enough that you seduced me and insisted on

the abortion for the sake of our careers. It was your ego-
tistical jealousy that finally destroyed me. You couldn't
stand the fact that Stacey Steele was the *real* star of *The
Agency,* and not Harrison Dane. So you pulled strings until
you got me written out of the series. Then you did your best
to ruin my career afterward."

"I don't feel very good," Webley muttered. "I think I
might be getting sick."

"Hoping for a last-second rescue?" Stacey Steele selected a scalpel from the tray, and bent over him. Webley
had a breathtaking glimpse through the cut-out of *LOVE,*
and then the blade touched his eye.

The police were already there by the time Elisabeth Kent got
home. Neighbors' dogs were barking at something in the
brush below her house; some kids went to see what they
were after, and then the police were called.

"Did you know the man, Miss Kent?"

Miss Kent nodded her double chins. She was concentrat-
ing on stocking her liquor cabinet with the case of generic
gin she'd gone out to buy with the advance check Webley
had mailed her. She'd planned on fortifying herself for the
interview that might mean her comeback, but her aging
Nova had refused to start in the parking lot, and the road
call had eaten up the remainder of the check that she'd
hoped would go toward overdue rent for the one-story
frame dump. She sat down heavily on the best chair of her
sparsely furnished living room.

"He was some fan from back east," she told the inves-
tigating officer. "Wanted to interview me for some fan magazine. I've got his letter here somewhere. I used to be in
films a few years back—maybe you remember."

"We'll need to get in touch with next of kin," the detective
said. "Already found the cabbie who let him out here while
you were off getting towed." He was wondering if he had
ever seen her in anything. "At a guess, he waited around on
your deck, probably leaned against the railing—got a little
dizzy, and went over. Might have had a heart attack or
something."

Elisabeth Kent was looking at the empty Glenfiddich bottle and the two glasses.

"Damn you, Stacey Steele," she whispered. "Goddamn you."

A psychiatrist who became both publisher and writer of supernatural fiction, Wagner was born in Tennessee in 1945. Educated at Kenyon College and the University of North Carolina, he was a resident in psychiatry at John Unstead Hospital until 1975, when he became a freelance writer. An admirer of the pulps, especially Weird Tales, *Wagner writes in much the same vein. Many of his stories featuring the killer-warrior Kane are collected in* The Book of Kane. Legion from the Shadows *is based on the real-life legend of the Roman Ninth Legion, and* The Road of Kings *features Robert Howard's hero, Conan. Wagner's shorter works include the August Derleth Award-winner "Sticks," and a Kane story, "Two Suns Setting." His publishing firm, Carcosa House, won a World Fantasy Special Award for its production of four collections by Manly Wade Wellman (two volumes), E. Hoffman Price, and H. B. Cave. Wagner's most recent collection is* Why Not You and I?

If there is no pain or grief in Summerland, why was Charley King in such torment?

SEVEN

Summerland

Avram Davidson

Mary King said—and I'm sure it was true—that she couldn't remember a thing about the séance at Mrs. Porteous's. Of course no one tried to refresh her memory. Mary is a large woman, with a handsome, ruddy face, and the sound of that heavy body hitting the floor and the sight of her face at that moment—it was gray and loose-mouthed and flaccid—so unnerved me that I am ashamed to say I just sat there, numb. Others scurried around and cried for water or thrust cushions under her head or waved vials of ammoniated lavender in front of her, but I just sat frozen, looking at her, looking at Mrs. Porteous lolling back in the armchair, Charley King's voice still ringing in my ears, and my heart thudding with shock.

I would not have thought, nor would anyone else, at first impression, that the Kings were the séance type. My natural tendency is to associate that sort of thing with wheat germ and vegeburgers and complete syndromes of psychosomatic illnesses, but Charley and his wife were beef-eaters all the way and they shone with health and cheer and never reported a sniffle. Be exceedingly wary of categories, I told myself; despise no man's madness. Their hearty goodwill, if it palled upon me, was certainly better for my mother than another neighbor's whining or gossip would have been. The Kings, who were her best friends, devoted to her about 500 percent of the time I myself was willing to give. For years I had lived away from home, our interests and activities were too different, there seemed little either of us could do when long silences fell upon us as we sat alone. It was much better to join the Kings.

"Funny thing happened down at the office today—" Charley often began like that. Ordinarily this opening would have shaken me into thoughts of a quick escape. Somehow, though, as Charley told it, his fingers rippling the thick, iron-gray hair, his ruddy face quivering not to release a smile or laugh before the point of the story was revealed—somehow, it *did* seem funny when Charley told it. To me, the Kings were old people, but they were younger than my mother, and I am sure they helped keep her from growing old too fast. It was worth it to me to eat vast helpings of butter-pecan ice cream when the Real Me hungered and slavered for a glass of beer with pretzel sticks on the side.

If tarot cards, Rosicrucian literature, séances, and milder non-contortionistic exercises made an incongruous note in the middle-class, middle-aged atmosphere the Kings trailed with them like "rays of lambent dullness"—why, it was harmless. It was better to lap up pyramidology than lunatic-fringe politics. Rather let Mother join hands on the ouija board than start cruising the Great Circle of quack doctors to find a cure for imaginary backaches. So I ate baked alaska and discussed the I Am and astral projection, and said "Be still, my soul" to inner yearnings for highballs and carnal conversation. After all, it was only once a week. And I never saw any signs that my mother took any of it more seriously than the parchesi game which followed the pistachio or peanut-crunch.

I am an architect. Charley was In The Real Estate Game. A good chance, you might think, for one hand to wash the other, but it hardly ever happened that our commercial paths crossed. Lanais, kidney-shaped swimming pools, picture windows, copper-hooded fireplaces, hi-fi sets in the walls—that was my sort of thing. "Income property"—that was Charley's. And a nice income it was, too. Much better than mine.

How does that go?—Evil communications corrupt good manners?—Charley might have said something of that sort if I'd ever told him what Ed Hokinson told me. Hoke is on the planning commission, so what with this and that, we see each other fairly often. Coincidence's arm didn't stretch too long before Charley King's name came up between us. Idly talking, I repeated to Hoke a typical Charleyism. Charley had been having tenant trouble.

"Of course there are always what you might call the Inescapable Workings of Fate, which all of us are subject to, just as we are to, oh, say, the law of Supply and Demand," said Charley, getting outside some dessert. "But by and large whatever troubles people of that sort"—meaning the tenants—"think they have, it's due to their own improvidence, for they won't save, and each week or month the rent comes as a fresh surprise. And then you have certain politicians stirring them up and making them think they're badly off when really they're just the victims of Maya, or Illusion." Little flecks of whipped cream were on his ruddy jowels. Mary nodded solemnly, two hundred pounds of well-fed, well-dressed, well-housed approbation.

"Maya," said Hoke. "That what he calls it? Like to come with me and see for yourself? I know Charley King," Hoke said. In the end I did go. Interesting, in its own way, what I saw, but not my kind of thing at all. And the next day was the day Charley died. He was interred with much ceremony and expense in a fabulous City of the Dead, which has been too well described by British novelists for me to try. Big, jolly, handsome, life-loving Mr. Charley King. In a way, I missed him. And after that, of course, Mary and my mother were together even more. After that there was even less of the Akashic Documents or Anthroposophism or Vedanta, and more and more of séances.

"I know I have no cause to grieve," Mary said. "I know that Charley is happy. I just want him to tell me so. That's not asking too much, is it?"

How should I know? What is "too much?" I never do any asking, myself, or any answering for that matter.

So off they went, my mother and Mrs. Mary King, and— if I couldn't beg off—I. Mrs. Victory's, Mrs. Reverend Ella Maybelle Snyder's, Madame Sophia's, Mother Honeywell's—every spirit-trumpet in the city must have been on time-and-a-half those days. They got little-girl angels and old-lady angels. They got doctors, lawyers, Indian chiefs, and young boy-babies—they must even have gotten Radio Andorra—but they didn't get Charley. There were slate-

125

messages and automatic writings and ectoplasm enough to reach from here to Punxatawney, P. A., but if it reached to Charley he didn't reach back. All the mediums and all their customers had the same line: There is no grief in Summerland, there is no pain in Summerland—Summerland being the choice real estate development Upstairs, at least in the Spiritualist hep-talk. They all *believed* it, but somehow they all wanted to be assured. And after the séance, when all the spooks had gone back to Summerland, *what* a consumption of coffee, cupcakes, and cold cuts.

Some of the places were fancy: you bought "subscription" for the season's performance and discussed parapsychology over canapés and sherry. Mrs. Porteous's place, however, was right out of the 1920s, red velveteen *porteers* on wooden rings, and all. I almost fancied I could feel the ectoplasm when we came in, but it was just a heavy condensation of boiled cabbage steam and hamburger smoke.

Mrs. Porteous looked like a caricature of herself—down-at-hem evening gown, gaudy but clumsy cosmetic job, huge rings on each finger, and, *oh,* that *voice.* Mrs. Porteous was the phoniest-looking, phoniest-sounding, phoniest-*acting* medium I have ever come across. She had a lady-in-waiting: sagging cheeks, jet-black page-boy bob or bangs or whatever you call it, velvet tunic, so on.

"Dear friends," says the gentlewoman, striking a Woolworth gong, "might I have your attention please. I shall now request that there be no further smoking or talking whilst the séance is going on. We guarantee—*nothing.* We shall attempt—*all.* If there is doubt—if there is discord—the spirits may not come. For there is no doubt, no discord, there is no grief nor pain, in Summerland." So on. Let us join our hands . . . let us bow our heads . . . I, of course, peeked. The Duchess was sitting on the starboard side of the incense, next to Mrs. Porteous, who was rolling her eyes and muttering. Then Charley King screamed.

It was Mrs. Porteous's mouth that it came from, it was her chest that heaved, but it was Charley King's voice—I know his voice, don't you think I know his voice? He screamed. My mother's hand jerked away from mine.

"*The fire! The fire! Oh, Mary, how it burns, how—*"

Then Mary fell forward from her seat, the lights went on,

went off, then on again, everyone scurried around except me—I was frozen to my seat—and Mrs. Porteous—she lay back in her arm chair. Finally I got to my feet and somehow we managed to lift Mary onto a couch. The color came back to her face and she opened her eyes.

"That's all right, dear," my mother said.

"Oh my goodness!" said Mary. "What happened? Did I faint? Isn't that silly. No, no, let me get up; we must start the séance."

Someone tugged at my sleeve. It was the Duchess.

"Who was that?" she asked, looking at me shrewdly. "It was her husband, wasn't it? Oh-yes-it-twas! He was burned to death, wasn't he? And he hasn't yet freed himself from his earthly ties so he can enter Summerland. He must of been a skeptic."

"He didn't burn to death," I said. "He fell and broke his neck. And he wasn't a skeptic."

(Hoke had said to me: "Of course the board was rotten; the whole house was rotten. All his property was like that. It should have been condemned years ago. No repairs, a family in each room, and the rent sky-high—he must have been making a fortune. You saw those rats, didn't you?" Hoke had asked. "Do you know what the death rate is in those buildings?")

The Duchess shook her head. Her face was puzzled.

"Then it couldn't of been her husband," she said. "There is no pain," she pointed out reasonably, "in Summerland."

"No," I said to her. "No, I'm sure there isn't. I know that."

But I knew Charley King. And I know his voice.

Talking dragons, the Civil War, and lethal old ladies are among the subjects of Avram Davidson's memorable tales. Born in Yonkers, New York, in 1923, he was educated at New York University, Yeshiva University, and Pierce College. He served in the Navy during World War II, and fought on the Israeli side in the 1948-49 Arab-Israeli War. A scholar and critic, he began publishing fiction in the 50s, and soon began winning prizes for his richly textured work: a Hugo in 1958, Edgars in 1961 and 1976, World Fantasy Awards in 1976 and 1978. His works also include fact-crime such as Crimes and Chaos, *and science fiction such as the Nebula nominee* Rogue Dragon, What Strange Stars and Skies, *and* Vergil in Averno.

Documentary filmmaker Gerald Sebastian was positive he had found Atlantis beneath China's fierce Takla Makan desert. He never even once considered that Atlantis—or whatever it was—might not want to be found.

EIGHT

The Courts of Xanadu
Charles Sheffield

The eagle's way is easy. Strike north-north-west from Calcutta, to meet the international border close to the little Indian town of Darbhanga. Fly on into Nepal, passing east of Kathmandu. After another hundred miles you encounter the foothills and then the peaks of the Himalayan range. Keep going—easy enough when you fly with the wings of imagination. You traverse silent, white-capped mountains, the tallest in the world, float on across the high plateau country of Tibet, and come at last to the Kunlun Mountains. Cross them. You are now in China proper, at the southern edge of the *Takla Makan Shamo,* one of the world's fiercest deserts, a thousand miles from east to west, five hundred from north to south.

If you are driving, or walking on real feet, you have to do things rather differently. The Himalayas are impassable. The Tibetan border is patrolled. Travel in the Tibetan interior is restricted.

Gerald Sebastian made the trip to the Takla Makan in two different ways. The first time he was alone, traveling light. He sailed from Calcutta to Hong Kong, flew to Beijing, and then took the train west all the way to Xinjiang Province. He was a celebrity, and his presence was permitted, even encouraged. However, his trip south from Urumqi, into the fiery heart of the Takla Makan desert, was not permitted. It was difficult to arrange, and it took a good deal of bribery.

Today's Chinese, you will be told by their government, do not accept tips or bribes. Just so.

Sebastian's second visit to the *Takla Makan Shamo* had

to be very different. His three-week disappearance on the first trip had left the Chinese authorities uneasy; they did not want him back. For his part, he did not want anyone in China to know of his presence. This time he also had four people with him, and he needed a mass of equipment, including two large, balloon-wheel trucks.

The trucks were the obvious problem; the four people— five, if one includes Sebastian himself—would prove a worse one. The group consisted of the following: one world-famous explorer and antiquarian, Gerald Sebastian; one wealthy, decorative, and determined woman, Jackie Sands; one NASA scientist, Dr. Will Reynolds, as out of place on the expedition as a catfish on the moon; one China expert, Paddy Elphinstone, fluent in the *Turkic* language spoken in Xinjiang Province, and in everything else; and one professional cynic, con-man, and four-time loser, convinced in his heart that this expedition would be his fifth failure.

How is it possible to know what a man believes in his heart?

It is time for me to step out of the shadows and introduce myself. I am Sam Nevis. I was along on this expedition because I knew more about treasure-hunting, wilderness excavation, and survival in the rough than the rest of Sebastian's helpers put together—which was not saying much. And by the time that we were assembled in Sebastian's hotel room in Rawalpindi, ready to head north-east out of Pakistan, I already knew that the expedition was going to be a disaster.

It was not a question of funds, which is where three of my own efforts had failed. Gerald Sebastian had enough silver-tongued persuasiveness for a dozen people. How else could a man raise half a million dollars for an expedition, without telling his backers what they would get out of it?

I had seen him cast his spell in New York, three months earlier, and knew I had met my master. He was a bantam-weight, silver-haired and hawk-nosed, with a clear-eyed innocence of manner I could never match.

"*Atlantis*," he had said, and the word glowed in the air in front of him. "Not in the middle of the Atlantic Ocean, as Colonel Churchward would have you believe. Not at Thera, or Crete, in the Mediterranean, as Skipios claims. Not among the Mayans, as Doctor Augustus Le Plongeon asserts. But *here*, where the world has never thought to look." He whipped out the map, placed it on the table, and set his right index finger in the middle of the great bowl of Xinjiang Province. "Right here!"

There were half a dozen well-dressed men and two women sitting at the long conference room table. They all craned forward to stare at the map. "Takla—Makan—Shamo," read one of them slowly. He was Henry Hoffman, a New York real estate multimillionaire who also happened to be Mr. Jackie Sands. He was seventy-five years old, and she was his third wife. He leaned closer to the map, peering through strong bifocals. "But it's marked as a *desert*."

"Exactly what it is." Gerald Sebastian had paused, waiting for the faces to turn back up to meet his eyes. "That's what the word *shamo* means, a sand desert—as distinguished from a pebble desert, which is a *gobi*. This is desert, extreme, wild, and uninhabited. But it wasn't always a desert, any more than there were always skyscrapers here on Manhattan. You have to look *under* the dunes, a hundred feet down. And then you will see the cities. Cities *drowned by sandstorms,* not by water."

He reached into his case and pulled out another rabbit: the images taken by the Shuttle Imaging Radar experiments. He slapped them onto the table, and turned to Will Reynolds. "Doctor Reynolds, if you would be kind enough to explain how these images are interpreted. . . ."

Reynolds coughed, genuinely uncomfortable at explaining his work to a group of laymen. "Well—uh—see, this is a strip taken by a synthetic aperture radar, the Shuttle Imaging Radar, on board the Shuttle Orbiter." He worked his hands together and cracked the knobby finger joints. Will Reynolds was a stork of a man, with a long neck, great ungainly limbs, and a mop of black hair. "It's sort of like a photograph, but it uses much longer wavelengths, microwaves rather than visible light. Centimeters, rather than micrometers. So it doesn't just see what's *on* the surface. Where the ground is dry, it sees *under* the surface, too. And in a real desert, where there's been no rain for years or decades, it can see a long way down. Tens of meters. Here's some earlier SEASAT and SIR-A shots of the Sahara Desert, where it hasn't rained and you can clearly see the old river courses, far below the surface sand dunes. . . ."

His hesitancy disappeared as he slipped into his special subject, and he was off and running.

Gerald Sebastian did not interrupt. He would not dream of interrupting. It was pure flummery, the oldest and best con-man style, with the right amount of technical and authentic detail to make it persuasive. Will Reynolds could not be bought, that was obvious. But he could be *sold*, and Sebastian had sold him on the project. Now he was showing the radar images of the Takla Makan, pointing out what seemed to be regular geometric figures under the sand dunes, where no such figures could be expected.

Those shapes looked like the natural cracking patterns of drying clay to me, but no one around the table suggested that. What do investment bankers, art museum patrons, and the rest of the New York *glitterati* know about clay cracks? And what do they care, when it's only half a million dollars at stake, and you might be part of the team that finds Atlantis? Nothing could beat that as cocktail party conversation. Sebastian knew his pigeons.

Very well; but what was I doing, following Sebastian on his wild chase to the world's most bleak and barren desert? I was a professional, a fundraiser and a treasure-hunter myself.

To understand that, you have to remember an old gold-miners' story. Two prospectors were out in the American West, late in the nineteenth century; they had looked for gold unsuccessfully for forty years. They had dug and panned and surveyed one particular valley from end to end, and found not an ounce of gold anywhere in it. Finally, they decided that there were better ways to get rich. They left the valley they had explored so carefully and so unproductively, and headed for the nearest big town. There they put every cent they had into buying provisions, horses, and wagons, and they both set up stores.

Then they started spreading the story: the world's biggest gold find had just been made, back in the valley they had come from. If you went for a stroll there, you would stumble over fist-sized nuggets of twenty-four carat.

The run on horses, wagons, and supplies was incredible. Everybody in town wanted to dash off to the wilderness and stake a claim. The two old prospectors had cornered the market for transportation and supplies, and they could name their price. They sold, and sold, and sold, until at last one of them found he had only one horse and one wagon left. He jumped into the wagon, whipped up the horse, and started to drive out of town. As he did so, he found he was running side by side with his old friend, also with horse and wagon.

"Where you heading?"

"Back to the valley—to get the gold!"

"Yeah!"

So I was along on Sebastian's ride. And I was sure that the same ghosts of golden discovery must fill and dominate the fine, phantasmagoric mind of Gerald Sebastian. He and I were cut from the same bolt of cloth. As the poet laureate of all confidence tricksters and treasure-seekers puts it, we were "given to strong delusion, wholly believing a lie."

In my own defense, let me point out that the full insanity of the enterprise was not obvious at once. It became apparent to me only when we assembled in Hong Kong, prior to flying to Pakistan.

There, in the Regent Hotel in Kowloon, looking out over Hong Kong Harbor with its crowded water traffic, I tried to buy Jackie Sands a drink. A dry martini, perhaps, which is what I was having. Paddy Elphinstone, our China expert, had warned me that it would be my last chance at a decent alcoholic cocktail for quite a while.

Jackie smiled and ordered an orange juice. It was predictable. She was dark-haired, clear-skinned, and somewhere between thirty-eight and forty-four. Her hair stood out in a black cloud around her head, her eyes were bright, and she was so healthy-looking it was disgusting. She seemed to glow. If she had ever tried alcohol, it must have been as a long-ago experiment.

"Gerald is entitled to his opinion," she was saying. "But I have my own. I didn't come here expecting to find Atlantis. And I'm sure we won't find Atlantis."

"Then what will we find?" I asked the question, but young Paddy Elphinstone seemed even more interested in the answer. He had been drinking before we arrived, then accepted the drink that Jackie refused and quadrupled it. As the waiters went by, he gabbled at them in their own tongues, Tamil and Malay and Thai and Mandarin and Cantonese. Now he was leaning forward, his chin low down toward the table top, staring at Jackie.

"Visitors," she said. "Old visitors."

Paddy laughed. "Plenty of those, to the Takla Makan. Marco Polo wandered through there, and the Great Silk Road ran north and south of it. The technology for horizontal well drilling in Turpan was imported all the way from Persia."

"I mean older than that. And farther away than that." Jackie reached out and put a carefully manicured, red-nailed hand on Paddy's. Wasn't she the woman I had imagined for twenty years, wandering the world at my side, the competent, level-headed companion that I had never managed to attract?

Her next words destroyed the fancy. "Visitors," she said. "Long, long ago. Aliens, from other stars. Beings who found the desert like home to them. They came, and then they left."

"Pretty neat trick," said Paddy. He was leaning back now, too drunk to pretend to sobriety. "Sure that they left, are you? Damn neat trick, if they did. D'yer know what Takla Makan means, in the local Turkic?"

I was sure that Jackie didn't. I didn't, either. I knew that Paddy had that incredible gift for languages, learning them as easily and idiomatically as a baby learns to talk. But I didn't know until that moment that Paddy Elphinstone was also an alcoholic.

"Takla Makan," he said again, and closed his eyes. His thin, straw-colored hair sagged in a cowlick over a pale forehead. "*Takla Makan* means this, Jackie Sands: 'Go in, and you don't come out.'"

At its western edge China meets three other countries: the Soviet Union to the north, Pakistan to the south, and a thin strip of Afghanistan between. That east-stretching tongue of Afghanistan would provide the easiest travel route, but it and the Soviet Union are both politically impossible. With no real choice, and a need for secrecy above all, Gerald Sebastian had arranged that we would move into China through Pakistan.

We drove from Rawalpindi to Gilgit, skirting the heights of the Karakoram Range. At Gilgit we made our final refueling stop, six hundred gallons for the trucks' enlarged tanks. Then we took the old path into Xinjiang, just as though we were heading for Kashi, on the western edge of the Takla Makan desert. Five miles short of the Chinese border we left the road and veered right.

I probably took more notice of our path than the others, because I was driving the first truck with Will Reynolds as companion and navigator. He was following our progress carefully, tousled dark head bent over maps and a terminal that hooked him into the Global Positioning System satellites. He called the turns to me for more than seven hours. Then, as the sun of early May began to set and the first sand dunes came into sight to the northeast, he nodded and folded the map.

"We're two hundred miles from the border, and we ought to be out of the danger area for patrols. Sebastian said he wants to stop early tonight. Keep your eyes open for a little lake ahead; we're going to stay by it."

I nodded, while Will put the map away and pulled out one of his precious radar images. Every spare moment went into them. Now he was trying to pinpoint our position on the picture and muttering to himself about "layover" location problems.

The lake, thirty yards across and fed by a thin trickle in a bed of white gravel, appeared in less than a mile. While the other truck caught up with us, I hopped out and bent down by the soda-crusted lakeside. The water was shallow, briny, and heavy with bitter alkalines.

I spat it out. "Undrinkable," I said to Sebastian, as he moved to join me.

He didn't argue, didn't want to taste it for himself to make sure. He knew why he had hired me, and he trusted his own judgment. "I'll get the desalinization unit," he said. "Tell the others. A gallon per person, to do what you like with."

"Washing?"

He gave me a remote smile and gestured at the pool's still surface.

Dinner—my job and Paddy's, we were the hired help—took another hour, cooking with the same diesel fuel that ran the motors and would power the hoist derrick. By the time we were finished eating, the first stars were showing. Fifteen minutes later the tents were inflated and moored. The trucks, packed with supplies and equipment, were emergency accommodation only.

We sat on tiny camp stools arranged in a circle on the rocky ground. Not around the romantic fire of Sebastian's movies—the nearest tree was probably three hundred miles away—but around a shielded oil lamp, hanging on a light tripod. Gerald Sebastian was in an ebullient mood. He had wandered around the camp, putting everything that appealed to his eye onto videotape, and now he was ready to relax. He was a rarity among explorers, one who did all his own camerawork and final program composition. He would add his commentaries back in America.

"The hard part?" he said, in answer to a question from Jackie. "Love, we're done with the hard part. We know where we're going, we know what we'll find there, we're all equipped to get it."

"What is it, d'you think?" said Paddy in a blurry voice. His words to me in Hong Kong concerning access to alcoholic drinks in China applied, I now realized, only to others. Paddy had brought along his own bottled supply, and from the way he was acting it had to be a generous one.

Instead of replying, Sebastian stood up and walked off to the trucks. He was back in a couple of minutes carrying a big yellow envelope. Without a word he slipped out half a dozen photo prints and passed them around the group. I felt the excitement goosepimpling the hair on my forearms. Sebastian had shown me pictures when we first talked, and I gathered he had shown others to Jackie Sands and Will Reynolds. But like a showman shining the spotlight on a different part of the stage for each different audience, he showed each set of listeners what it wanted to hear—and only that. I had asked a dozen times for more details, and always he had said, "Soon enough you'll see—when we get to Xinjiang." I had no doubt that even now there was another folder somewhere, one that none of us would see.

Back in the United States, Sebastian had produced for me only two photographs, of a ruby ring set in thick gold, and of a flat golden tablet the length of a man's hand, inscribed with unfamiliar ideographs. I couldn't relate either of those to Atlantis, but of course I didn't care. Atlantis was somebody else's part of the elephant.

The picture in my left hand was not one I had seen before. It was clear, with excellent detail and color balance, good enough to be used on one of Gerald Sebastian's TV documentaries. Some day it might be. For I was staring at a green statue, with a meter ruler propped alongside to show the scale, and although in fourteen years of wasted wandering I had seen the artifacts of every civilization on Earth, this, whatever it might be, was unlike any of them.

It was man-sized, and must have weighed a quarter of a ton. The plumed helmet and tunic might be Greek or Cretan, the sandals Roman. The face had the Egyptian styling, while the sword on the heavy buckled belt was vaguely central Asian. And if I stretched my imagination, I could see in the composed attitude of the limbs the influence of Indonesia and of Buddhism. Put the pieces together, and the sum was totally strange.

Strange, but not enough to excite me. The picture in my right hand did that. It was an enlargement of the statue's ornate belt. The buckle looked like the front of a modern hand calculator, with miniature numerals, function keys, and display screen. Next to it, attached to the belt but ready to be detached from it, was a bulbous weapon with sights, trigger, and a flared barrel. It was not a revolver, but it looked a lot like a power laser.

First things first. "Do you have the statue?" I asked, before anyone else could speak.

He had assumed his old seat in the circle. "If I did, I would not be here." He was sitting as immobile as a statue himself. "And if I thought I could obtain it alone, none of you would be here. Let me tell you a story. It concerns my earlier trip into the Takla Makan, and how I came to make it."

137

The lamp caught the keen profile and the dreamer's brow. The moon was rising. Far away to the northeast, the first desert dunes were a smoky blur on the horizon.

"I thought I knew it all," he said. "And then, three years ago, I was called in to help the executor of an estate in Dresden. Dull stuff, I thought, but an old friend called in a favor. You may ask, as I did, why me? It turned out that the old lady who died was a relative of Sir Aurel Stein, and she mentioned my name in her will." Paddy Elphinstone started, and Sebastian caught the movement. "That's right, Paddy, there's only one of him." He turned to the rest of us. "Aurel Stein was the greatest Oriental explorer of his time. And this was his stamping-ground"—he gestured around us—"for forty years, in the early part of this century. He covered China, Mongolia, and Xinjiang—Sinkiang, the maps called it in his day—like nobody else in the world. He lived in India and he died in Kabul, but he left relatives in Germany. It was more than a pleasure to look at that house in Dresden. It was an *honor.*

"Before I'd been in that place for an hour, I knew something unusual had been thrown my way. But it was a couple more days before I realized how exciting it was." He tapped the photographs on his knee. "Stein drew the statue, and described its dimensions. The pen-and-ink drawing was in the old lady's collection. Sir Aurel told in his journal exactly where he had found it, in a dry valley surrounded by dunes. He gave the location—or to be more accurate, he described how to reach the spot from Urumqi and the Turpan Depression. He knew it was an oddity and he couldn't identify its maker, but it was far too heavy to carry. Sixty years ago, that statue's belt didn't send its own message. Electronic calculators and power lasers didn't exist. So he left it there. He was content with the drawing, and he didn't set any great value on that. It could take an inconspicuous place in his works, and end up in the possession of an old German lady, dying in her late eighties in a Dresden rowhouse."

It was hard to be specific, but there was something different about Gerald Sebastian. I felt an openness, an eagerness in him since he had entered China, something that was quite different from his usual public persona. Evaluating his performance now, I decided that he was a little too obsessive to appeal to his own backers. He and Will Reynolds were brothers under the skin.

"I went there," he said. "Three hundred miles south of Urumqi, just as Sir Aurel Stein said, to the middle of the worst part of the desert. Of course, I didn't *expect* to find the statue. Chances were, if it were ever there, it was long gone. I knew that, so I went inadequately prepared and I didn't think through what I would do if I found it. But I had to look. Sam will understand that, even if the rest of you don't." He nodded his head at me, eyes unreadable in the lamplight. "Well, the valley was there, half filled with drifting sand. And I didn't have equipment with me. I spent one week digging—scrabbling, that's a better word—then I was running short of water." He slipped the photographs back into their envelope and stood up abruptly. "The statue was there. I found it on my last day. There was a gold tablet and a ruby ring, attached to the belt, and I took those. Then I photographed it, and I covered it with sand. It will be there still. We're going to lift it out this time and put it on the truck. And when we get it, we'll take it back for radioactive dating. My guess is that it is more than seven thousand years old."

He walked away, outside the circle of lamplight, over behind the two balloon-wheeled trucks. After a few seconds Jackie Sands followed him. Paddy was off in an alcoholic world of his own, eyes closed and mouth open. I looked at Will Reynolds, sitting hunched forward and tugging at his finger joints.

"Give me a hand to get Paddy to his tent, would you? It's getting cold, and I don't think he'll manage it on his own."

Will nodded and moved to the other side of Paddy. "I've seen it, you know," he said, as we lifted, one to each arm.

I paused. "The statue?"

"Naw." He gave a snuffling laugh. "How the hell would I see the statue? The *valley*. It shows on the radar images, clear as day. And there's structure underneath it—buildings, a whole town, buried deep in the sand. I saw 'em, before I'd ever met Gerald Sebastian."

"He contacted you?"

"No. I wrote to him. You see, after I interpreted the images and realized what I might be seeing, I asked the applications office at Headquarters for field trip funding, to collect some ground truth. And they *bounced* it—as though it was some dumb boondoggle to get me a trip to China!" Between us, we stuffed Paddy Elphinstone into his tent and zipped the flap. If he wanted to undress that was his own affair. "That made me so mad," said Will, "I thought, damn you bureaucrats. If you don't want this, there's others might. I'd seen one of Sebastian's travel programs about China, and I wrote to him. The hell with NASA! We'll find that city without 'em."

Will turned and lurched off toward his own tent. He had the height of a basketball player and none of the coordination.

Well, I thought, that's another piece of the elephant accounted for. So far as Will Reynolds was concerned, this illegal journey to China's western desert was just a field trip, a way to gather the data that justified his own interpretation of satellite images. I wondered, had Sebastian talked of Sir Aurel Stein's legacy in Dresden, and the follow-up trip to the Takla Makan desert *before* Will Reynolds had shown him those radar images? My skeptical soul assured me that he had not.

And yet I couldn't quite accept my own logic. While Sebastian had been speaking about Aurel Stein, a disquieting thought had been creeping up on me. From the day I was recruited by him, I had been sure that he and I had the same motives. Sure, he was smoother than I was, but inside we were the same. Now I wasn't sure. He was so terribly convincing, so filled with burning curiosity. Either his interest in exploration was powerful and genuine—or he was better at the bait-and-catch funding game than anyone in history. Was it somehow possible that *both* were true?

I lit a black Poona cheroot and stood there in the lamplit circle, noticing the temperature dropping fast around me. In this area, it would be well below freezing before dawn, and then back up to a hundred degrees by the next afternoon. I zipped up my jacket and started to put away the cooking equipment. With Paddy gone for the night, the number of hired help on the party was down to one.

The evening was not yet over. Before I had time to finish tidying up, Jackie Sands reappeared from the direction of the trucks. She was wearing a fluffy wool sweater, as dark, tangled, and luxuriant as her hair. She made no attempt to help—I wondered if she had ever in her whole life cleared up after dinner—but sat down on one of the camp stools.

"Destroying your lungs," she said.

"Do you tell that to your hubby, too?"

There was a flash of teeth, but I couldn't see her facial expression. "It's not worth telling things to Henry. He stopped accepting inputs years ago on everything except stocks and bonds."

"Does he smoke?"

"Not any more. Doctor's orders."

"So he *does* accept other inputs."

This time a chuckle accompanied the gleam of teeth. "I suppose he does. But not from me."

I flicked the cigar stub away and watched its orange-red spark cartwheel across the dusty surface. "That's one nice thing about deserts. No fire hazard." I sat down on a camp stool opposite her. "What can I do for you, Mrs. Hoffman?"

"Miss Sands. I don't use my husband's name. Do you have to be so direct?"

"It's nearly ten-thirty."

"That's not late."

"Not for Manhattan. But social functions end early in the Takla Makan. I have to be up at five. And it's getting cold."

"It is." She snuggled deeper into her sweater. "I thought this was supposed to be a hot desert. All right, straight to business. I know why Gerald Sebastian organized this expedition. He did it for fame and fortune, equal parts. I know why Will Reynolds came along; he wants to protect his scientific reputation. And I understand Paddy. He's a born explorer, along for the sheer love of it, and if he doesn't drink himself to death he'll be world famous before he's forty. But what about you, Sam? You sit and listen to everybody else, and you hardly say a word. What's your motive for being here?"

"Why do you want to know? And if it comes to that, what's your motive?"

"Mm. You show me yours and I'll show you mine, eh?" She stared straight into the lamp and pursed her lips. "You know, being on an expedition like this is a bit like being on a

141

small cruise ship. After a few days, you start to tell near-strangers things you wouldn't admit to your family."

"I don't have a family."

"No?" Her eyebrows arched. "All right then, I'll do it. I'll play your game. A swap. Who first?"

"You."

"You're a hard man, Sam-I-Am. Lordie. Where should I begin? Do you know what SETI is?"

"Settee? Like couch?"

"No. SETI, like S-E-T-I—the Search for Extra-Terrestrial Intelligence. Heard of it?"

"No. I'm still looking for signs of intelligence on Earth. What is it, some sort of game?"

"Not to me. Just think what it will mean if we ever find evidence that there are other intelligent beings in the universe. It will change everything we do. Change the basic way we think, maybe stop us all blowing ourselves up. I believe the work is enormously important, and for nearly five years I've been giving money to promote SETI research."

"Henry's money?"

She sat up a little straighter. "My allowance. But most of the research work is highly technical, with radio receivers and electronics and signal analysis. I can't even understand how my money is spent."

"Which makes it sound like a classic rip-off."

"It does sound like that, I admit. But it's not."

Her voice was totally earnest. Unfortunately, that's one prime qualification to be a total sucker. "You *think* it's not," I said.

"Put it that way if you want to. I've never regretted giving the money. But then I heard about this expedition, and it really made me think. Sebastian says he has found Atlantis, with a technological civilization as advanced as ours. But I say, it's just as likely he found evidence of *visitors* to the Earth, ones who came long ago."

"And just happened to look exactly like humans? That's too implausible."

"Not if they were truly advanced. Beings like that would be able to look just as they wanted to look. Anyway, Sam, you're on the wrong side of the argument. Suppose there's

142

only a one-in-a-thousand chance that what we are looking for is evidence of aliens. I'm still better off spending my money coming here, to do something myself, rather than being a little bit of something I don't even understand. Don't you agree?"

"Oddly enough, I do. It's one of the golden rules: stay close to the place your money is spent."

"But you don't accept the idea of visitors to this planet?"

"I don't reject it. I just say it's improbable."

"Right. But it's possible." She sounded short of breath. "And that's what I think, too. So that's me, and that's why I'm here, and the only reason I'm here. Now how about you?"

I didn't want to talk, but now I seemed committed to it. I lit another cigar and blew smoke toward the half-moon. "I'm going to be a big disappointment to you," I said, with my face averted. "You're on an expedition with a world-famous traveler and television celebrity, a NASA scientist, and a born explorer. I'm the bad apple in the barrel. You see, I'm a treasure hunter. I came with Gerald Sebastian for one simple reason: there's a chance—an outside chance, but a hell of a lot better than the odds that you'll find your extraterrestrials—that I'm going to walk away from this holding a whole basket of money. That's why I'm here."

"I don't believe you!"

I shrugged. "I knew you wouldn't. I didn't think you'd like it, and you don't. But it's true."

"You may have convinced yourself that it's true, but it isn't." She sounded outraged. "My God, if all you wanted was money, there are a hundred easier ways to get it. Play the stock market, work in a casino, go into the insurance business. You don't have to come to the ends of the earth to make money. I don't think you know your own motivation, or you want to hide it from me."

I threw away my second cigar—this one much less than half-smoked. "Miss Sands, how long have you been married?"

"Why, four years, I suppose. Five years in August. Not that I see why—"

"Do you love Henry Hoffman?"

"What! I—of course I do. I *do*. And it's no damned business of yours."

"But you left him for months to come on this expedition."

"I told you why!"

"Right. Do you enjoy sleeping with him? Never mind, ignore that, and let's assume you do. You're quite right, it *is* no business of mine. All I'm trying to say is that people do a lot of different things to make money, and it's no one else's concern *why* they do it. And sometimes the obvious assumptions about why people do things are right, and sometimes they are quite wrong. So why won't you believe me, when I tell you that I'm here for the simplest possible reason, to make my fortune?"

But she was on her feet, swiveling around and heading fast for the dark bulk of the trucks. "Damn you," she said as she walked away. "My marriage is fine, and anyway it's none of your bloody business. Keep your big nose out of it."

She was gone, leaving me still with the clearing-up to take care of. Before I did that I picked up the lamp and went off to look for the cigar I had thrown away. The way things were going, before the end of this expedition I might be craving a half-smoked cigar.

I slept poorly and woke at dawn. When I emerged from my tent Paddy already had the stove going and water heated for coffee. Apparently he was one of those unfortunates who never suffer a hangover, which made his long-term prospects for full alcoholism all too good. One good hangover will keep me sober for months. He nodded at me cheerfully while he shaved. "Sleep well?"

"Lousy. I thought I could hear noises outside the tent— like people talking. I guess I was dreaming."

"No. You *were* listening to *them*." Paddy pointed his razor at the sand dunes to the north. "It's called *mingsha*— singing sand. It will get worse when we move deeper into the Takla Makan."

"I'm not talking about sand dunes, Paddy. I'm talking about *people*. Conversations, whistling, calling to animals. I even heard somebody playing the flute."

"That's right." He was intolerably perky for the early morning. "Hold on a minute." He put his razor down on the little folding table that held his coffee, towel, soap, and a cheese sandwich, and ran off to dive into his tent. A second later he reappeared with a paperback book in his hand.

"We're not the first people to visit this place, not by a long shot. It was a big obstacle for two thousand years on the Great Silk Road, and all the travelers skirted it either north or south. Marco Polo came by the Takla Makan seven hundred years ago, when he was traveling around on Kubla Khan's business. He called it the Desert of Lop. Here's what he says about the desert."

While I poured sweetened black coffee for myself, Paddy found his place in the book and began to read aloud. " 'In this tract neither beasts nor birds are met with, because there is no kind of food for them. It is asserted as a well-known fact that this desert is the abode of many evil spirits, which lure travelers to their destruction with extraordinary illusions . . . they unexpectedly hear themselves called by their own names, and in a tone of voice to which they are accustomed. Supposing the call to proceed from their companions, they are led away from the direct road and left to perish. At night, they seem to hear the march of a large cavalcade.' And here's another choice bit. 'The spirits of the desert are said at times to fill the air with the sounds of all kinds of musical instruments'—there's your flute, Sam— 'and also of drums and the clash of arms.' And it wasn't only Marco Polo. A Chinese monk, Fa Xian, passed this way in the fifth century, and he wrote that there were 'evil spirits and hot winds that kill every man who encounters them, and as far as the eye can see no road is visible, only the skeletons of those who have perished serve to mark the way.' "

Paddy closed his book and grinned happily. "Good stuff, eh? And nothing has changed. At least we know what we're in for over the next few weeks." He went to put the book back in his tent.

The dust-red sun was well above the horizon now, and the other three team members emerged from their tents within a couple of minutes of each other. Between cooking breakfast and striking camp, Paddy and I had no more chance for talk.

Gerald filmed our activities and the scenery around us, then disappeared into the second truck. But Jackie Sands gave me an extra nice smile and even helped collect the breakfast plates. Whatever had annoyed her so last night was apparently all forgotten or forgiven.

She had discarded yesterday's shirt and jeans in favor of a long, loose-fitting dress of white cotton and thick-soled leather sandals. The clothes made good hot-weather sense. So did the different hair styling, smoothing the viper's nest of tangles to long, dark curls. But she had also applied heavy makeup and bright lipstick, and that was not so smart. I wondered if she would keep it up when we melted in the heart of the desert and the trucks' inside temperature soared over a hundred and ten.

And then I noticed the dark rings under her eyes, which makeup could not quite hide. Like me, Jackie had apparently suffered a disturbed night.

We were on our way by six. We planned to drive only in the early morning and late afternoon, resting through the worst heat of midday. Today we would be penetrating the true dune country of the desert. I thought that in spite of Gerald Sebastian's optimism, the tough part of the expedition was just beginning.

We drove almost due north, while the land ahead turned to rolling sand hills, enormous, lifeless, seemingly endless. Dun-colored, distinct, and sun-shadowed, each dune rose five or six hundred feet above the dead plain. By nine o'clock their profiles smoked and shimmered in dust and heat haze. It was easy to see why travelers regarded this desert as featureless and impassable. The dunes moved constantly, shaped by wind, creeping across the arid landscape. Nothing could grow here, nothing provided permanence.

And Will Reynolds, seated at my side, was in his element. His space images revealed the contour of every dune. He had known, before he left Washington, their extent, their shape, and their steepness. Months ago he had sat at his desk and plotted an optimum route, weaving us north to Gerald Sebastian's destination on an efficient and sinuous path that took advantage of every break in the dune pattern.

Now he was finally able to apply his knowledge. As I drove, and the thermometer above the truck's dashboard climbed implacably through the nineties, Will chuckled to himself and called out compass headings. At a steady twenty-five miles an hour, we snaked our way forward without a hitch.

Other than an occasional tamarisk bush, we saw nothing and no one. A billion Chinese people lived far to the east, on the alluvial plains and along the fertile river valleys, but no one lived here. This land made Tibet's high plateau appear lush and fertile, even to China's central development committee. According to Gerald Sebastian, the danger of our discovery was too small to worry about.

By ten-thirty, there was no scrap of shade from even the steepest of the dunes. We halted, raised the parasol over both trucks, and settled down to wait. That gave me my first chance to talk to Sebastian alone since we had stopped for dinner last night.

I followed him as he prowled outside the shady zone with his video camera. He spoke with his eye still to the viewfinder. "All right, Sam. Say it."

"You're the one who has to say it."

He turned to face me, squinting up at me in the strong sun. "I don't understand. What do you want?"

"An explanation." We automatically walked on up the dune, farther out of earshot of the others. The heat of the sand burned through our shoes. "Last night, you told us all that you took the ruby ring and the gold tablet from the statue on your last trip."

"Quite right, I said that. And it's quite true."

"So why didn't Sir Aurel Stein do the same thing, when *he* found and drew a picture of the statue?"

He looked me in the eye, the honest stare that was part of his stock-in-trade. "I don't know, Sam. All I can tell you is that he didn't take them. Naturally, I asked myself the same question."

"And how did you answer it?"

"First, I thought that maybe he planned to return for the statue itself, and so he left everything else behind, too. Then

147

when Xinjiang was closed to foreigners, in 1930, he couldn't go back. It's a weak argument, I know, because we all carry what we can, and only leave behind what we can't haul with us. My second explanation is not much better. Aurel Stein didn't show the tablet and ring in his drawing; therefore, they were not there when he explored the valley. Someone else was there between his visit and mine. I'm sure you see what's wrong with that idea."

"People take things from archeological sites. They don't leave them there."

"Exactly!" There was a furious, frenzied energy to Gerald Sebastian now, an effervescence that had not been there before we reached the Takla Makan. But he was not worried, only excited. "So what is the explanation? Sam, that's what we're going to find out. And this time, we didn't come lacking equipment."

He was not referring to the pulleys, hoist, and derrick on the truck. So what was it? I knew the complete inventory of the truck I was driving. Maybe Paddy Elphinstone could tell me about the other one.

"Don't worry, Sam," Sebastian was saying. "If I knew what had happened, I would have told you." He was interrupted by a cry from the camp. Jackie Sands was standing out from under the parasol, calling and waving her arms at us. We ran back to her.

"It's Will Reynolds," she said as soon as we were close enough. "He was sitting next to me, and suddenly he started to speak. He sounded all slurred, as though he was drunk. Then he tried to stand up and fell off his chair. I think he had a stroke. He's unconscious."

He wasn't, not quite. When we got to him his eyes were rolling from side to side under half-open lids and he was muttering to himself. I sniffed his breath, felt his pulse, then touched my fingers to his forehead.

"Not a stroke. And not drunk. He's overheated—get his shirt open and bring some water. Where the devil is Paddy?"

Before I had an answer to that question, Will Reynolds was sitting up and looking about him. We had damp cloths on his wrists, temples, and throat.

"What happened?" he said.

"What do you remember?" I wanted to be sure that he was functioning normally.

"Over there." He pointed up at the brow of a dune, into the eye of the sun. "I saw them marching over the top of it and I stood up to shout to you and Gerald. Then I woke up here."

"Saw who?" said Jackie. She looked at me. "I was sitting there, and I didn't see a thing."

"The patrol, or whatever it was. A line of men and pack-horses and camels, one after another, parading across the top of the dune. There must have been fifty of them." He turned to Gerald. "That's one idea of yours out of the window. You said there was a negligible chance that we'd have trouble with Chinese patrols, and we run into one the first day. I guess they didn't see us down here." He tried to stand, then swayed and leaned back against me. "What's happened to me?"

"Just rest there," I said. "You're all right, Will. You've got a slight case of heatstroke. Take it easy today, and tomorrow you'll be back to normal."

The nature of his overheated fancy worried me. Had he, half-asleep, somehow overheard Paddy reading to me this morning, and built the idea of desert caravans into his subconscious? Now Paddy himself was returning from almost the direction that Will had pointed, shuffling along between two dunes and wearing a coolie hat that covered his head and shielded his shoulders. His walk told me that he was not sober.

"Where have you been?" Sebastian's voice was more than excited. It was demented.

Paddy's face had a blurry, unfocused look. "I thought I saw something." He made a vague gesture behind him. "Out there, between the dunes. Some*body*," he corrected, with the precision of the drunkard.

Add that to Will Reynolds' statement, and you had something to catch Sebastian's full attention.

"Who was it?"

Paddy shook his head, but before the gesture was complete Sebastian was running off between the dunes, following the weaving line of Paddy's footsteps. Then he went scrambling up the steepest slope of the nearest mountain of sand. Three minutes later he was back, slithering down amid a great cloud of dust.

"Of all the bloody bad luck!" When he got too agitated his upper-class accent began to fall apart. "One patrol per thousand square miles, and we run smack into it."

"You saw it?" I asked.

"I saw their dust, and that was enough." He ran to the camp and began to throw things anyhow into the trucks. "Come on, we're getting out of here. If we head north we can run clear of them."

I folded down the parasol. "What about Reynolds? He's not fit to navigate."

"He can travel in the second truck." Sebastian hesitated for a moment, staring first at Paddy and then at Jackie. I could read his thoughts. Who was going to drive that one, if he navigated for me?

"Will Reynolds has the track through the dunes clearly marked on his radar images," I said. "I'm pretty sure Miss Sands could call the turns for me."

"Do it." The trucks were loaded, and already he was hustling dazed Will and drunk Paddy into the second one. "And don't stop unless you need to consult with us. We'll be right behind you."

I swung up into the driver's seat and put my hand on the dashboard. We were in the hottest part of the afternoon. The grey exposed metal would blister skin. As Jackie moved to the seat beside me, and muttered her protest at the heat of the leather, I leaned out again. "What time do you want to make camp?" I called to Sebastian. "Sunset?"

"No. There should be a decent moon tonight. Keep going as long as you can see and stay awake." The engine behind me started, growling into low gear. His voice rang out above it. "There may be other patrols. We have to reach that valley—*soon*."

For the first hour it was the silence of people with too much to say. Jackie kept her head down, pored over the images, and called off the turns clearly and correctly. I stared at the land ahead, drove, sweated, and wondered why I had such a terrible headache.

"Will you do me a disgusting favor?" I asked at last.

"What? While you're driving?"

"Dig down into the knapsack behind you, and give me a cigar."

"Yuck."

When she reached out to put the lit cheroot in my mouth I turned to nod my thanks. She had wiped the makeup off her face with paper towels, and patches of sweat discolored the armpits and back of her white cotton dress. The dress itself had become dust-grey. Trickles of perspiration were running down her brow and cheeks.

"It will start to cool off in about two hours," I said.

"Two more hours of this. God." While I was still looking at her, she reached up with both hands and pushed the mass of dark hair deliberately off her head.

"You wear a wig," I said brainlessly.

"No. I wear six of them. A look for all occasions. Or almost all." She sighed and ran her hands through her hair. "My God, that feels good."

Her hair was short, almost boyish, a light blond showing the first lines of grey. Without the wig her face had a different shape, and oddly enough she looked younger.

She stared back at me with only a trace of embarrassment. "Well, Sam-I-Am, there's the dreadful truth. Next comes the glass eye and the wooden leg."

"Slipping down the ladder rung by rung. Have a cigar."

"I've not come to that yet. But I'd sell my best friend for a glass of chilled orange juice." She laughed. "You know, it's hard on Will, but I'm glad that I'm not riding in that other truck. Paddy's sloshed all the time, and I think Gerald is going crazy."

Her cheerful manner didn't quite convince.

"You had a fight with Gerald," I said.

"Why do you say that?"

"Guessing. You were both too keen for you to ride with me. And you looked exhausted this morning. You had a fight with him last night, after you left me."

"No. After dinner, and before I sat with you by the lamp. I suppose that's why I came to you—I wanted to avoid more contact with him."

"Thanks."

"It worked. He didn't try to come to my tent. But I had a

terrible night anyway. I'm normally a great sleeper. Head on pillow, and I'm gone. Only last night. . . ."

With most people I'd have suggested a sleeping pill. Jackie would no doubt have given me a lecture on drug abuse.

"Horrible dreams!" she went on. "I got up feeling like a wet Kleenex."

"Me too. Did you hear things outside?"

"Yes!"

"People talking, and animals, and music?" I slowed the truck and stared at her.

She frowned back at me. "No. Nothing like that. I heard storm noises, and rushing water, and horrible sounds like buildings falling over. In fact, in the middle of the night I was so scared I opened my tent and looked out to see what was happening. I thought there must be flash floods or something. But everything outside was quiet. I decided I must have been asleep without knowing it. And yet I still couldn't sleep. What's happening, Sam? Is it all nerves?"

Before I would accept that, I'd believe something more mundane, like bad food or water. Or even—I couldn't stop the thoughts—deliberate drugging or poisoning. Gerald Sebastian controlled all the water supply from the distillation unit. *Was* it no more than alcohol with Paddy, and heat stroke with Will Reynolds?

"You said Gerald was going crazy. What did you mean by that, Jackie?"

And now she did seem embarrassed. Her eyes moved to stare at the truck's radiator emblem. "I wish I hadn't said that, even though it's true enough. I don't think you have a very good opinion of me. So it probably won't surprise you to find out that Gerald and I are lovers."

"Surprise, no. Upset, maybe."

A quick sideways flash of her eyes in my direction. "Thanks, Sam. That's kind when I'm not looking my best. You know, that's the first nice thing you've said to me. You pretend to be a human icicle, but you're not. I'm glad. But I want you to know that Gerald wasn't the reason I'm on this expedition. I'm serious about the SETI work, and I wanted to come here long before he and I started anything."

"I believe you. Henry doesn't know?"

"Know, or care. He's fascinated by Gerald, thinks he's brilliant."

"So do I. He is."

"The Gerald Sebastian that I met in New York certainly was. He knew where he was going, how to get there, just what he wanted."

"Present company included?"

"I guess so. But once we reached Pakistan he changed completely. He's a monomaniac now. All day yesterday in the truck, while he drove, he talked and talked and talked."

"Of course he did. Jackie, this is his baby."

"You don't understand. He didn't talk about the expedition, the way he had in Hong Kong. Or rather he did, but not in a sensible way. He went on and on about *Atlantis*—about the rivers and lakes there, and the flower gardens, and fruit trees, and white sailboats moving along streets like Venetian canals. Sam, he was totally dippy. As though he thought he had been there himself, and knew just what it was like. I tried to tell him he had to get hold of himself, but it was useless. He couldn't stop. And Paddy was no help at all. He just sat there in the truck with a dreamy look on his face."

I remembered my discussion with Gerald Sebastian regarding Aurel Stein's failure to take the ring and gold tablet from the statue. He had seemed wildly excited, but as rational as you could ask. "I'm sorry, Jackie. I can't see Sebastian that way."

"Nor could I, three days back. Sam, he's your colleague and your boss. But Gerald and I were *lovers,* for heaven's sake. Less than a week ago we couldn't get enough of each other. But last night after dinner, when we went to his tent. . . ."

I could complete that thought, and also the whole proposition. Gerald hadn't wanted to make love to Jackie; Jackie needed her self-esteem; therefore, something must be seriously wrong with Gerald.

"Oh, don't be an idiot, Sam." And I hadn't said a word. "It's not that he's tired of me, or got other things on his mind. Anway, I wouldn't get bent out of shape about Gerald and sex. I'm telling you, he's gone *crazy.*"

It was her inconsistency that convinced me. She had

wanted Sebastian in her tent right after dinner, but later she wanted to avoid him altogether.

Perfect, I thought. I'm on an expedition with a crazy leader, a drunk interpreter, a brain-fried navigator, and a wild lady who thinks we will find little green men in the middle of the Takla Makan. Disaster on wheels.

And with all that to worry about, what thought poked its way again and again into my forebrain? Of course. It was Jackie's comment that I was a human icicle.

We had stopped talking. Maybe she thought I didn't believe a word she'd said, and was waiting for a chance to talk about her with Sebastian. Maybe she felt as exhausted as I did. My head was still aching, and I drove by instinct, following the route that Jackie gave me without thinking or caring where it led. The sun set, the moon came up, and we were able to cruise on without stopping. The temperature went from hot to cool to cold. About eight-thirty, Jackie stirred in her seat.

"I can go without dinner, Sam, but I have to have warm clothes. My legs are beginning to freeze. You have to stop."

I emerged from my reverie. The dunes were all around us. At night they became frozen ocean breakers, looming high and dark above the moving truck. Sometimes my tired eyes could see long shapes scudding across their flanks. Was this the illusion that had fueled Gerald Sebastian's sea-fantasies?

"How much farther to go?"

Jackie had put her wig on again and sat hugging herself. "No more than forty miles. Two hours, at the rate we've been going. But I don't care. I want to stop and rest."

I let us coast to a halt. "Gerald will never agree to it. When he's this close he'll want to get there tonight. In less than two hours the moon will set and it will be too dark to drive."

"We'll be there in the morning."

Jackie didn't understand treasure-hunters. The idea of camping here, when we were so close to the valley. . . .

Gerald popped out of the cabin of the other truck almost before it had stopped moving. "What's the problem?" His voice echoed off the dunes and he ran to peer in at us. "Why are you stopping?"

"My eyes," I said. "They're so tired I'm seeing double. And I'm cold and hungry. We have to take a break."

Jackie said nothing, but her hand touched my arm in appreciation.

"But we're almost there!" said Sebastian. "It's a straight run from here, a child could drive it."

"I know, but I need rest—and so do you."

He turned to stare at the moon. I could see his face, and although it was tired and lined his expression was perfectly sane. "Twenty minutes," he said after a moment. "That will give us time to eat. Then—"

"No." Jackie did not raise her voice. "You can do what you like, Gerald, but I'm not going any farther tonight. And Will Reynolds should be asleep in his tent, not jolting around in a truck. If you want to go on, you'll do it without Will and me."

There was a moment when I thought Sebastian would explode at her. Then he nodded, lowered his head, and marched without a word to the other truck.

I could never earn a living as a fortune-teller. My premonition had told me that we were in for a grim evening. Instead it proved to be the most peaceful few hours since we had left Hong Kong.

Will Reynolds was fully recovered. Paddy was semi-sober. And Gerald Sebastian hid any angry feelings he had toward Jackie under icy politeness. Only his eyes betrayed him. They turned, at every gap in the conversation, to the north. On the other side of those moonlit dunes, less than forty miles away, lay his obsession. I could share his feelings.

We had halted at about eight forty-five. At nine-fifteen, when we had finished a meal of hot tinned beef and biscuits, Sebastian wandered away from the lamplight and stood looking wistfully up at the haloed moon. It was setting, and a northern breeze veiled its face with fine sand.

Abruptly he swung around and walked back to us. "I'm going on, Sam," he said to me. "I have to go on. You follow me tomorrow morning."

His voice carried the command of the expedition's leader. Jackie looked at me to raise an objection. I could not. I knew the desire too well. All I could do was wish that I could go with him.

"You have only one more hour of moonlight," I said.

"I know." He picked up a gallon container of water and climbed into the truck that I had been driving. "You're in charge here. See you tomorrow."

The truck rumbled away between the mountains of sand. We watched it leave in silence, following it with our ears for what felt like minutes. When the last faint mutter of the engine was lost, I was able to pick up in the new silence the sounds of the cooling landscape around us. It was the *mingsha* again, the song of the dunes as they lost their heat to the stars. There were faint, crystalline chimes of surface slidings, broken by lower moans of movement deep within the sandhills. It was easy to imagine voices there, the whistle and call of far-off sentinels.

"The dragon-green, the luminous, the dark, the serpent-haunted sea," said Paddy suddenly. He was gazing out beyond the circle of lamplight, and his eyes were wide. Without another word he stood up, turned, and went off to his own tent.

We stared after him. Within a couple of minutes Will Reynolds rose to his feet. He shivered, snorted, and glared at the fading moon. "Seen that in New Mexico," he said. "Dust halo. Sandstorm on the way. It'll be a bugger. Gotta get some sleep." He lurched away.

And then there were two. Jackie and I sat without speaking while the night grew colder and the sands murmured into sleep. "Did you understand what Paddy said?" she said at last.

I shook my head. Our thoughts had been running along in parallel. "He seemed to be talking about the sea, too, but we're in one of the driest places in the world. Will Reynolds made a lot more sense. I've seen that haloed moon myself in desert country. It's caused by a high dust layer. If there's a sandstorm on the way we have to start early tomorrow, or Sebastian may be in trouble. We have all the food and the water distillation unit on this truck."

We left the camp just as it stood, the lamp still burning, and walked across to Jackie's tent. There we hesitated.

"Good night, Sam," she said at last. "I don't know if I'll be able to sleep, but sweet dreams."

"And you, Jackie." Then, as she was putting her dark head into the tent, "I have some Halcion here. Sleeping tablets. If you'd like one."

She paused and pulled her head out of the tent. Then she held out her hand. "Just this once. Don't get me into bad habits."

"Tomorrow, your first cigar." I watched as she closed the tent, then walked back to turn out the lamp. The moon was on the horizon, a smoky, grey blur. Overhead no stars were visible. By the time that I stepped into my tent and climbed into my sleeping bag the night was totally dark.

Sleep is mystery, a force beyond control. The previous night, with nothing to worry about, I had been restless. To-night, hours away from what could be the greatest event of my life, I put my head down and enjoyed the dreamless, uninvaded slumber that we mistakenly assign to small children. I did not stir until Paddy unzipped my tent and an-nounced that I would miss coffee and eggs if I didn't get a move on. Then I woke from a sleep so deep that for a mo-ment I had no idea where I was.

Neither Paddy nor Will seemed to remember anything strange about their last night's behavior. We were in the truck before six-thirty, facing north into a cold, grit-filled wind. Visibility was down to less than two hundred yards and we would be reduced to map and compass. It promised to be slow work, and I intended to drive carefully. This truck contained a hundred pounds of plastic explosive, and no one knew why Gerald Sebastian had brought it. Plastic is safe enough without a detonator, everyone tells you so, but it makes an uncomfortable travel companion.

I asked Will, bent over his image, for a first direction. And it was then, as I slipped into first gear and looked beyond the closest dunes to a red-brown sky, that I learned my mis-take.

Sleep had not been without dreams, and Gerald Sebas-tian's vision was a strong one—strong enough to infect oth-ers. Night memories came flooding back to me.

157

It was evening, with sunset clouds of red and gold. I stood next to the green statue, but it was no longer a lonely mono-lith half-buried in grey sand. Now it formed part of a great line of identical statues, flanking an avenue beside a broad canal. Laden pack animals walked the embankment, cam-els and donkeys and heavy-set horses, and I heard the jingle of metal on carved leather harnesses. A flat-bottomed boat eased along past me. The crew were tall, fair-skinned women with braided amber hair, singing to the music of a dreamy flute player cross-legged in the dragon's-head bow. Beyond the embankment, as far as I could see, buildings of white limestone rose eighty to a hundred feet above the water. They were spired and windowless, mellow in the late sunlight. The wind was at my back. I could smell apple blossom and pear blossom from the dwarf trees that grew between the statues.

I moved forward along the pebbled embankment. In half a mile the canal broadened to a lake bordered by lotus plants and water-lilies. Although the waters stretched to the purple haze of the horizon, I knew that they were fresh, not salt.

On the quiet lake, their sails dipping rose-red in the eve-ning sun, moved dozens of small boats. It was obvious that they were pleasure craft, sailing the calm lacustrine waters for pure enjoyment.

As I watched, there was a sudden shivering of the land-scape. The sky darkened, there was the sound of thunder. The buildings trembled, the road cracked, lake waters gathered and divided. The dream shattered.

"Sam!" The shout came from Jackie and Paddy in the back seat. I found we were heading at a thirty degree angle up the side of a dune, four-wheel drive scrabbling to give purchase on the shifting sands. A second before we tipped over I brought us around to head down again.

"Sorry!" I raised a hand in apology and fought back to level ground, horribly aware of our explosive cargo. "Lost concentration. It won't happen again."

Will had just got round to looking up. "North-west, not north," he said calmly. "Look, there's his tracks. Follow them where you can."

To our left, almost hidden by blown sand, I saw the

ghostly imprints of balloon tires. New sand was already drifting in to fill them. I followed their line and increased our speed. In full day, the temperature in the truck began to inch higher.

After another ten miles the tire tracks faded to invisibility. But by that time we were on the final stretch, a long, north-running ridge that led straight to the valley. Less than an hour later we were coasting down a shallow grade of powdery white sand that blew up like smoke behind us.

"Half a mile," said Will Reynolds. "Look, all the contours are right. There's a whole city underneath us, deep in the sand." He thrust an image under my nose. It showed a broad pattern of streets, picked out as dark lines on a light background. I thought I recognized the curving avenues and the sweep of a broad embankment, and saw again in my mind the white sails and the laden animals. But I had no time for more than a moment's glance. Then my attention moved to the valley ahead of us.

He was there. So was the truck. And so was the statue. When we turned the final lip of the valley I could see the green warrior standing waist-deep in a great pit. Sebastian must have been working all night to dig it clear. Now he was leaning over the back of the truck, so uniformly covered in white dust that he was himself like a stone statue. The derrick had already been swung out over the rear of the truck. Chains were clinched around the statue's broad belly and hooked to iron cables over the pulley. Red sticks of explosive stood near it on the sand, with detonators already in place.

Our diesel made plenty of noise but Sebastian did not seem to hear us. He was working the engine on the back of his truck. As Will Reynolds and I jumped down from the front seat there was a chattering of gears and the scrape and clatter of chains. The statue moved a little, altering its angle. The sound of the engine growled to a deeper tone. The chains groaned, the statue tilted and began to lift.

I understood the plastic explosive now, but it would be unnecessary. The statue was not anchored at its base. It moved infinitely slowly, but it moved, inching up from the depths. Sand fell away from it, and after a few more seconds the ponderous torso was totally visible.

159

Will and I slowed our pace down the slope. There was every sign that Sebastian had matters under full control. At the same time, I marveled that he could have done so much, alone, in such a short time. The valley was perhaps a quarter of a mile long and a hundred yards across. And the white sand was everywhere, a uniform layer of unguessable depth. Judging from its general level, no more than the top of the statue's head would have peered above it when the truck first arrived. To reach the point where the chains and tackle could be attached, Gerald Sebastian must have moved many tons of dry sand.

When we were still twenty yards away, and while Paddy behind me was calling out to the unheeding Sebastian, I looked along the line of the valley. In my mind I saw a hundred companion statues stretched beneath the lonely desert. As I stared, some final load of sand was shed at the figure's base. There was a faster whirring of gears, the cable moved quickly, and the whole statue was suddenly hanging in midair. Suspended on the flexible cable, the body turned. The blind, angry gaze swung to meet me, then on to survey the whole valley.

I did not think it then, but I thought of it later. And I understood it for the first time, that simple epitaph of Tamburlaine the Great: "If I were alive, you would tremble."

As the swinging statue completed its turn, to look full on Gerald Sebastian, many things happened at once.

The sky darkened and the air filled with a perfume of apple and pear blossom, one moment before the plastic explosive by the pit blew up. A flash of white fire came from it, brighter than the sun. It blinded me. When I could see again, the statue was no longer hanging from the chains. It stood on the ground, eight and a half feet high, and towered into a leaden sky. As I watched, it moved. It turned, and took one ponderous, creaking step toward Gerald Sebastian.

He screamed and backed away, lifting his hands in front of his face. But he no longer stood on powdery desert sand. He stood on a broad avenue, at the brink of a great lake bordered by apple groves. The statue took another lumbering step forward. Gerald Sebastian seemed unable to turn and run. He backed into the lake, among the lotus flowers and lilies, until the water was to his knees. Then he himself became a statue, frozen, mouth agape.

The face of his pursuer was hidden from me, but as it bent forward to stare into Sebastian's eyes I heard a cruel, rumbling laugh. I ran forward across the avenue to the edge of the lake, as a great green hand reached out and down. Sebastian was lifted, slowly and effortlessly. He hung writhing in midair, the grip around his throat cutting off his new screams.

The other hand reached forward. Sebastian's jacket was ripped from his body. Carved jade fingers stripped from beneath his shirt a ruby ring and an engraved gold tablet, and tucked them into the statue's buckled belt. "Xe ho chi!" growled a deep voice. The meaning was unmistakable: "Mine!"

There was a roar of triumph. "Ang ke-hi!" Then the statue was wading into the water, still holding Gerald Sebastian in its remorseless grip. I ran after them, splashing through the blooming water-lilies. Soon I was waist-deep in the cool lake. I halted. The green colossus strode on into deepening waters, still carrying Sebastian. As his head dipped toward the surface he gave one last cry of terror and despair. The statue raised him high in the air, then plunged him under with terrible violence. He did not reappear.

The head swung to face the shore. The blind gaze focused, found me. The wide mouth grinned in challenge.

I turned and fled from the lake, blundering up onto the embankment with its line of fruit trees. The statue was out of the water now, striding back toward me. I ran on, to cower against the shelter of a squat grey obelisk. As my soaked clothing touched its stone base there was a second burst of white light. I became blind again, blind and terror-stricken. The statue was stalking the embankment. I could hear the clanking tread of its progress.

Where could I hide, where could I run to? Again I tried to flee. Something was clutching me, holding me at thigh level.

Sight returned, and with it the beginnings of sanity. I saw a stone statue before me, but it stood silent and motionless. On its belt sat a ring of ruby fire and an engraved gold tablet.

Beyond the silent effigy I saw for one moment the faint outlines of white buildings, cool green water, and a hundred tiny sails. A freshwater wind blew on my face, filled with lotus blossoms. But in moments, that vision also faded. Superimposed on its dying image appeared once more the dry, dusty valley, deep in the sterile desert. Another few seconds, and the ghostly outline of a truck flickered back into existence, then steadied and solidified. Its chains and tackle hung free, unconnected to the ancient statue beneath the derrick.

I stared all around me. Will Reynolds had fallen supine on the sand, face staring up at the overcast sky. Paddy was on his knees in front of me (but when had he run past me?), hands clapped over his ears. And it was Jackie, also on her knees, who was clutching me around the legs. She crouched with her face hidden against my thigh.

I began to stagger forward, pulling free of Jackie's grip. For Gerald Sebastian had reappeared. He was thirty yards away, face-down on the loose sand. But unlike Will he was not lying motionless. He was *swimming,* propelling himself toward me across the level surface with laborious strokes of arms and legs, striking out for an unseen shore. His breath came in great, shuddering spasms, as though he had long been deprived of air. Perhaps he had. His mouth was below the surface and he was choking on sand.

A few yards from him—unexploded and untouched— lay the sticks of red plastic.

I knelt by his side, turning his head so that he could breathe, and found that the eyes looking into mine were empty, devoid of all thought or awareness. And as I knelt there, clearing sand from his gaping mouth, sudden bright marks touched his upturned face. I heard a pattering on the dusty desert floor.

I stared up into the sky. In that valley, in the fiercest depths of the *Takla Makan Shamo,* a hundred-year event was taking place. It was raining.

Paddy Elphinstone had seen an army of warriors, swords unsheathed, sweeping down on us from across the valley. He had known that he was about to die. Jackie saw a city, perhaps the same one I had seen, but it was writhing and collapsing in the grip of a huge earthquake, while she was sliding forward into a great abyss that opened in the surface.

Will Reynolds, God help him, could not tell what vision had gripped him. Like Gerald Sebastian, he was *elsewhere,* in a mental state that permitted no communication with other humans.

When the rain shower was over I searched that valley from end to end, looking for anything out of place. There was the quiet, dusty slope, merging into the dunes in all directions. There was the truck, just where Gerald Sebastian had left it. There was the pit with the statue at its center, rapidly filling with new sand. A ruby ring and an engraved gold tablet were attached to the buckled belt. I took two steps that way, then halted. As I watched the sand steadily covered them. In the whole valley, nothing moved but the trickling sands.

With two terribly sick men in my charge, I had no time for more exploration. We had to leave, and I had to make a decision: would we drive north or south? In other words, would Will and Gerald receive treatment in China, or would we try to get them home through Pakistan to the United States?

Maybe I made the wrong choice, maybe it was the cowardly choice. I elected to run for home. With me driving one truck and Paddy, shocked to sobriety, the other, we set off southwest as fast as we could go. We drove night and day, cutting our sleep down as far as we dared and keeping ourselves going on strong coffee that we brewed by the gallon. Paddy leaned on me, I leaned more and more on Jackie. I said more to her in two days than I had said to anyone in forty years. Necessary talk. I brought us out, but she kept me sane.

Sixty hours later we were in Rawalpindi, and I was buying airline tickets for the long flight home.

New York again. I told the backers of the expedition the unpleasant truth: that we had taken nothing from the valley, and they had nothing to show for all their investment. They were perhaps a little upset by that, but they were far more upset when they heard what had happened to Will and Gerald, and read the medical prognoses. Either might recover, but no one could predict how or when. Henry Hoffman showed what a gentleman he was by arranging perpetual medical care at his expense for as long as the two might need it.

I went home. And it was then that I discovered I had lied—accidentally—to our financial backers. While we were still traveling I had looked at the videocamera tapes made by Sebastian on the trip, including one taken in the valley itself. It showed the same bleak desert that I remembered so well, dry sand and barren rock.

In addition to the videotapes, Gerald Sebastian had also shot several rolls of film, but I had no way of developing those until we returned home and I could get to a photolab. The films, with whatever latent images might be on their exposed surfaces, did not seem to me a high-priority item. I left them in the bottom of my luggage. At last, four days after I returned to my apartment in Albuquerque, I went to my modest photolab and developed them.

Five rolls showed Hong Kong and Pakistan, and our entry to western China. The sixth was different. I stared at the pictures for half an hour. And then I went to the telephone and placed a call to Jackie Sands in Manhattan. We talked for four hours, while little by little it dawned on me how much I had been missing her.

"I know," she said at last. "I feel the same. We could talk forever, but I'm going to hang up now. Don't do anything silly, Sam. I have to see you, and I have to see it. I'll be on the next plane out."

She had to see what I had hardly been able to describe: the sixth film. There were just three exposures on it. The first was of the green statue, with only its head showing above the sand. In the other two, the statue was uncovered to waist level. It filled most of the frame, with an expression on its face that I could only now read *(If I were alive, you would tremble)*. But there was enough space at the edges for something else to show: not the dry grey of desert sands, but the cool green of water; and on the surface of that water, dwarfed by distance and slightly out of focus, a score of tiny white sails, delicate as butterfly wings. At the very edge of the frame was a hint of a broad embankment, curving away out of sight.

Jackie's plane would not arrive for another five hours, but I drove at once to the airport. I thought about her while I waited, and about one other thing. Gerald Sebastian had expected to find Atlantis. Jackie had sought aliens. Had they in one sense both been right?

There is nothing more alien to a modern American than yesterday's empires, with their arbitrary imperial powers, their cruelty, and their casual control over life and death. Humans make progress culturally, as well as technologically. Progress in one field may be quite separate from advances in the other. Suppose, then, the advanced civilization of an Atlantis; it might have technology far beyond our own, but it would have the bloody ways of a younger race. What would you expect from its emperors?

In ancient Egypt, Cheops had his Great Pyramid; Emperor Qin had his terracotta army of ten thousand at Xian. But their technology was simple, and their monuments limited to stone and clay. Imagine a great khan, king of Atlantis, with powerful technology wedded to absolute rule. How would he assure his own memory, down through the ages?

I can suggest one answer. Imagine a technology that can imprint a series of images; not just on film, or a length of tape, but on an entire land, with every molecule carrying part of the message. The countryside is saturated with signal. But like a picture on an undeveloped film, the imprint can lie latent for years or thousands of years, surviving the change from fertile land to bleak desert, until the right external stimulus comes along; and then it bursts forth. Atlantis, or Xanadu, or whatever world is summoned, appears in its old glory. To some, that vision may be beautiful; to others, it is intolerable. The great khan, indifferent to suffering, laughs across the centuries and inflicts his legacy.

An idea, no more; but it fills my mind. And how can I ever test it? Only by going back to that lonely valley in the Takla Makan, providing again the stimulus of disturbance, and waiting for the result.

I would love to do it, whatever the risk. The opportunity exists. Jackie told me on the phone that Henry Hoffman, indulgent as ever, was not disappointed by the last expedition. He would be willing to finance another trip to the Takla Makan; and he will let me lead it.

An attractive offer, since to raise that much money myself would take years. To search for Xanadu. How can I say no?

And yet it is not simple; for Jackie and I know the rules, even though we have never discussed them. We must begin right, or not at all. I am not Gerald Sebastian. If I let myself take Henry's money, I cannot also take his wife.

I made the decision sound difficult, but it is actually very easy. I learned the answer in the Takla Makan, and it is the only answer: for access to its rarest treasures, life offers but a single opportunity.

Xanadu has waited for thousands of years; it must wait a few years longer.

A professional scientist turned writer, Charles Sheffield is often ranked with Arthur C. Clarke for his science fiction adventures that are solidly backed with accurate scientific knowledge. Born in England, he was educated at St. John's College, and is a past president of the American Astronautical Society, president of the Science Fiction Writers of America (1985), and vice president of the Earth Satellite Corporation. His first story, "What Song the Sirens Sang," appeared in 1977, and his books include The Web Between the Worlds, The MacAndrews Chronicles, *and* Between the Strokes of Night.

Actress Sheila DeVore insisted that to portray murderess Meg Peyton she would have to wear the same wig Meg had worn. Miss DeVore also insisted on ignoring all the warnings that came with the wig.

NINE

A Wig for Miss DeVore
August Derleth

Sheila DeVore was a glamour girl whose platinum blonde hair and languorous smile outshone any other's on the silver screen. Quite a girl! She occupied more attention in the minds of thousands of young and old men than she had any right to occupy. She had eyes of baby blue with a come-on slant, and she had curves that haunted many an uneasy dreamer. Her pictures were on the screen magazines, on the cigarette ads ("Miss DeVore smokes nothing but Flambeaux! 'I never assume a role until I am assured my supply of Flambeaux is at hand to protect my throat, my bronchial tubes, and my photogenic value.'"), and even on the confession magazine covers; and she was the subject of an oft-reprinted biography telling all about her beginnings, her debut into society, her escape from the rich home that had been hers, her longing for fame, to do her part for society by entertaining the millions of underprivileged, etc., etc.

A beautiful story! Unfortunately, it sprang full-bodied from the imagination of her publicity agent.

Actually, Sheila DeVore was born plain Maggie Mutz in a little Missouri town whose chief claim to fame was that an Indian chief had once stopped there on his way to be massacred. She was a mistress of false frontage, and knew how to hog any picture in which she took part, throwing around her curves (which were the only genuine thing about her) in a way calculated to distract the attention of anything human from the only real acting in the picture—not Miss DeVore's, of course. She had a background which would have put Herbert Asbury's Hatrack into a wild scramble for her humble fame, and even now she was the subject and the object of plenty of gossip—some self-initiated. Publicity, after all, being what it is, and considered so necessary. Among her intimates in Hollywood she was fondly known by a five-letter word which the law says it is illegal to call anyone no matter how many witnesses are ready to testify.

She forgot her parents and let her father die in the poor-farm. She divorced her first—and only—husband, and ruined his reputation. She could not bear to let alone the poor deluded promoter who was responsible for putting her on the road to fame, but managed to shorten his life by a prolonged suit for the return of such money as she had paid him in that first flush of gratitude which accompanied sight of her name in bright lights. She was as selfish as an inhibited packrat, and had never heard of moral scruples. As for ethics—there was no room for ethics in her profession. She was, in short, one of those people for whom there does not seem to be any excuse for permitting them to continue an existence which is giving them no pleasure, and is burdening others far too much. However, on the other side of the ledger, there were those countless thousands of palpitating hearts in the darkened theatres of the land, watching that curvaceous morsel of femininity fling her weight around in picture after picture, loving and being loved, as if it were all the real thing and Miss DeVore were not getting a cool four grand a week to play roles which women like her and all female cats are by nature fully qualified to play without acting.

And at the moment, too, there was Herbert Bleake. Herbert was a good natured, addlepated playboy, who saw Sheila DeVore's toothsome map in a screen magazine and immediately took a plane out to Hollywood to see her. Sheila would never have seen him, but her publicity agent saw him first. After all, that story about the attempted robbery of her apartment had already been forgotten, and that touching release about how Sheila had given a ten thousand dollar home to her old mother (complete with picture, posed by an underpaid extra and a rented house, her real mother having been dead five years) was getting pretty well around, and it was time for something new in the life of the darling of America's repressed males. So Herbert was it; he was seized upon by the publicity agent, photographed descending from a liner of the air, shown with a great armful of flowers, and finally, with Sheila DeVore, all for the purpose of screaming headlines: "Rich Playboy Makes Beeline for Hollywood After Seeing DeVore's Pix!"

What a story!

For weeks Sheila DeVore's publicity agent could count upon seeing that inane and rather vacuous face looking out from behind that armful of roses, or fatuously at Sheila, staring up from the newspapers and magazines, and after that, there was always the run-around that could be given the gossip columnist, Arabella Bearst. She would be good for a couple hundred lines about the tantalizing possibilities of Sheila DeVore's engagement, wedding to, and break with Herbert Bleake to keep the matter running through all the yellow sheets for two months thereafter—if Sheila DeVore could hold out that long—which was doubtful.

In any case, there was Herbert, and Sheila had to treat him with a modicum of decency, however difficult it might be, while she devised some way to get rid of him. Preferably something spectacular—like a brawl at the Actors' Lagoon, when the photographers were present. Alas! for Herbert—he had his coming, and he might have known.

Sheila DeVore would never have believed that she had hers coming, too—long overdue, to be sure. And she would have burst into raucous Maggie Mutz laughter if someone had told her that Herbert was the instrument of fate, her nemesis, and so on. But there it was; the Fates had cut the pattern, and there was nothing to do but for the unwitting actors to play their parts.

Sheila had been cast in the role of Meg Peyton, the Soho murderess: four dead men, a leg show for the jury, and acquittal. A color picture for which she would need red hair, for the real Meg Peyton had worn red hair, and, moreover, she had worn a wig—brighter than auburn. She stamped her pretty foot and said she could not go into the role without the proper accoutrements—by which she meant the wig; and she ranted and raved for a day or so about the necessity of having it. She would have forgotten all about it, had her director not rebelled and said she should shut her silly mouth and get on to the work in hand. That was too much for her, and that night she poured her heart's desire into Herbert's flapping ears, and before dawn there was a cablegram on the way to Herbert's London agent, and within forty-eight hours more, Meg Peyton's wig had been leased for a huge sum from a London exhibitor and was on its way to Sheila DeVore.

Her publicity agent went into ecstasies.

Herbert was childishly happy.

Sheila preened herself and posed for some sober-faced pictures and gave out noble statements: "I could not feel that I could do my best work without something of this nature to inspire me!"

The wig arrived, was duly photographed on and off Sheila DeVore (good for several hundred rotogravure shots, and a dragged-out existence in the screen magazines), and the picture went into production. Sheila DeVore in *Soho Meg,* or *The Titian Murderess.*

Not a word about the letter that came with the wig. Sheila read it, committed it to memory, and destroyed it without saying anything about it. She did not think it important, and memorized it only because it was reasonably short and a little curious. Her publicity agent would have torn his hair if he could have realized what a first-rate story she was passing up. The letter concerned the real Meg Peyton, and said of her that she had not originally been anything more than a poor artist's model, but that, after the loss of her hair, she had acquired her red wig, and her change of character more or less coincided with that date. Moreover, there were certain suggestions which went over Sheila DeVore's head like a balcony. For instance—that the wig should not be worn more than a few minutes at a time; that it should be kept out of sight; that it had certain "properties" not subject to reasonable explanation. And so forth. Naturally, the fancies of its present owner were no concern of Sheila DeVore's.

The wig was really a beauty. It was made of real hair, beyond question; indeed, it seemed to have come from a single head—in what manner a sensitive person would not have wanted to guess. Moreover, it was beautifully preserved; in age, it was said to date far back, to certain Central

American Indians—which was completely beyond Sheila
DeVore's limited ken. In fact, it was such a striking thing that
Sheila DeVore painted her eyebrows and announced that,
in the custom of Charles Laughton and other notables, she
was going to wear the wig and impregnate herself with the
character of Meg Peyton, so that she could more effectively
portray her role—which she insisted upon treating as something to stand beside the roles of Lady Macbeth, Portia, and
Ophelia. With the cooperation of her agent, of course, and
of Herbert—though he was getting the brushoff but was not
at the moment sufficiently alert to correctly interpret the
signs. After all, he had done his work, and there was no
reason to be obtuse about it.

But Herbert was obtuse. He was so fatuous as to believe
he had won Sheila DeVore, and actually gave himself airs
on the strength of it. Sheila admitted to herself that he was
rapidly becoming a nuisance with whom she would have to
cope sooner or later. Fortunately—or unfortunately, as the
case may be—for Herbert, she was at the time much too
wrapped up in the titian wig, both figuratively and literally.

She went everywhere in the wig—with an entire new
wardrobe to go along. She was photographed from Hollywood to New York, getting out of the plane in Chicago,
eating at the Savoy, dancing at the Trianon, and, of course,
in various stills from the picture. It was wonderfully exciting,
and she felt an exhilaration she had never known before.
She felt something more, too—something that took possession of her in the few hours during which she was alone.

It was a curious delusion, or rather, a succession of delu-
sions, beginning with the conviction that she was not alone
in her rooms, that someone was there with her, someone she
could only fancy that she saw. Her fancies were real enough,
at any rate; once or twice she was certain she saw someone
lurking in the vicinity of the stand where she kept the wig; so
that presently she was convinced that someone meant to steal
her titian treasure. This hallucination made a wonderful press
release, though there was one annoying aftermath, when the
story got around to Meg Peyton's home town; that was an
urgent cablegram from Grigsby Heather, the owner of the wig,
that it be returned immediately.

171

*   *   *

Naturally, Sheila DeVore ignored Heather's unreasonable demand.

The hallucinations, however, increased, and one evening, when the picture had got about halfway along, she had a particularly strange experience. She was sitting at her dressing table preparing to go out, and had just adjusted the titian wig over her closely-cropped platinum hair, when she saw bending above her someone she at first took to be her maid. Indeed, she went so far as to give a casual order, when something about the creature's dress caught her eye: a colorful, spangled costume worn loosely over the shoulder in a kind of ceremonial manner, a band about its head; and at the same moment she was conscious of the face of a very old man, seamy with wrinkles, horny and swarthy, like a gypsy's face, and of the man's long, gnarled, titian hair. For just one instant she had this vision; then the creature at her back seemed to dissolve like a fog and settle down upon her to vanish into her own shapely chassis.

The most extraordinary thing about it was that, while at the moment of her vision, Sheila DeVore was frightened out of her small allotment of wits, as soon as the creature had made its strange disappearance, she was not at all disturbed: a transition so rapid that she had actually put out her hand to ring for her maid, and arrested her movement in midair, as the vision at her back vanished.

It was at about this time too that her intimates began to notice a change in Sheila DeVore. Her claws seemed to have grown sharper and more expert, even her most casual glance seemed dangerously predatory, and her manner, when she walked into a public place, was catlike, as if she were a huntress after bigger game than that which formerly interested her. But, of course, the most startling mutation which took place in the character of Sheila DeVore was a sudden, unprecedented craving for raw meat, preferably the comparatively fresh hearts of such fowl and animals as she was normally accustomed to eat in a more civilized fashion.

Even her publicity agent could not make use of this. Indeed, he did everything in his power to hush the matter up, but of course, there was Arabella Bearst, who had had her feelings hurt by Sheila (as who hadn't!), and she hinted at it in her column, so that millions of Americans read it and began to wonder.

By this time, Grigsby Heather was in a dither. He sent Herbert a long message saying flatly that Herbert must get the wig away from Miss DeVore at once, without delay, under pain of the gravest consequences. "The thing carries a revenant with it," he wrote. "And there is great danger in wearing it. I should never have permitted it to leave my possession, but I was assured that Miss DeVore would wear it only a short time each day." And so on. Herbert, being a rich playboy, looked upon any matter of the "gravest consequence," as something like a court battle; he had survived many of them, and estimated that he would survive this one, especially since it could be fought at long range. As for the "revenant," he wondered about that. Frankly, Herbert was far more educated in biological lines than in words of three-syllables. He looked it up in the dictionary. "One returned from the dead or from exile, etc." Not very illuminating, he thought. Undoubtedly Heather had got the wrong word.

Nevertheless, he asked his valet what a revenant was.

Unlike Herbert, his valet had several degrees, on the strength of which he had been hired. "A revenant is something left over," he explained. "Well, sort of like a ghost—if you know what I mean."

"No, I don't," admitted Herbert with that characteristic bluntness he could afford to manifest before those whose checks he signed.

"Well, it's like this. If I died, and left something of my character or personality in this room—why, that would be a revenant."

"I see," said Herbert.

He pondered this for a week, and then returned to his original hypothesis: that Heather had got hold of the wrong word—the imbecile!

Soon there came another letter from Heather, via Clipper. He said frankly that if it had not been for wearing the wig, Meg Peyton would never have committed those murders. Moreover, there was much more to those murders than ever got into print—a peculiarly horrible feature which was a

173

common practice among the priesthood of the Aztec Indians of Mexico in making the blood sacrifice to the Sun God.
Herbert's knowledge of the Aztecs was about as profound as
the average man's knowledge of outermost cosmos.

That lack was unfortunate for Herbert.

Things had come to a pretty pass indeed, insofar as
Sheila DeVore was concerned. Her passion for raw meat
was unabated, indeed—it was getting quite out of hand.
Moreover, she was becoming a veritable tower of self-
ishness: she was not to be crossed, not to be thwarted, not
to be gainsaid in anything. She fired her maid, her cook, her
housekeeper, her butler, and her gardener, and she was
alone on that fateful night when Herbert came to remon-
strate with her about this revolting habit of hers.

He rang the bell, but no one answered.

He peered in through the window, and saw her sitting at
her dressing table, titian wig and all. But that was not all he
saw. In the glass beyond her he saw a most awful caricature
of a face: not the face of a woman at all—but that of a
horrible, wrinkled old man, with incredibly evil eyes—and
worse—it was in that place where the face of Sheila DeVore
ought to have been. He cried out, and Sheila turned. Fortunately for Herbert's sanity, it was the familiar face that
looked out at him.

She came to let him in, rather petulantly, and then went
back to her dressing table, Herbert dogging her heels. But
she was not dressing. She was fascinated by a curious stone
instrument, like a horseshoe with a handle on it, which she
said she had been compelled to buy in an antique shop in
San Francisco only the previous day. It was like nothing
Herbert had ever seen before, but since Herbert's attention
had been exclusively for banks, women, yachts, and high
life in general, that was no wonder.

It was like nothing Sheila had ever seen before, either—
and yet, she could not help thinking, she had known the
feel of this tool before. She would know what to do with it if
the time came.

Clearly, it was psychologically the wrong moment for
Herbert to open up about his complaint. But he did, with a
witlessness characteristic of him. Sheila said not a word. She
turned around slowly and looked at him. One look out of

174

those eyes was enough to stop his words in his throat; they were not the eyes of Sheila DeVore—they were the eyes he had seen in the glass. He swallowed hard and got up.

With paralyzing rapidity Sheila struck.

Then, with the utmost composure, she proceeded to put to its designed use the curious instrument from the antique shop.

And she was sly. It was not until a week after the disappearance of her publicity agent, who made something of the same mistake Herbert did, that Herbert's body was discovered, and two days later, the agent's. That discovery rocked Hollywood, and then California, and then the nation, with repercussions that spread across the seas. One headline after the other—Star of Soho Meg Involved in Murder Mystery; Deaths Recall Meg Peyton Murders—and so on.

But always there was something concealed, something secret: a kind of hush-hush. Something that did not get out, though Arabella Bearst hustled her 350-pound self around to dig it out. Some juicy morsel of scandal that Arabella might miss. "The condition of the bodies." Something about the condition of the bodies. But no one would talk. Miss DeVore was clapped into quod, and from there was taken quietly to an asylum for the rest of her days.

Arabella Bearst was fit to be tied. And then Grigsby Heather hove onto the scene. At first he would say nothing. He got his wig; he shipped it back to London. But Arabella was not to be put off forever, and she was a master of the tripup. She cornered Heather one day at the railroad station and flashed the instrument "found in Miss DeVore's possession."

"How curious!" exclaimed Heather excitedly. "Wherever did you find it?"

"What is it?" asked Arabella, with her dimples at their best.

"Why, it's a sacrificial tool of the Aztec priests. Mexico, you know. That's the instrument with which they cut out the living hearts of their human sacrifices."

Arabella was a woman who never forgot a slight, however unimportant. And she had it in for Sheila DeVore, no matter where she was. As soon as possible her column blossomed out with a cutting little line: "Ask Sheila DeVore, one-time screen star, how she enjoyed the heart of Herbert Bleake!"

That was too much for even her employer.

If Sheila DeVore had been in any position to appreciate it, she would have enjoyed knowing that Arabella Bearst was in the market for a job, thanks to Sheila's titian wig.

Arabella Bearst's employer was needlessly impulsive. No one would have guessed from her column that, far from captivating the heart of Herbert Bleake—or for that matter, of her publicity agent—Sheila DeVore had followed the prevailing custom among the Aztecs—and eaten it, raw.

A man with three literary careers and an important figure in all of them, August Derleth was born in Wisconsin in 1903 and graduated from the University of Wisconsin in 1930. He sold his first story to Weird Tales *when he was fifteen and was soon a major contributor to that magazine. His work was encouraged by H. P. Lovecraft, and some of Derleth's best work is set in the Lovecraft universe. His novels include* The Trail of Cthulhu, *and his long series about consulting detective Solar Pons is collected in* The Solar Pons Omnibus. *His historical fiction series about Wisconsin, the Sac Prairie Saga, made him a noted regional novelist. His publishing firm, Arkham House, preserved the work of H. P. Lovecraft and formed the foundation of today's wide interest in supernatural work of high literary quality.*

Some of the movies playing at J.A. Bijou's were so old that the original prints no longer existed. Where were the new prints and the new scenes coming from?

TEN

One for the Horrors
David J. Schow

He recalled a half-column article that had said Stanley Kubrick postedited *A Clockwork Orange* by something like two-and-a-half minutes, mostly to deter jaded MPAA types from slapping it with an "X" rating, that probably would have murdered the film in 1971. It might have been consigned to art houses for eternity. Inconceivable.

Clay Colvin strolled through the theater waiting room with its yellowing posters of *Maitresse* and Fellini's *8½*. Wobbly borax tables were laden with graying copies of *Film Quarterly* and *Variety* and *Take One* amid a scatter of the local *nouveaux*-undergrounds—which, Clay thought, weren't really undergrounds anymore but "alternative press publications." More respectable; less daring, less innovative. Victims of progress in the same way this theatre differed from the big, hyperthyroid single-play houses with their $4.50 admissions.

Predictably, the wall was strewn with dog-eared lobby cards, one-sheets, and film schedules citing such theme-oriented programs as Utopian Directors, Oh-Cult and Modern Sex Impressionism. The front exit was a high-school-gym reject that had been painted over a dozen times or so, the color finally settling on a fingerprinty fire-engine red that also marred the tiny box window set into the door's center. Outside, worn stone-and-tile stairs spiraled beneath a pale metal canopy, down to the street and back into the world-proper.

Clay's wife of twenty-one years, Marissa, had died on October 17, 1976, about seventeen hours before his promotion to Western Division Sales Manager finally came through. It would have been the upward bump that would embellish their life together. Her reassurances that the position would be awarded to him "sometime soon" were devoted and unflagging; her belief in him was never half-hearted, not even when her hospital bills had become astronomical. Clay dined on soups and kept a stiff upper.

Guilt at her passing was the last thing Clay would allow himself, for Marissa would not have permitted it. What surprised him was the way he settled into a regimen during the next six months: 8-to-5 with overtime on each end, mail stop, and then filling the several hours hitherto devoted to the hospital stop. As substitutes, Clay either took work home, or went to a movie, or a bar, or tried a bit of television or a dollop of reading matter (*damned if you can't make fifty pages a night, old man,* he chided himself) prior to slumber in a bed realistically too big for a single person the likes of Clay Francis Colvin, Jr.

A birthday and a half later saw more impressive sales rosters and salary hikes for Clay. A bit more hair and vision lost. Unlike Marissa, his checking account had bounced back robustly. His new gold wire-prims were respectably costly. Comparatively frugal since Marissa's death, he splurged on a Mercedes and fought the cliche of a widower faced with the steep side of late middle age. Although he looked a bit rheumy-eyed in the mirror, he eventually concluded that he had been dealt to fairly.

It had been an unusually productive Wednesday, and upon spotting a Xerox place during his drive home, Clay pulled over to duplicate some documents he'd forgotten to copy at the office. From his cater-corner viewpoint, the block consisted of the Xerox shop, flanked by a pair of health food restaurants, a hole-in-the-wall ten-speed store, a pizzeria, and a place called Just Another Bijou—it seemed that the business establishments on the periphery of the university district were the only places open after six o'clock. In the Xerox shop, a thumbtacked flyer caught Clay's eye. He scanned a list of features and discovered the theatre he had seen was referred to as J.A. Bijou's. The bill for the night highlighted Fredric March in *Death Takes a Holiday* and *Anthony Adverse,* the latter Clay knew to feature a neat Korngold score. He knew both films—of course—and the

178

jump from Xerox shop and dull evening to the lobby of J.A. Bijou's was a short, easy one.

Clay enjoyed himself. More importantly, he came back to the theatre, and without his vested business suit.

What there was: Theatre-darkness and old cinema chairs of varied lineage and age, in wobbly rows, and comfortably broken-in. Loose floor boltings. The mustiness of old cushions; not offensive, but rather the enticing odor of a library well-stocked with worthwhile classics. Double-billed tidbits like *Casablanca* and *The Maltese Falcon* together, for once, or the semiannual Chaplin and Marx orgies. Clay favored Abbott and Costello; J.A. Bijou's obliged him. Homage programs to directors, to stars, and on one occasion to a composer (Bernard Herrmann). Also cartoon fests, reissues, incomprehensible foreign bits, and the inevitable oddball sex-art flicks, which Clay avoided. But the oldies he loved and the better recent items insured his attendance. It was a crime not to plunk down two bucks—or $1.50 before six P.M.— to escape and enjoy, as Clay had done frequently in the five months between *Anthony Adverse* and tonight's offering, Kubrick, who had wound up in an art house, censors or no. Clay enjoyed himself—it was all he required of J.A. Bijou's. He never expected that anything would be required of him, nor did he expect to be blown away in quite the fashion everyone was during the following week.

Clay had an affection for Dwight Frye's bit parts, and Fritz in *Frankenstein* was one of his best. After Renfield, of course. It was opening night of a week's worth of Horror Classics, and Clay was in enthusiastic attendance. He, like most of the audience, would cop to a bit of overfamiliarization due to used car screenings on the tube after midnight.

There were some unadvertised Fleischer Betty Boops and the normal profusion of trailers before the shadow-show commenced. *Frankenstein* had been the *Exorcist* of its heyday, evoking nausea and fainting and prompting bold warnings on screen and ominous lobby posters. Many houses in the 1930s offered battle-ready ambulances and cadres of medics with epsoms primed. Then came the obsessed censors, cleavers raised and hair-triggered to hack out nastiness . . . quite an uproar.

Soon after Colin Clive's historic crescendo of *"It's alive!"* filtered into J.A. Bijou's dusty green curtains, Clay's eyelids began a reluctant, semaphoric flutter. His late hours and his full workload were tolling expertly, and he soon dozed off during the film, snapping back to wakefulness at intervals. His memory filled in the brief gaps in plot as he roller-coastered from the blackness to the screen and back. It was a vaguely pleasing sensation, like accomplishing several tasks at once. Incredibly, he managed to sleep through the din of the torture scene and the monster's leavetaking from the castle. He was wakened by a child's voice instead of noise and spectacle.

"Will you play with me?"

The voice of the girl—little Maria—chimed as she addressed the mute, lumbering Karloff. She handed him a daisy, then a bunch, and demonstrated that they floated on the surface of the pond by which they both sat.

"See how mine floats!"

Together the pair tossed blooms into the water, and for the first time a smile creased the Monster's face. Having expended all his daisies, he gestures and the girl walks innocently into his embrace. He hefts her by the arms and lofts her high and wide into the water. Her scream is interrupted by sickly bubbling.

Clay was fully awake now, jolted back in his seat by an image that was the essence of horror—the Monster groping confusedly toward the pond as it rippled heavily with death. There was something odd about the scene as well; the entire audience around Clay, veterans all, shifted uneasily. A more familiar tableau would soon have the girl's corpse outraging the stock villagers, but for now there were only the Monster and the horrible pond, on which the daisies still floated.

The scene shifted to Elizabeth in her wedding gown, and the crowd murmured. It had been a premiere, of sorts.

Clay dreamt, peacefully. He became aware of impending consciousness as per his usual waking-up manner, a rush of images coming faster and faster and why not a pretty girl?

And up he sat. For the first time, he thought of the drowning scene in *Frankenstein*. Clay shook his head and rolled out of bed into the real world.

Next on the roster was *King Kong*.

The college kid who vended Clay's ticket that evening after work was gangly and bearded, his forehead mottled, as though by a pox. Five years ago, Clay would have dismissed him as a hippie; ten years, a queer. Now hippies did not exist and he regarded the gay community with a detached, *laissez-faire* attitude. He queued before the cramped snackbar to provision himself.

He had taken a dim view of the uninspired "remake" of the 1933 RKO Studio's *King Kong*—in fact, had avoided an opportunity to see it for free. The chance to again relish the original on a big screen was pleasant; in this one, unlike the new version, the only profiteering fame-grubbers were the characters on the screen.

Clay conjured various other joys of the original while conversing with the lobby-smokers: the glass-painted forests, the delightfully anachronistic dinosaurs of Skull Island. He was told that this was not a "butchered" print, that is, not lacking scenes previously excised by some overzealous moralist in a position of petty authority—shots of Kong jawing a squirming man in tight closeup, picking at Fay Wray's garments with the simian equivalent of eroticism, and a shot of Kong dropping a woman several stories to her death were all intact.

This time around, Clay was more palpably disturbed. He clearly recalled reading an article on *King Kong* concerning scenes that had never made it to the screen in the *first place*—not outtakes, or restorative footage, or Band-Aids over some editor's butchery—and among those were bits that were *now* streaming out of J.A. Bijou's projection booth.

Carl Denham's film crew was perched precariously atop a log bridge being shaken by an enraged King Kong. One by one, the marooned explorers plummeted, howling, into a crevasse and were set upon greedily by grotesque, truck-sized spiders. *It stopped the show*, the film's original producer had claimed, over forty-five years ago. It was enough justification to excerpt the whole scene; no audience had ever seen it, because it would have stopped the show.

It certainly does, thought an astonished Clay, as he watched the men crash to the slimy floor of the pit. Those who survived the killing fall confronted the fantastic black horrors; not only giant spiders but shuffling reptiles and chitinous scorpions the size of Bengal tigers. The audience sat, mouths agape.

New wonders of Skull Island manifested themselves: A triceratops with a brood of young, plodding along via stop-motion animation, and a bulky-horned mammal Clay later looked up in a paleontology text and found out it was an Arsinoittherium. Incredible.

"Where did you come across this print?" he questioned the bearded kid, with genuine awe. He was not alone. Fans, buffs, and *experts* had been drilling him since the beginning of the week, and the only answer he or the other staff could offer against the clamor was that they had nothing to do with it. The films came from the normal distribution houses, the secretaries of which were unable to fathom what the J. A. Bijou employees were babbling about, when they phoned long-distance—an expense just recently affordable. Word of mouth drew crowds faster than Free Booze or Meet Jesus signs, and the theatre's limited capacity was starting to show the strain of good business. No one else had ever seen these films. In all of history.

And instead of acting then, when he should have, Clay was content to sit, and be submissively amazed by the miracle.

Recently, two 1950s science fiction flicks had been shunted into a two-and-a-half hour timeslot on Sunday afternoon television. A quick check of a paperback TV-film book revealed their total running time to be 160 minutes. The local independent station not only edited the films to accommodate the inadequate time allotment, but shaved further in order to squeeze in another twenty minutes of used-car, rock-and-roll, pimple-killing, free-offer, furniture-warehouse, Veg-o-Matic madness per feature. Viewers were naturally pissed, but not pissed enough to lift their telephones. The following week boasted the singularly acrobatic feat of Tod Browning's *Dracula* corking a one-hour gap preceding a "Wild King-dom" rerun.

Edited for Television notices always grated Clay's nerves when they intruded in video white across the bottom of his 24-inch screen. The J.A. Bijou wonderfulness was a kind of vengeance realized against the growly box; a warm, full-belly feeling. No one seemed to realize that the J.A. Bijou prints were also of first-rate, sterling caliber and clarity, lacking even a single ill-timed splice. They were all too stunned by the new footage. Justifiably.

Clay sat and viewed Fredric March again, but this time as Dr. Jekyll, mutating for the first time into the chunky fiend Hyde *without* the crucial potion—a scene never released, along with another sequence where Jekyll witnessed the bloody mauling of a songbird by a cat, a scene that serves as the catalyst for another gruesome transformation.

He watched a print of Murnau's premier vampire movie, *Nosferatu*—not the remake—clearly not from the 1922 pirate negatives; in short, an impossibility. Bram Stoker's widow had recognized Murnau's film as an unabashed plagiarism of her husband's novel, *Dracula,* and won the right in court to have all extant prints and negatives of *Nosferatu* destroyed. The film survived only because film pirates had already hoarded illegal prints, and it was from these less-than-perfect "originals" that all subsequent prints came. Yet what Clay watched was a crystal-sharp, first-generation original, right down to the title cards.

He saw Lon Chaney, Jr., as Lawrence Stewart Talbot, wrestling a cathedral-sized grizzly bear in *The Wolf Man.* Not the remake. He watched a version of *Invasion of the Body Snatchers* a full five minutes longer than normal. Not the remake.

He saw Janet Leigh's naked breasts bob wetly as she cowered through her butcher-knife finish in an incarnation of Hitchcock's *Psycho* that was one whole reel more complete. He wondered idly when they would get around to grinding out a tacky remake of *this* classic as well, before he actually thought about it and realized that second-rate producers had been trying and failing for years.

The blanket denials by the film outlet that had shipped the entire festival as a package deal were amusing to hear, as related by J.A. Bijou's staff. The most the tinny voices from LA would concede was that *maybe* the films had come out of the wrong vault. That other phone calls were being made to them, along with lengthy and excited letters, was undeniable.

This expanding miracle had hefted an unspoken weight from Clay's shoulders. It was overjoy, giddiness, a smattering of cotton-candied jubilation, a reappearance of fun in his life, sheer and undeniable. A shrink would delve so far beyond this simple idea that Clay would become certifiable; so, no shrinks. Accept the fun, the favor.

The "favor" of J.A. Bijou's was, Clay reasoned, repayment to him, personally, for his basic faith in the films—a faith that endured the years, and that he allowed to resurface when given an opportunity. This made sense to him, though he did not totally comprehend the *why*, yet. He did toy with the phrasing, concocting impressive verbiage to explain away the phenomena, but he always looped back around to the simplicity of his love for the films. He was one with the loose, intimate brotherhood that would remain forever unintroduced, but who would engage any handy stranger in a friendly swap of film trivia.

He felt that, despite his happiness, the picture was still incomplete. The miracle of the films he was viewing was a kind of given. *Given A, B then follows.* . . . He discussed his idea with other (unintroduced) J.A. Bijou regulars. Had anyone the power to inform him of the turn of events to follow, Clay would have thought them as whacko as his imaginary psychiatrist would have diagnosed him. If he had told anyone. He didn't.

The projection booth of J.A. Bijou's was a cluttered, hot closet tightly housing two gargantuan, floor-mounted 35 mm. projectors and a smaller 16mm. rig, along with an editing/winding table and a refugee barstool. Knickknacks of film equipment were jumbled together on tiers of floor-to-ceiling shelving. Homemade, egg-carton soundproofing coating the interior walls, throwing soft green shadows under a dim work light. The windows were opaqued with paint and the floors were grimy. A large cardboard box squatted to receive refuse film just beneath a rack on which hung the horribly over-used Coming Attractions strips that got spliced hundreds of times per month, it seemed.

J.A. Bijou's air conditioning system was almost as old as the vintage brownstone that housed the theatre. The first time it gave up the ghost was during the mid-Thursday afternoon showing of *Psycho,* just as Vera Miles began poking about the infamous Bates mansion. There was a hideous shriek as metal chewed rudely into metal, followed by a sharp spinning that wound down with a broken, wagon-wheel clunk. The audience nearly went through the ceiling, and afterward, everyone laughed about the occurrence as things were makeshifted back to order.

The insulation on the cooler's motor held out until Friday night, for the benefit of the overflow audience. The years of humid dampness and coppery, wet decay had been inexorable. The engine sparked and shorted out, fuses blew, and as the blades spun down a second time, the theatre filled up with acrid electrical smoke, from the vents.

Gray smoke wafted dreamily around near the ceiling as the exits were flung open. A few moved toward the fresher air, but most kept stubbornly to their prize seats, waiting.

In the darkness of the booth, the projectionist had concluded that a melted hunk of old film might be jamming the film gate, and was leaning over to inspect it when the lights went out. Sitting in the dark, he groped out for his Cinzano ashtray and butted his Camel as a precaution against mishaps in the dark.

It did not do any good.

When the cardboard film bin later puffed into flames, the projectionist had temporarily abandoned the booth in search of a flashlight. The preview strips quickly blackened, cured, and finally ignited, snaking fire up to the low ceiling of the booth. The eggcartons blossomed a dry orange. The wooden shelves became fat kindling as the roomful of celluloid and plastic flared and caused weird patterns of light to coruscate through the painted glass. It took less than thirty seconds for the people sitting in front of the booth to notice it, dismiss it, and finally check again to verify.

The projectionist raced back. When he yanked open the door, the heat blew him flatly on his ass. People were already panicking toward exits; Clay rose from his seat and saw.

The bearded kid had already scurried to the pizzeria to trip the local fire alarm. Nobody helped the projectionist.

185

The sudden chaos of the entire scene remained as a snapshot image in Clay's mind as he rapidly located a fire extinguisher, tore it from its wall-mount, and hurried to the booth. A crackerbox window blew outward and the fire licked out of the opening, charring the wall and lighting up the auditorium.

Lightly dazed, the projectionist was up and had one foot wedged over the threshold of the booth entrance, but the sheer heat buffeted him back as he exhausted his own tiny CO_2 cannister. He yelled something unintelligible into the fire, then he stepped back, fire-blind and nose-to-nose with Clay, shouting for him to get out.

Clay haltingly approached the gaping doorway and nozzled his larger extinguisher into the conflagrant oven. A better inferno could not have been precipitated if the Monster himself had tipped an ancient oil-lamp into dry straw. Clay's effort reduced the doorway to smoke and sizzle, and he stepped up in order to get a better aim on the first projector, which was swathed in flames. He took another excruciating step inside.

The Monster, having tried his misunderstood best, always got immolated by the final reel. Friday night's screening of *Psycho* keynoted the close of the horror classics festival at J.A. Bijou's. Clay understood, as he moved closer to the flaming equipment and films. It would not hurt much.

Above the booth, a termite-ridden beam exploded into hot splinters and smashed down through the ceiling of the booth, showering barbeque sparks and splitting the tiny room open like a peach crate. It was a support beam, huge, weighty and as old as the brownstone, and it impacted heavily, crushing the barstool, collapsing the metal film racks, and wiping out the doorway of the booth.

It was a perfect, in-character finish, complemented by the welling sound of approaching sirens.

One of the health food places threatened a lawsuit after the fire marshal had done *his* job—J.A. Bijou's had been unsafe all along, etcetera. Negligence, they claimed.

The festival package of films was gone, gone to scorched shipment cans and puddles of ugly black plasma. When the projection booth died, so did they, even though they were being stored at the theatre manager's house for safekeeping. They had been, after all, perfect prints, and the door-locks at J.A. Bijou's had not yet been updated against a particular kind of desperate collector.

Now the new sprinkler and air conditioning systems were in. The new projection booth was painted and inspected; the new equipment, spotless and smelling of lubricant. J.A. Bijou's insurance, plus the quick upsurge in income, sparked financial backing sufficient to cause its rebirth in time for the following semester at the university.

With the new goods in place and all tempers balmed, the projectionist's somewhat passionate tale of an unidentified customer supposed to have died in the blaze was quickly forgotten or attributed to his excited state during the crisis. He steadfastly insisted that he had witnessed a death, and maintained his original story without deviation despite the fact that no corpse or suggestion of a corpse had ever been uncovered in the wreckage. No one had turned up tearfully seeking dead relatives.

But no one could explain about the films, either. And from opening night onward, none of the J.A. Bijou staffers bothered to consider why, on fullhouse nights (weekends, for the college crowd), the ticket count always came up two seats short. Nor could they give a solid, rational reason explaining why J.A. Bijou's was the sole theatre—in the universe, apparently—that regularly featured peculiar, never-before-seen cinema gems. The phone voices still had no answers.

The bearded kid suggested that J.A. Bijou's had a guardian spirit.

Clay relished the cool anonymity of the darkened theatre. As always, the crowds were friendly, but unintroduced. The film bond held them together satisfactorily without commitment. He had been cussing/discussing the so-called *auteur* theory with a trio of engineering majors seated behind him, when the house lights dimmed. You never learned their names.

The first feature was *The Man Who Would Be King,* starring Humphrey Bogart and Clark Gable. Clay had not decided what the second feature would be, yet.

Marissa returned, with the popcorn, as the trailers commenced.

David J. Schow was born in 1955 in Marburg, West Germany. A German child adopted by American parents, he was raised in the United States and attended the University of Arizona until 1978 when he dropped out to begin writing. In Los Angeles, he wrote sixteen novels under pen names, all of them film tie-ins. A respected film historian, Schow wrote The Outer Limits: The Official Companion. *His short stories of supernatural horror include "Red Light," "Pamela's Gift," and "Monster Movies" (featured in his collection* Lost Angels). *He edited* Silver Scream, *an anthology of horror stories about the movies, which appeared in 1988 along with his mystery novel* The Kill Riff. *In 1990,* Weird Tales *ran a special David J. Schow issue.*

Jaimie considered himself lucky to have won the elegant Bel Air home in a poker game. Now if he could just convince his girlfriend that there was absolutely nothing wrong with the swimming pool. . . .

ELEVEN

The Pool

William F. Nolan

As they turned from Sunset Boulevard and drove past the high iron gates, swan-white and edged in ornamented gold, Lizbeth muttered under her breath.

"What's the matter with you?" Jaimie asked. "You just said 'shit,' didn't you?"

"Yes, I said it."

"Why?"

She turned toward him in the MG's narrow bucket seat, frowning. "I said it because I'm angry. When I'm angry, I say shit."

"Which is my cue to ask why you're angry."

"I don't like jokes when it comes to something this important."

"So who's joking?"

"You are, by driving us here. You *said we were going to* look at our new house."

"We are. We're on the way."

"This is *Bel Air,* Jaimie!"

"Sure. Says so, right on the gate."

"Obviously, the house isn't in Bel Air."

"Why obviously?"

"Because you made just $20,000 last year on commercials, and you haven't done a new one in three months. Part-time actors who earn $20,000 a year don't buy houses in Bel Air."

"Who says I bought it?"

She stared at him. "You told me you *owned* it, that it was yours!"

He grinned. "It is, sweetcake. All mine."

"I hate being called 'sweetcake.' It's a sexist term."

"Bull! It's a term of endearment."

"You've changed the subject."

"No, *you* did," he said, wheeling the small sports roadster smoothly over the looping stretch of black asphalt.

Lizbeth gestured toward the mansions flowing past along the narrow, climbing road, castles in sugar-cake pinks and milk-chocolate browns, and pastel blues. "So we're going to live in one of these?" Her voice was edged in sarcasm.

Jaimie nodded, smiling at her. "Just wait. You'll see!"

Under a cut-velvet driving cap, his tight-curled blond hair framed a deeply tanned, sensual actor's face. Looking at him, at that open, flashing smile, Lizbeth told herself once again that it was all too good to be true. Here she was, an ordinary small-town girl from Illinois, in her first year of theater arts at UCLA, about to hook up with a handsome young television actor who looked like Robert Redford and who now wanted her to live with him in Bel Air!

Lizbeth had been in California for just over a month, had known Jaimie for only half that time, and was already into a major relationship. It was dreamlike. Everything had happened so fast: meeting Jaimie at the disco, his divorce coming through, getting to know his two kids, falling in love after just three dates.

Life in California was like being caught inside one of those silent Chaplin films, where everything is speeded up and people whip dizzily back and forth across the screen. Did she *really* love Jaimie? Did he *really* love her? Did it matter?

Just let it happen, kid, she told herself. Just flow with the action.

"Here we are," said Jaimie, swinging the high-fendered little MG into a circular driveway of crushed white gravel. He braked the car, nodding toward the house. "Our humble abode!"

Lizbeth drew in a breath. Lovely! Perfect!

Not a mansion, which would have been too large and too intimidating, but a just-right two-story Spanish house topping a green-pine bluff, flanked by gardens and neatly trimmed box hedges.

"Well, do you like it?"

She giggled. "Silly question!"

"It's no castle."

"It's perfect! I hate big drafty places." She slid from the MG and stood looking at the house, hands on hips. "Wow. Oh, wow!"

"You're right about twenty-thou-a-year actors," he admitted, moving around the car to stand beside her. "This place is way beyond me."

"Then how did you . . . ?"

"I won it at poker last Thursday. High-stakes game. Went into it on borrowed cash. Got lucky, cleaned out the whole table, except for this tall, skinny guy who asks me if he can put up a house against what was in the pot. Said he had the deed on him and would sign it over to me if he lost the final hand."

"And you said yes."

"Damn right I did."

"And he lost?"

"Damn right he did."

She looked at the house, then back at him. "And it's legal?"

"The deed checks out. I own it all, Liz—house, gardens, pool."

"There's a *pool?*" Her eyes were shining.

He nodded. "And it's a beaut. Custom design. I may rent it out for commercials, pick up a little extra bread."

She hugged him. "Oh, Jaimie! I've always wanted to live in a house with a pool!"

"This one's unique."

"I want to *see* it!"

He grinned and then squeezed her waist. "First the house, *then* the pool. Okay?"

She gave him a mock bow. "Lead on, master!"

Lizbeth found it difficult to keep her mind on the house as Jaimie led her happily from room to room. Not that the place wasn't charming and comfortable, with its solid Spanish furniture, bright rugs, and beamed ceilings. But the prospect of finally having a pool of her own was so delicious that she couldn't stop thinking about it.

"I had a cleaning service come up here and get every-thing ready for us," Jaimie told her. He stood in the center of the living room, looking around proudly, reminding her of a captain on the deck of his first ship. "Place needed work. Nobody's lived here in ten years."

"How do you know that?"

"The skinny guy told me. Said he'd closed it down ten years ago, after his wife left him." He shrugged. "Can't say I blame her."

"What do you know about her?"

"Nothing. But the guy's a creep, a skinny creep." He flashed his white smile. "Women prefer *attractive* guys."

She wrinkled her nose at him. "Like *you*, right?"

"Right!"

He reached for her, but she dipped away from him, pull-ing off his cap and draping it over her dark hair.

"You look cute that way," he said.

"Come on, show me the pool. You promised to show me."

"Ah, yes, madame . . . the pool."

They had to descend a steep flight of weathered wooden steps to reach it. The pool was set in its own shelf of wood-land terrain, notched into the hillside and screened from the house by a thick stand of trees.

"You never have to change the water," Jaimie said as they walked toward it. "Feeds itself from a stream inside the hill. It's self-renewing. Old water out, new water in. All the cleaning guys had to do was skim the leaves and stuff off the surface." He hesitated as the pool spread itself before them. "Bet you've never seen one like it!"

Lizbeth never had, not even in books or magazine photos.

It was *huge*, at least ten times larger than she'd expected, edged on all sides by gray, angular rock. It was designed in an odd, irregular shape that actually made her . . . made her . . . suddenly made her. . . .

Dizzy. I'm dizzy.

"What's wrong?"

"I don't know." She pressed a hand against her eyes. "I . . . I feel a little . . . sick."

"Are you having your . . . ?"

"No, it's not that. I felt fine until. . . ." She turned away toward the house. "I just don't like it."

"What don't you like?"

"The pool," she said, breathing deeply. "I don't like the pool. There's something wrong about it."

He looked confused. "I thought you'd *love* it!" His tone held irritation. "Didn't you just tell me you always wanted. . . ."

"Not one like this," she interrupted, overriding his words. "Not *this* one." She touched his shoulder. "Can we go back to the house now? It's cold here. I'm freezing."

He frowned. "But it's *warm*, Liz! Must be eighty at least. How can you be cold?"

She was shivering and hugging herself for warmth. "But I am! Can't you feel the chill?"

"All right," he sighed. "Let's go back."

She didn't speak during the climb up to the house.

Below them, wide and black and deep, the pool rippled its dark skin, stirring, sluggish, patient movement in the windless afternoon.

Upstairs, naked in the Spanish four-poster bed, Lizbeth could not imagine what had come over her at the pool. Perhaps the trip up to the house along the sharply winding road had made her carsick. Whatever the reason, by the time they were back in the house, the dizziness had vanished, and she'd enjoyed the curried chicken dinner Jaimie had cooked for them. They'd sipped white wine by a comforting hearth fire and then made love there tenderly late into the night, with the pulsing flame tinting their bodies in shades of pale gold.

"Jan and David are coming by in the morning," he had told her. "Hope you don't mind."

"Why should I? I think your kids are great."

"I thought we'd have this first Sunday together, just the two of us; but school starts for them next week, and I promised they could spend the day here."

"I don't mind. Really I don't."

He kissed the tip of her nose. "That's my girl."

"The skinny man. . . ."

"What about him?"

"I don't understand why he didn't try to sell this house in the ten years when he wasn't living here."

"I don't know. Maybe he didn't need the money."

"Then why bet it on a poker game? Surely the pot wasn't anywhere near equal to the worth of this place."

"It was just a way for him to stay in the game. He had a straight flush and thought he'd win."

"Was he upset at losing the place?"

Jaimie frowned at that question. "Now that you mention it, he didn't seem to be. He took it very calmly."

"You said that he left after his wife split. Did he talk about her at all?"

"He told me her name."

"Which was?"

"Gail. Her name was Gail."

Now, lying in the upstairs bed, Lizbeth wondered what had happened to Gail. It was odd somehow to think that she and the skinny man had made love in this same bed. In a way, she'd taken Gail's place.

Lizbeth still felt guilty about saying no to Jaimie when he'd suggested a post midnight swim. "Not tonight, darling. I've a slight headache. Too much wine, maybe. You go on without me."

And so he'd gone on down to the pool alone, telling her that such a mild, late-summer night was just too good to waste, that he'd take a few laps around the pool and be back before she finished her cigarette.

Irritated with herself, Lizbeth stubbed out the glowing Pall Mall in the bedside ashtray. Smoking was a filthy habit—ruins your lungs, stains your teeth. And smoking in bed was doubly stupid. You fall asleep . . . the cigarette catches the bed on fire. She *must* stop smoking. All it took was some real will power, and if. . . .

Lizbeth sat up abruptly, easing her breath to listen. Nothing. No sound.

That was wrong. The open bedroom window overlooked the pool, and she'd been listening, behind her thoughts, to Jaimie splashing about below in the water.

194

Now she suddenly realized that the pool sounds had ceased, totally.

She smiled at her own nervous reaction. The silence simply meant that Jaimie had finished his swim and was out of the pool and headed back to the house. He'd be here any second.

But he didn't arrive.

Lizbeth moved to the window. Moonlight spilled across her breasts as she leaned forward to peer out into the night. The pale mirror glimmer of the pool flickered in the darkness below, but the bulk of trees screened it from her vision.

"Jaimie !" Her voice pierced the silence. "Jaimie, are you still down there?"

No reply. Nothing from the pool. She called his name again, without response.

Had something happened while he was swimming? Maybe a sudden stomach cramp or a muscle spasm from the cold water? No, he would have called out for help. She would have heard him.

Then . . . what? Surely this was no practical joke, an attempt to scare her? No, impossible. That could be cruel, and Jaimie's humor was never cruel. But he might think of it as fun, a kind of hide and seek in a new house. *Damn him*!

Angry now, she put on a nightrobe and stepped into her slippers. She hurried downstairs, out the back door, across the damp lawn, to the pool steps.

"Jaimie! If this is a game, I don't like it! Damn it, I *mean* that!" She peered downward; the moonlit steps were empty. "*Answer* me!"

Then, muttering "Shit!" under her breath, she started down the clammy wooden steps, holding to the cold iron pipe rail. The descent seemed even more precipitous in the dark, and she forced herself to move slowly.

Reaching level ground, Lizbeth could see the pool. She moved closer for a full view. It was silent and deserted. Where was Jaimie? She suddenly was gripped by the familiar sense of dizzy nausea as she stared at the odd, weirdly angled rock shapes forming the pool's perimeter. She tried to look away. And *couldn't*.

It wants me!

That terrible thought seized her mind. But what wanted her? The pool? No . . . something *in* the pool.

She kicked off the bedroom slippers and found herself walking toward the pool across the moon-sparkled grass, spiky and cold against the soles of her bare feet.

Stay back! Stay away from it!

But she couldn't. Something was drawing her toward the black pool, something she could not resist.

At the rocks, facing the water, she unfastened her night-robe, allowing it to slip free of her body.

She was alabaster under the moon, a subtle curving of leg, of thigh, of neck and breast. Despite the jarring hammer of her heart, Lizbeth knew that she had to step forward into the water.

It wants me!

The pool was black glass, and she looked down into it, at the reflection of her body, like white fire on the still surface.

Now . . . a ripple, a stirring, a deep-night movement from below.

Something was coming—a shape, a dark mass, gliding upward toward the surface.

Lizbeth watched, hypnotized, unable to look away, unable to obey the screaming, pleading voice inside her: *Run! Run!*

And then she saw Jaimie's hand. It broke the surface of the pool, reaching out to her.

His face bubbled free of the clinging black water, and acid bile leaped into her throat. She gagged, gasped for air, her eyes wide in sick shock.

It was *part* Jaimie, part something else!

It smiled at her with Jaimie's wide, white-toothed open mouth, but, oh God! only *one* of its eyes belonged to Jaimie. It had three others, all horribly different. It had *part* of Jaimie's face, *part* of his body.

Run! Don't go to it! Get away!

But Lizbeth did not run. Gently, she folded her warm, pink-fleshed hand into the icy wet horror of that hand in the pool and allowed herself to be drawn slowly forward. Downward. As the cold, receiving waters shocked her skin, numbing her, as the black liquid rushed into her open mouth, into her lungs and stomach and body, filling her as a cup is filled, her final image, the last thing she saw before closing her eyes, was Jaimie's wide-lipped, shining smile— an expanding patch of brightness fading down . . . deep . . . very deep . . . into the pool's black depths.

Jan and David arrived early that Sunday morning, all giggles and shouts, breathing hard from the ride on their bikes.

A whole Sunday with Dad. A fine, warm-sky summer day with school safely off somewhere ahead and not bothering them. A big house to roam in, and yards to run in, and caramel-ripple ice cream waiting (Dad had promised to buy some!), and games to play, and. . . .

"Hey! Look what I found!"

Jan was yelling at David. They had gone around to the back of the house when no one answered the bell, looking for their father. Now eight-year-old Jan was at the bottom of a flight of high wooden steps, yelling up at her brother. David was almost ten and tall for his age.

"What is it?"

"Come and see!"

He scrambled down the steps to join her.

"Jeez!" he said. "A pool! I never saw one *this* big before!"

"Me neither."

David looked over his shoulder, up at the silent house.

"Dad's probably out somewhere with his new girlfriend."

"Probably," Jan agreed.

"Let's try the pool while we're waiting. What do you say?"

"Yeah, let's!"

They began pulling off their shirts.

Motionless in the depths of the pool, at the far end, where rock and tree shadows darkened the surface, it waited, hearing the tinkling, high child voices filtering down to it in the sound-muted waters. It was excited because it had never absorbed a child; a child was new and fresh—new pleasures, new strengths.

It had formed itself within the moist deep soil of the hill, and the pool had nurtured and fed it, helping it grow, first with small, squirming water bugs and other yard insects. It had absorbed them, using their *eyes* and their hard, metallic bodies to shape itself. Then the pool had provided a dead bird, and now it had feathers along part of its back, and the bird's sharp beak formed part of its face. Then a plump gray rat had been drawn into the water, and the rat's glassy eye became part of the thing's body. A cat had drowned here, and its claws and matted fur added new elements to the thing's expanding mass.

Finally, when it was still young, a golden-haired woman, Gail, had come here alone to swim that long-ago night, and the pool had taken her, given her as a fine new gift to the thing in its depths. And Gail's long silk-gold hair streamed out of the thing's mouth (one of its mouths, for it had several), and it had continued to grow, to shape itself.

Then, last night, this man, Jaimie had come to it. And his right eye now burned like blue phosphor from the thing's face. Lizbeth had followed, and her slim-fingered hands, with their long, lacquered nails, now pulsed in wormlike convulsive motion along the lower body of the pool-thing.

Now it was excited again, trembling, ready for new bulk, new lifestuffs to shape and use. It rippled in dark anticipation, gathering itself, feeling the pleasure and the hunger.

Faintly, above it, the boy's cry: "Last one in's a fuzzy green monkey!"

It rippled to the vibrational splash of two young bodies striking the water.

It glided swiftly toward the children.

A professional artist turned novelist and screenwriter, William F. Nolan has had a strong influence on the science fiction field. Born in Missouri in 1928, he was educated at the Kansas City Art Institute, San Diego State College, and Los Angeles City College. He worked at various jobs before becoming a full-time writer in 1956. His most famous novels are Logan's Run *and its two sequels, which are set in a future America devoted to youth. His stories of horror show the same stylistic brilliance and suspense. Many are featured in his collection* Things Beyond Midnight.

Jimmy Rogers did not go to the movies to watch the films. He went to search for a girl—an extra—who continued to appear in crowd shots, even though she had died in 1930.

TWELVE

The Movie People
Robert Bloch

Two thousand stars.

Two thousand stars, maybe more, set in the sidewalks along Hollywood Boulevard, each metal slab inscribed with the name of someone in the movie industry. They go way back, those names; from Broncho Billy Anderson to Adolph Zukor, everybody's there.

Everybody but Jimmy Rogers.

You won't find Jimmy's name because he wasn't a star, not even a bit player—just an extra.

"But I deserve it," he told me. "I'm entitled, if anybody is. Started out here in 1920 when I was just a punk kid. You look close, you'll spot me in the crowd shots in *The Mark of Zorro*. Been in over 450 pictures since, and still going strong. Ain't many left who can beat that record. You'd think it would entitle a fella to something."

Maybe it did, but there was no star for Jimmy Rogers, and that bit about still going strong was just a crock. Nowadays Jimmy was lucky if he got a casting call once or twice a year; there just isn't any spot for an old timer with a white muff except in a western barroom scene.

Most of the time Jimmy just strolled the Boulevard; a tall, soldierly erect incongruity in the crowd of tourists, fags, and freakouts. His home address was on Las Palmas, somewhere south of Sunset. I'd never been there but I could guess what it was—one of those old frame bungalow court sweatboxes put up about the time he crashed the movies and still standing somehow by the grace of God and the disgrace of the housing authorities. That's the sort of place Jimmy stayed at, but he didn't really *live* there.

Jimmy Rogers lived at the Silent Movie.

The Silent Movie is over on Fairfax, and it's the only place in town where you can still go and see *The Mark of Zorro*. There's always a Chaplin comedy, and usually Laurel and Hardy, along with a serial starring Pearl White, Elmo Lincoln, or Houdini. And the features are great—early Griffith and DeMille, Barrymore in *Dr. Jekyll and Mr. Hyde*. Lon Chaney in *The Hunchback of Notre Dame*, Valentino in *Blood and Sand,* and a hundred more.

The bill changes every Wednesday, and every Wednesday night Jimmy Rogers was there, plunking down his ninety cents at the box office to watch *The Black Pirate* or *Son of the Sheik* or *Orphans of the Storm*.

To live again.

Because Jimmy didn't go there to see Doug and Mary or Rudy or Clara or Gloria or the Gish sisters. He went there to see himself, in the crowd shots.

At least that's the way I figured it, the first time I met him. They were playing *The Phantom of the Opera* that night, and afterwards I spent the intermission with a cigarette outside the theatre, studying the display of stills.

If you asked me under oath, I couldn't tell you how our conversation started, but that's where I first heard Jimmy's routine about the 450 pictures and still going strong.

"Did you see me in there tonight?" he asked.

I stared at him and shook my head; even with the shabby hand-me-down suit and the white beard, Jimmy Rogers wasn't the kind you'd spot in an audience.

"Guess it was too dark for me to notice," I said.

"But there were torches," Jimmy told me. "I carried one."

Then I got the message. He was in the picture.

Jimmy smiled and shrugged. "Hell, I keep forgetting. You wouldn't recognize me. We did *The Phantom* way back in '25. I looked so young they slapped a mustache on me in Makeup, and a black wig. Hard to spot me in the catacombs scenes—all long shots. But there at the end, where Chaney is holding back the mob, I show up pretty good in the background, just left of Charley Zimmer. He's the one shaking his fist. I'm waving my torch. Had a lot of trouble with that picture, but we did this shot in one take."

200

In weeks to come I saw more of Jimmy Rogers. Sometimes he was up there on the screen, though truth to tell, I never did recognize him; he was a young man in those films of the twenties, and his appearances were limited to a flickering flash, a blurred face glimpsed in a crowd.

But always Jimmy was in the audience, even though he hadn't played in the picture. And one night I found out why.

Again it was intermission time and we were standing outside. By now Jimmy had gotten into the habit of talking to me and tonight we'd been seated together during the showing of *The Covered Wagon.*

We stood outside and Jimmy blinked at me. "Wasn't she beautiful?" he asked. "They don't look like that any more."

I nodded. "Lois Wilson? Very attractive."

"I'm talking about June."

I stared at Jimmy and then I realized he wasn't blinking. He was crying.

"June Logan. My girl. This was her first bit, the Indian attack scene. Must have been seventeen—I didn't know her then; it was two years later we met over at First National. But you must have noticed her. She was the one with the long blonde curls."

"Oh, *that* one." I nodded again. "You're right. She was lovely."

And I was a liar, because I didn't remember seeing her at all, but I wanted to make the old man feel good.

"Junie's in a lot of the pictures they show here. And from '25 on, we played in a flock of 'em together. For a while we talked about getting hitched, but she started working her way up, doing bits—maids and such—and I never broke out of extra work. Both of us had been in the business long enough to know it was no go, not when one of you stays small and the other is headed for a big career."

Jimmy managed a grin as he wiped his eyes with something which might once have been a handkerchief. "You think I'm kidding, don't you? About the career, I mean. But she was going great, she would have been playing second leads pretty soon."

"What happened?" I asked.

The grin dissolved and the blinking returned. "Sound killed her."

"She didn't have a voice for talkies?"

Jimmy shook his head. "She had a great voice. I told you she was all set for second leads—by 1930 she'd been in a dozen talkies. Then sound killed her."

I'd heard the expression a thousand times, but never like this. Because the way Jimmy told the story, that's exactly what had happened. June Logan, his girl Junie, was on the set during the shooting of one of those early *All Talking-All Singing-All Dancing* epics. The director and camera crew, seeking to break away from the tyranny of the stationary microphone, rigged up one of the first traveling mikes on a boom. Such items weren't standard equipment yet, and this was an experiment. Somehow, during a take, it broke loose and the boom crashed, crushing June Logan's skull.

It never made the papers, not even the trades; the studio hushed it up, and June Logan had a quiet funeral.

"Damn near forty years ago," Jimmy said. "And here I am, crying like it was yesterday. But she was my girl. . . ."

And that was the other reason why Jimmy Rogers went to the Silent Movie. To visit his girl.

"Don't you see?" he told me. "She's still alive up there on the screen, in all those pictures. Just the way she was when we were together. Five years we had, the best years for me."

I could see that. The two of them in love, with each other and with the movies. Because in those days, people *did* love the movies. And to actually be *in* them, even in tiny roles, was the average person's idea of seventh heaven.

Seventh Heaven, that's another film we saw with June Logan playing in a crowd scene. In the following weeks, with Jimmy's help, I got so I could spot his girl. And he'd told the truth—she was a beauty. Once you noticed her, really saw her, you wouldn't forget. Those blonde ringlets, that smile, identified her immediately.

One Wednesday night Jimmy and I were sitting together watching *The Birth of a Nation.* During a street shot, Jimmy nudged my shoulder. "Look, there's June."

I peered up at the screen, then shook my head. "I don't see her."

"Wait a second—there she is again. See, off to the left, behind Walthall's shoulder?"

There was a blurred image and then the camera followed Henry B. Walthall as he moved away.

I glanced at Jimmy. He was rising from his seat.

"Where you going?"

He just marched outside.

When I followed I found him leaning against the wall under the marquee and breathing hard; his skin was the color of his whiskers.

"Junie," he murmured. "I saw her—"

I took a deep breath. "Listen to me. You told me her first picture was *The Covered Wagon*. That was made in 1923. And Griffith shot *The Birth of a Nation* in 1915."

Jimmy didn't say anything. There was nothing to say. We both knew what we were going to do—march back into the theatre and see the second show.

When the scene screened again, we were watching and waiting. I looked at the screen, then glanced at Jimmy.

"She's gone," he whispered. "She's not in the picture."

"She never was," I told him. "You know that."

"Yeah." Jimmy got up and drifted out into the night, and I didn't see him again until the following week.

That's when they showed the short feature with Charles Ray—I've forgotten the title, but he played his usual country-boy role, and there was a baseball game in the climax with Ray coming through to win.

The camera panned across the crowd sitting in the bleachers, and I caught a momentary glimpse of a smiling girl with long blonde curls.

"Did you see her?" Jimmy grabbed my arm.

"That girl—"

"It was Junie. She winked at me!"

This time I was the one who got up and walked out. He followed, and I was waiting in front of the theatre, right next to the display poster.

"See for yourself." I nodded at the poster. "This picture was made in 1917." I forced a smile. "You forget, there were thousands of pretty blonde extras in pictures, and most of them wore curls."

He stood there shaking, not listening to me at all, and I put my hand on his shoulder. "Now look here—"

"I *been* looking here," Jimmy said. "Week after week,

year after year. And you might as well know the truth. This ain't the first time it's happened. Junie keeps turning up in picture after picture I know she never made. Not just the early ones, before her time, but later, during the twenties when I knew her, when I knew exactly what she was playing in. Sometimes it's only a quick flash, but I see her—then she's gone again. And the next running, she doesn't come back.

"It got so that for a while I was almost afraid to go see a show—figured I was cracking up. But now you've seen her too. . . ."

I shook my head slowly. "Sorry, Jimmy. I never said that." I glanced at him, then gestured towards my car at the curb. "You look tired. Come on, I'll drive you home."

He looked worse than tired; he looked lost and lonely and infinitely old. But there was a stubborn glint in his eyes, and he stood his ground.

"No, thanks. I'm gonna stick around for the second show."

As I slid behind the wheel, I saw him turn and move into the theatre, into the place where the present becomes the past and the past becomes the present. Up above in the booth they call it a projection-machine, but it's really a time-machine; it can take you back, play tricks with your imagination and your memory. A girl dead forty years comes alive again, and an old man relives his vanished youth. . . .

But I belonged in the real world, and that's where I stayed. I didn't go to the Silent Movie the next week or the week following.

And the next time I saw Jimmy was almost a month later, on the set.

They were shooting a western, one of my scripts, and the director wanted some additional dialogue to stretch a sequence. So they called me in, and I drove all the way out to location, at the ranch.

Most of the studios have a ranch spread for western action sequences, and this was one of the oldest; it had been in use since the silent days. What fascinated me was the wooden fort where they were doing the crowd scene—I could swear I remembered it from one of the first Tim Mc-Coy pictures. So after I huddled with the director and scribbled a few extra lines for the principals, I began nosing around behind the fort, just out of curiosity, while they set up for the new shots.

Out front was the usual organized confusion; cast and crew milling around the trailers, extras sprawled on the grass drinking coffee. But here in the back I was all alone, prowling around in musty, log-lined rooms built for use in forgotten features. Hoot Gibson had stood at this bar, and Jack Hoxie had swung from this dance-hall chandelier. Here was a dust-covered table where Fred Thomson sat, and around the corner, in the cutaway bunkhouse—

Around the corner, in the cutaway bunkhouse, Jimmy Rogers sat on the edge of a mildewed mattress and stared up at me, startled, as I moved forward.

"You—?"

Quickly I explained my presence. There was no need for him to explain his; casting had called and given him a day's work here in the crowd shots.

"They been stalling all day, and it's hot out there. I figured maybe I could sneak back here and catch me a little nap in the shade."

"How'd you know where to go?" I asked. "Ever been here before?"

"Sure. Forty years ago in this very bunkhouse. Junie and I, we used to come here during lunch break and—"

He stopped.

"What's wrong?"

Something *was* wrong. On the pan makeup face of it, Jimmy Rogers was the perfect picture of the grizzled western old timer; buckskin britches, fringed shirt, white whiskers and all. But under the makeup was pallor, and the hands holding the envelope were trembling.

The envelope—

He held it out to me. "Here. Mebbe you better read this."

The envelope was unsealed, unstamped, unaddressed. It contained four folded pages covered with fine handwriting. I removed them slowly. Jimmy stared at me.

"Found it lying here on the mattress when I came in," he murmured. "Just waiting for me."

"But what is it? Where'd it come from?"

"Read it and see."

As I started to unfold the pages, the whistle blew. We both knew the signal; the scene was set up, they were ready to roll, principals and extras were wanted out there before the cameras.

Jimmy Rogers stood up and moved off, a tired old man shuffling out into the hot sun. I waved at him, then sat down on the moldering mattress and opened the letter. The handwriting was faded, and there was a thin film of dust on the pages. But I could still read it, every word. . . .

"Darling: I've been trying to reach you so long and in so many ways. Of course I've seen you, but it's so dark out there, I can't always be sure, and then too you've changed a lot through the years.

"But I *do* see you, quite often, even though it's only for a moment. And I hope you've seen me, because I always try to wink or make some kind of motion to attract your attention.

"The only thing is, I can't do too much or show myself too long or it would make trouble. That's the big secret— keeping in the background, so the others won't notice me. It wouldn't do to frighten anybody, or even to get anyone wondering why there are more people in the background of a shot than there should be.

"That's something for you to remember, darling, just in case. You're always safe, as long as you stay clear of close-ups. Costume pictures are the best—about all you have to do is wave your arms once in a while and shout, 'On to the Bastille,' or something like that. It really doesn't matter except to lip readers, because it's silent, of course.

"Oh, there's a lot to watch out for. Being a dress-extra has its points, but not in ballroom sequences—too much dancing. That goes for parties, too, particularly in a DeMille production where they're 'making whoopee' or one of von Stroheim's orgies. Besides, von Stroheim's scenes are always cut.

"It doesn't hurt to be cut, don't misunderstand about that. It's no different than an ordinary fadeout at the end of a scene, and then you're free to go into another picture. Anything that was ever made, as long as there's still a print available for running somewhere. It's like falling asleep and then having one dream after another. The dreams are the scenes, of course, but while the scenes are playing, they're real.

"I'm not the only one, either. There's no telling how many others do the same thing; maybe hundreds for all I know, but I've recognized a few I'm sure of, and I think some of them have recognized me. We never let on to each other that we know, because it wouldn't do to make anybody suspicious.

"Sometimes I think that if we could talk it over, we might come up with a better understanding of just how it happens, and why. But the point is, you *can't* talk, everything is silent; all you do is move your lips, and if you tried to communicate such a difficult thing in pantomine, you'd surely attract attention.

"I guess the closest I can come to explaining it is to say it's like reincarnation—you can play a thousand roles, take or reject any part you want, as long as you don't make yourself conspicuous or do something that would change the plot.

"Naturally, you get used to certain things. The silence, of course. And if you're in a bad print, there's flickering; sometimes even the air seems grainy, and for a few frames you may be faded or out of focus.

"Which reminds me—another thing to stay away from, the slapstick comedies. Sennett's early stuff is the worst, but Larry Semon and some of the others are just as bad; all that speeded-up camera action makes you dizzy.

"Once you can learn to adjust, it's all right, even when you're looking off the screen into the audience. At first the darkness is a little frightening—you have to remind yourself it's only a theatre and there are just people out there, ordinary people watching a show. They don't know you can see them. They don't know that as long as your scene runs, you're just as real as they are, only in a different way. You walk, run, smile, frown, drink, eat. . . .

"That's another thing to remember, about the eating. Stay out of those Poverty Row quickies where everything is cheap and faked. Go where there's real set-dressing, big productions with banquet scenes and real food. If you work fast, you can grab enough in a few minutes, while you're off-camera, to last you.

"The big rule is, always be careful. Don't get caught.

There's so little time, and you seldom get an opportunity to do anything on your own, even in a long sequence. It's taken me forever to get this chance to write you—I've planned it for so long, my darling, but it just wasn't possible until now.

"This scene is playing outside the fort, but there's quite a large crowd of settlers and wagon train people, and I had a chance to slip away inside here to the rooms in back—they're on camera in the background all during the action. I found this stationery and a pen, and I'm scribbling just as fast as I can. Hope you can read it. That is, if you ever get the chance!

"Naturally, I can't mail it—but I have a funny hunch. You see, I noticed that standing set back here, the bunkhouse, where you and I used to come in the old days. I'm going to leave this letter under the mattress, and pray.

"Yes, darling, I pray. Someone or something *knows* about us, and about how we feel. How we felt about being in the movies. That's why I'm here, I'm sure of that; because I've always loved pictures so. Someone who knows *that* must also know how I loved you. And still do.

"I think there must be many heavens and many hells, each of us making his own, and—"

The letter broke off there.

No signature, but of course I didn't need one. And it wouldn't have proved anything. A lonely old man, nursing his love for forty years, keeping her alive inside himself somewhere until she broke out in the form of a visual hallucination up there on the screen—such a man could conceivably go all the way into a schizoid split, even to the point where he could imitate a woman's handwriting as he set down the rationalization of his obsession.

I started to fold the letter, then dropped it on the mattress as the shrill scream of an ambulance siren startled me into sudden movement.

Even as I ran out the doorway, I seemed to know what I'd find; the crowd huddling around the figure sprawled in the dust under the hot sun. Old men tire easily in such heat, and once the heart goes. . . .

Jimmy Rogers looked very much as though he were smiling in his sleep as they lifted him into the ambulance. And I was glad of that; at least he'd died with his illusions intact.

"Just keeled over during the scene—one minute he was standing there, and the next—"

They were still chattering and gabbling when I walked away, walked back behind the fort and into the bunkhouse.

The letter was gone.

I'd dropped it on the mattress, and it was gone. That's all I can say about it. Maybe somebody else happened by while I was out front, watching them take Jimmy away. Maybe a gust of wind carried it through the doorway, blew it across the desert in a hot Santa Ana gust. Maybe there *was* no letter. You can take your choice—all I can do is state the facts.

And there aren't very many more facts to state.

I didn't go to Jimmy Rogers' funeral, if indeed he had one. I don't even know where he was buried; probably the Motion Picture Fund took care of him. Whatever *those* facts may be, they aren't important.

For a few days I wasn't too interested in facts. I was trying to answer a few abstract questions about metaphysics—reincarnation, heaven and hell, the difference between real life and reel life. I kept thinking about those images you see up there on the screen in those old movies; images of actual people indulging in make-believe. But even after they die, the make-believe goes on, and that's a form of reality too. I mean, where's the border line? And if there is a border line—is it possible to cross over? *Life's but a walking shadow—*

Shakespeare said that, but I wasn't sure what he meant.

I'm still not sure, but there's just one more fact I must state.

The other night, for the first time since Jimmy Rogers died, I went back to the Silent Movie.

They were playing *Intolerance,* one of Griffith's greatest. Way back in 1916 he built the biggest set ever shown on the screen—the huge temple in the Babylonian sequence.

One shot never fails to impress me, and it did so now; a wide angle on the towering temple, with thousands of people moving antlike amidst the gigantic carvings and colossal statues. In the distance, beyond the steps guarded by rows

209

of stone elephants, looms a mighty wall, its top covered with tiny figures. You really have to look closely to make them out. But I did look closely, and this time I can swear to what I saw.

One of the extras, way up there on the wall in the background, was a smiling girl with long blonde curls. And standing right beside her, one arm around her shoulder, was a tall old man with white whiskers. I wouldn't have noticed either of them, except for one thing.

They were waving at me. . . .

"I have the heart of a little boy," Bloch once said. "I keep it in a glass jar on my desk." His joke is almost as famous as his novel Psycho, *which was made into the Alfred Hitchcock film. Born in Chicago in 1917, Bloch sold his first story two months after high school graduation. He was strongly influenced by the work and correspondence of H. P. Lovecraft, but Bloch developed a new style, fresh and modern. His most famous short story is "Yours Truly, Jack the Ripper." The success of* Psycho *led to a career in screenwriting, including scripts for episodes of* Star Trek *and the* Alfred Hitchcock Hour. *Later works include* Psycho House, Lori, *and a limited edition of his* Collected Stories. *Bloch is the winner of a Hugo for "That Hell-Bound Train, and was awarded the 1975 Lifetime Achievement Award of World Fantasy.*

Acknowledgments